SOPHIE STREET

A Pendragon Island Story

SOPHIE STREET

A Pendragon Island Story

Grace Thompson

This first world edition published in Great Britain 1999 by
SEVERN HOUSE PUBLISHERS LTD of
9–15 High Street, Sutton, Surrey SM1 1DF.
This first world edition published in the USA 1999 by
SEVERN HOUSE PUBLISHERS INC., of
595 Madison Avenue, New York, NY 10022.

British Library Cataloguing in Publication Data

Thompson, Grace
  Sophie Street
  1.   Pendragon Island (Imaginary place) - Fiction
  2.   Domestic fiction
  I.   Title
  823.9'14 [F]

  ISBN 0 7278 5433 X

Typeset by Hewer Text Ltd., Edinburgh, Scotland.
Printed and bound in Great Britain by
MPG Books Ltd, Bodmin, Cornwall.

One

R hiannon and Charlie Bevan looked across at 7 Sophie
Street and held each other close.

"Not another row," Charlie muttered.

"Perhaps they're just arguing about who makes the early morning tea," Rhiannon said hopefully. "Come on, Charlie, it's time to
wake Gwyn." She made her way to the bathroom and washed
quickly before calling her stepson and reminding him that if he
stayed in bed any longer he'd miss breakfast. That usually worked.

Charlie and his son, Gwyn, worked at Windsor's garage and
had to leave the house before eight o'clock. Rhiannon worked in
Temptations, the sweetshop on the corner, and didn't need to
leave the house before five minutes to nine. "I think I'll pop over
and see Mam," she said as she began preparing breakfast ten
minutes later. "I dread to think of those two separating again."
She sighed. "Why can't they behave?"

"The thought of having your father back as our lodger is
daunting," said Charlie, adding, "I think we'd threaten to
emigrate if it came to that!"

Charlie and Gwyn were leaving to cycle to the garage when
they saw Lewis storming out of number seven. "All right?"
Charlie called.

"No it isn't!" Lewis Lewis snapped. "I told her. I told her to
buy batteries for the torch and she forgot again. She won't carry
one and I think she should on these dark mornings and evenings.
I can't give her and Sian Weston a lift if I'm out of town, can I?
And she should always have a decent torch in her pocket. D'you
think she'll listen? No!"

Darting back into the house, Charlie came out and handed a

1

small torch to his father-in-law. "Give her this, we've got a couple more. And please, Father-in-law, don't frighten us by shouting at each other like that. Rhiannon always expects the worst; that you and her mam will separate again."

"And I'll end up living with you?" Lewis grinned. "I think that's one reason why Dora took me back, mind, so I wouldn't be a nuisance to you and Rhiannon." He was chuckling as he went back inside to give Dora the torch.

Dora Lewis ran the Rose Tree cafe near the lake, with her friend, Sian Weston. They had both been keen on cooking and when the opportunity came to develop their skills and begin a small business, they had taken it. Both had been separated from their husbands at the time: Lewis had gone to live with his long-time mistress Nia Williams who had subsequently died, and Sian's husband, Islwyn, had gone to live with *his* mistress, Margaret Jenkins of Montague Court.

"How are things with you and Lewis?" Sian asked as they took the first batch of scones out of the oven and put in a second baking.

"All right, I suppose, but we're still a bit touchy with each other. Like this morning he flared up because I said I didn't need to carry a torch. Daft, eh?"

"Not really, Dora. At least it shows he cares for you, wants to keep you safe. I don't think Islwyn would ever have been that thoughtful. He was more likely to grumble that I hadn't reminded *him* to carry one!"

Someone rattled the door and Dora looked up, her eyes bright, ready to complain. "Who can that be? It's clear we aren't open yet. Ten o'clock it says on the notice."

"It might be that Carl Rees," Sian said, going to open the door, wiping her floury hands down her sides. "Him that's going to repair the windowframe, remember?"

She was right, and a tall, dark-haired young man came in carrying a carpenter's tool bag.

"Is it all right to start on the repair now?" he asked. "I should get the wood patched and the prime coat on by lunchtime, then I'll be back tomorrow to finish painting it. Right?"

"Who is he?" Dora asked, when the young man was outside, with a cup of tea and a sandwich provided.

"He lives in Bella Vista Road. You know," Sian laughed, "the road with the beautiful view – of the new factory!"

"A bedsit?"

"Yes. I don't know much else except that he does work for Jennie Francis, her that opened a paint and wallpaper shop and hoped to take trade from Westons. No chance of that, with my niece Joan and your son Viv managing Westons, is there?"

"On to a loser before she started," Dora agreed.

"Carl Rees is very secretive by all accounts, but good at what he does. Carpentry mostly, but other jobs as well. It was Jennie Francis who recommended him to us. He does carpet fitting for her – when she manages to sell any, poor dab. I think things are going hard for her."

When most people living in Pendragon Island needed paint, wallpaper, carpets or small items of furniture they went to Westons. For the remaining few, Jennie Francis's small shop on a side road not far from the church was an alternative. Jennie stocked fewer lines but was willing to collect their requirements from the wholesalers and deliver them the same day. In this she was helped, not by her husband, who worked in the shipping offices on the docks, but by a casual worker, Carl Rees.

Carl fitted carpets, collected and delivered paint and wallpaper and would even decorate rooms, if required. He also did small carpentry jobs, like fitting shelves and making cupboards, tending to prefer this more skilled work to the mundane collection and delivery service Jennie required.

Jennie had begun her business with the assumption that her personal service and the smallness of her enterprise would wean people away from the larger and still expanding Westons. Part of her conviction had been based on the fact that Arfon Weston had been charged with theft and arson, having set fire to his own premises to recover insurance money when his business was failing. In this conviction she had been wrong.

For a while customers had trickled in, some out of curiosity, some to buy, but most had preferred the wider choice of Westons. She was having to face the fact that, unless she could find a way of increasing her sales, she would soon have to close.

Arfon Weston's large shop was managed by Viv Lewis and his wife, Joan, who was Arfon's granddaughter. Together Viv and Joan had rebuilt the business, raising it from just an outlet for wallpaper and paint, to a successful furniture showroom as well. Lucky Arfon Weston, Jennie sighed.

She was checking the totals on her till roll and writing them into her account book preparing to close for the day. She knew she would have to spend the evening working on her accounts, trying to decide whether to ask for a further loan or gradually close down the business. Carl came in, having washed the van and collected together the rubbish – wrappings, unwanted advertising boards, oddments of carpet and underlay – left from the day's jobs. Two bedrooms fitted from small remnants, with not enough profit to pay for Carl's time.

"I might have to close before the end of next month, Carl," she said, as he picked up his coat and shrugged it on. "I'm sorry."

"Can't you sell it as a going concern? Better than closing it I'd have thought." He looked down at her from his six feet four, his dark eyes softening, as pity for her disappointment filled his mind. She had worked so hard, and even tried a bit of cheating, getting information about the plans being made by Westons, and offering makes of carpet before they added them to their stock, but it had been hopeless. He'd always thought it would fail. Westons, with the go-ahead Viv Lewis in charge, was impossible to fight.

"What about your old man, won't he chip in a bit more? You could branch out into something that will bring people in."

"Such as?" she asked wearily. "Viv Lewis has done it all."

"Why not specialise in carpets and curtains and forget the rest? You could employ a professional designer."

"Too expensive."

"Someone young and not yet greedy?"

She shook her head. "I just don't have the capital." Or the support, she added silently.

When Carl had gone she sat for a long time looking at the sales and measuring the stock, working out the possible reductions if she were to have a sale. An hour passed and another, and it was almost eight o'clock when she came to with a shock and hurried from the shop. Peter would have a late dinner again and he hated eating later than seven. Her thoughts changing direction, she busied herself working out a meal that could be quickly prepared. She decided on cold meats, salad and coleslaw, even though the weather on this January day was more suitable to something hot. Unable to enthuse over the mundane subject of food, she switched back to thinking about the business.

She thought about Carl's suggestion as she drove home. Curtains and carpets would make a natural combination, and it would be a relief to forget about wallpaper and paints and the boring accessories that went with them, but where would she find the money to expand? Advertising would be costly too but, without it, nothing she did in her out of the way premises would succeed.

Expand or give up? Her mind was going round and round considering the alternatives. As she opened the front door, she heard her husband in the kitchen and called, "Peter? Sorry I'm late, darling, I was talking to Carl."

"You've forgotten about this evening then?"

Puzzled, she went to the kitchen door and saw that Peter was dressed in his best suit and obviously ready to go out. But where? He was standing, eating an untidily made sandwich and leaning over the sink to avoid marking his clothes. His eyes were shooting arrows of anger in her direction. The fact she had forgotten was clear on her face.

"Don't worry, Jennie, I'll go on my own. Again."

"I'm sorry, I—" How could she admit she had no idea where they were supposed to be going?

"The leaving do?" he supplied. "The leaving do for Freddy Parker?"

"Give me twenty minutes and I'll be ready." She turned to go upstairs but he threw down the sandwich and caught hold of her arm, thin, bony and suddenly repulsive to him. "Don't bother."

5

He released his hold of her as though throwing her from him, and left the room. "Don't wait up. I plan to be very late."

He didn't slam the door when he left – that was something Peter never did – but Jennie opened it and called after him, "Give my best wishes to Freddy." Then *she* slammed it.

She had a bath and, in her dressing gown, sat and went through the books once more. The loan from Peter's parents was the biggest problem. They insisted on regular weekly payments and it was draining her. Instead of adding to her stock, she was having to pay them back and, although she knew they would have to be paid, she wondered whether they could be persuaded to delay any repayments for six months, to give her a chance to get things on a stronger footing. On impulse she phoned them.

After the usual rather formal pleasantries, she began to explain about the need to plough back any profits until the business was on its feet but Peter's father cut her short.

"Sorry, Jennie, but Mum and I have been discussing this and we think its time our loan was repaid in full."

"What? But you promised to accept weekly instalments until the shop was comfortably paying its way!"

"We went to Westons today and had a chat with Viv Lewis and that smart wife of his, Joan. She was a Weston you know, and is a very competent business woman. It's so smart, that store, and they offer a good service. You should see their stock too. Marvellous it is. You can't compete with them whatever we do to help."

"Why did you go there? They probably thought you were spying."

"I didn't say who we were, of course, but from what Viv Lewis said, you don't stand a chance. The position of your shop is wrong: too far from the shopping centre, without any passing trade. And you can't offer a wide enough choice. Besides, Westons sell so many other things, and Joan Lewis offers a design and advisory service. Mum and I think you should sell while you've still got something to sell. Sorry, Jennie, but that's what we think."

Jennie sat with her eyes staring, unseeing, at the books in front of her, feeling as though she had taken a beating. She ached so much that she didn't think she had the strength to go up the stairs to bed. The day's post was piled up on the hall table. Peter rarely opened it, preferring to leave it to her to sort out. Forcing herself to leave her chair she gathered it up and took it upstairs planning to glance through it in bed.

Bank statements, gas and electricity bills she put on one side for Peter to deal with, advertisements and prospective distributers wanting an order, she threw onto the floor. The last one she opened and unfolded with curiosity. The letter was from the landlord of her shop, reminding her that the lease was soon ending and asking for confirmation of another year's tenancy. She had six weeks to decide what she was going to do, but ten seconds were enough. Without Peter's parents continuing to lend her the money she had no choice, she would have to close.

Another new business in Pendragon Island was showing none of the problems experienced by Jennie Francis. Edward Jenkins, previously of Montague Court, had opened a sports shop and it was increasing its turnover month by month. Mair Gregory worked for Edward full time and had never been happier. She had once worked as a maid for the Westons in their large house overlooking the docks, but Gladys and Arfon's demands had been too much for her. Life in the sports shop was more interesting and far better paid.

Mair was twenty-two and not yet married. She'd had several boyfriends but none of them suited her. She lived at home with her father, who was a police constable, and was quite content. When she married she was determined not to become a housewife and mother with nothing more in her life than the weekly routine of what she saw as drudgery. Working as a maid for Gladys Weston had made her realise that for most women, life offered nothing more than being an unpaid servant. That wasn't for her. Rich, he'd have to be, she laughingly told Edward when the subject of her boyfriends came up. "Rich, and boring, so no one else will want him, and at least fifty years old!"

But when Carl Rees came in late one afternoon, she thought

she might change her mind. He was very tall, towering over her and filling the shop with his size. The day was gloomy and outside it was raining as though it would never stop. The shop was dark, even with the lights blazing in an attempt to add cheer, but he looked huge and to her, attractive and utterly fascinating in a 'Heathcliff' kind of way. The winter weather no longer seemed important. Edward smiled knowingly and stood back for her to attend to him.

"Do you have fishing gear?" Carl asked and, unexpectedly shy, Mair showed him the section where the rods and reels and accessories were displayed.

"Fond of fishing are you?" she asked stupidly, as he tried out the whip of a fly-fishing rod.

"Why else d'you think I'm buying?"

"For a present? Hanging about waiting for the rain to stop?" she snapped back, embarrassment making her angry.

"Sorry. Yes, I do like fishing and I want a beach rod, but I was looking at the fly rods out of curiosity."

"I expect you know Viv Lewis who works for the Westons then, if you like fishing? He and Jack Weston are always off hoping to catch fish for supper."

"I wouldn't think Viv had much time, running that busy shop."

"I don't think he goes as often as he used to. Both he and Jack Weston are married now so things have changed for them."

"Where do they go?" Carl asked. If Jennie was closing down then it might be a good idea to get to know the manager of Westons. They were sure to use more than one carpet fitter at times.

"The docks after mullet, the river after sewen. And salmon when they get a chance."

"I'll have a word, see if they can recommend a good spot."

He didn't buy the rod. Thinking it might be worth a second visit to talk to Mair again, he made an excuse and said he'd be calling in the following day, about lunchtime. "You can share my sandwiches if you like," he said, with a grin that weakened her knees.

8

"I go home most days," she said, then added, "Except Saturdays. We're too busy for more than a quick snack then. I usually go to the cafe."

"Saturday it is," Carl said, then wondered why he had bothered. Mair didn't look the sort who was ready for some fun. She was attractive enough, plump, just as he liked them. But as he was unable to consider more than a brief fling and no commitment, she was worth a second visit.

On Saturday, they ate in a small corner cafe some distance from where she worked. Best if they weren't seen together. She was amusing, describing the customers and their wants, explaining about how she had started working for Edward Jenkins.

"You still live at home?" Carl asked.

"There's just me and Dad," she told him. "He's a policeman and he works shifts, so I have to stay and look after him. I don't know what will happen when I get married," she added coyly, and Carl swiftly changed the subject. Even on a first meeting that was dangerous ground.

Viv Lewis knew Carl Rees by sight although they had never spoken. He had watched the progress of Jennie Francis's business with interest although he no longer had fears of her overtaking Westons. He had started managing the company after a series of disasters had brought it to the brink of closure. With Joan Weston helping, and eventually marrying him, he had worked to bring Westons into its present successful position as the first place people came when they were redecorating and refurnishing.

Seeing Carl walk in that Saturday afternoon carrying a new fishing rod and reel, he went to speak to him. Small, like his mother Dora and with her red hair, Viv no longer felt his lack of height to be a disadvantage. He was king of this particular castle and he made sure everyone knew it.

"Come to see how it's done?" he asked as he approached Carl. "Or some lessons in fishing?"

"Both I suppose." Carl grinned. "I fancy a bit of fishing and thought to go off to one of the beaches. What d'you think?"

"I think you're fishing for ideas to take back to Miss Francis."

9

"It's Mrs. And, no, I wanted to see your set-up, I admit that, I might be looking for extra work, fitting carpets and some carpentry, you know, shelves and the like. But I was hoping for a bit of information on the best spots for a bit of sport. I hear that you and Jack Weston are the local experts."

"Us and the Griffiths brothers, yes, I suppose we are. Jack and I are the legal side and the Griffiths brothers more the 'what the hell' brigade."

"I've heard about the wild Griffiths boys. Often in court for fighting I understand. I'd like to meet them," Carl said, matching Viv's smile. "They'll be the ones to show me the best spots for some catches but, fishing aside, will you bear me in mind when you're short of a carpet fitter?"

"I'd have to see your work first."

Carl took out a notebook and offered it to Viv. "These are some of my customers. I'm sure any of them will let you have a look-see, and you can judge for yourself."

"Meet me in the Railwayman's's tonight and we'll talk about it," Viv said, turning to attend to a nearby customer. Carl nodded and went out. A date with Mair for Sunday afternoon and an arrangement to discuss work with Viv Weston. Not a bad day's work. Learning that Mair's father worked shifts and was sometimes out all night was an added bonus to the promise in Mair's eyes. Mair for amusement and Viv opening the way to earn more money. Yes, things were looking up. He only had to persuade Jennie to sell her stock at a low price and he'd consider himself very fortunate. Hope after months of misery.

Jennie and Peter had hardly exchanged a word since the evening when he had gone out without her. She had said nothing about his father's ultimatum regarding the loan and she didn't attempt to discuss her decision to close down the business. What was the point? All he'd say was, told you so, and remind her how foolish he thought his parents had been to lend her the money in the first place. She'd heard it so often before and knowing he had been proved right only added to the misery of her failure. She would ring the bank first thing on Monday morning and make an appointment to discuss the best way of sorting out the closing down of her shop. The stock was not large, most of her orders were taken from pattern books, but there were tins and tins of paint and dozens of rolls of wallpaper, besides several rolls of carpets and a dozen or so rugs. A sale was a possibility, but it would be rubbing salt into her wound to advertise a closing-down sale.

"I'll buy the stock," Carl offered when she told him her decision on Monday morning. "I'll give you what you paid plus a little extra, how's that?"

Jennie regretted being so open with Carl regarding her situation, he would know the mark-up to the last penny and she wouldn't be able to argue. She had made so many mistakes.

"Perhaps I'll have a sale, at least that will bring the customers in, if only to search for a bargain."

"Take you a couple of weeks, mind. And then you'd be left with your least popular colours," he warned.

"Wait until I've seen the bank manager, then I'll decide, Perhaps he'll have a better idea. But thanks," she added, wondering with some bitterness why she was thanking him for taking advantage of her predicament.

Two hours later she walked back into the shop, knowing that even if she accepted Carl's offer and sold him all her stock, she still wouldn't have enough to pay her creditors and settle the loan from Peter's parents. She had to find a way of retrieving more of her money.

Leaving Carl to look after the shop she went to see Viv Lewis in Weston Wallpaper and Paint Store. The woman who came forward obviously knew her because, although there were other people in the store needing assistance, Joan Lewis, Viv's wife, came to her at once.

"Mrs Francis? How can we help?"

"I'd like to talk to your husband if he has a moment. Later today will do if he's busy."

"My husband is busy, but I am not!" Joan's voice was sharp. She had no patience with people who thought she was the lesser partner simply because she was a woman. Really, Mrs Francis should know better having taken on a business herself.

"Sorry," Jennie said quickly. "What I meant was that I would like to talk to you both, if that's possible."

"Viv will be back in half an hour, will that suit?" Joan's voice was still sharp, and Jennie knew she hadn't been forgiven.

"That will be fine, and thank you."

Rather than go back to her shop for ten minutes or so, Jennie went to the Blue Bird cafe and joined the morning shoppers gathered there. Monday wasn't a busy time but three tables were occupied. While she waited for her tea and toast, Jennie looked around at the other customers and recognised Gladys Weston, her loud voice penetrating the rest of the chatter to announce that her darling granddaughter, Megan, was getting married at Easter, to one of the Jenkinses of Montague Court. Jennie knew that was no longer true. Edward Jenkins had once owned the rather grand old house but it had been sold and he now ran a very successful sports shop on the High Street. Jennie smiled and admired the old woman for putting up a front, when everyone knew that her granddaughter, Megan Fowler-Weston had a child, a little girl of about five months old called Rosemary, and the man she was marrying was not the father.

Poor Glady Weston. She'd had such hopes of her twin granddaughters, only to face Joan marrying Viv Lewis, one of their employees and helping him to manage the shop she and her husband, Arfon, owned. Now the other one, Megan, had an illegitimate child and was marrying the owner of a sports shop. Not an emporium or a store, but a shop. So common, she thought, even if Edward was a Jenkins of Montague Court.

Knowing Gladys Weston was aware of her and knew who she was, Jennie smiled and said, "Good morning," as she left. Gladys responded rather cautiously. Then, as Jennie left the cafe, she turned to her companion, her shoulders curled protectively against being overheard, her face wearing a look that showed she was ready to impart some gossip.

"You know who that is, don't you? The woman who thought she could do better than the Westons, that's who! She took on more than she could manage there, I can tell you!"

12

Jennie heard this and smiled grimly. There was nothing better than the failure of an impertinent upstart to create gossip. It was something she'd have to accept over the next few weeks.

Viv and Joan Lewis were waiting in their office, which overlooked the sales floor when Jennie returned and was shown up by an assistant.

"Mrs Francis. Do sit down. How can we help?" Joan asked.

"I've decided to sell up," Jennie began, her voice bold but her heart thumping. If only they would agree to buy her stock, she might come out of this with only a small debt. "I wondered whether you would like to look at my stock and consider buying it?"

Viv and Joan both shook their heads sorrowfully and Jennie had the the firm conviction that they had been expecting this and had prepared their response.

"I'm sorry, but we have all the stock we need and we deal straight from the wholesalers wherever possible to avoid overstocking," Viv replied.

"It isn't all that much, and I don't expect to make anything, just clear the shop and give up the lease." She looked at them, unable to hide her distress. "Will you at least look at it?" She fumbled in her handbag and handed Joan a list. "That's all the good stuff. I know you wouldn't want to bother with small offcuts, small room sizes, or some of the older tins of paint. I thought I'd have a sale to dispose of those."

Joan and Viv glanced at each other and Jennie felt a surge of hope.

"All right," Viv said, "on the understanding that we aren't promising anything, we'll come at lunchtime and have a look."

"Thank you." She stood up and Viv stepped past her and opened the door. She walked out on the edge of tears. If she had done what she had originally planned and not been talked into stocking paint and paper, if Peter had been more supportive, if she had borrowed from someone other than his father, if, if, if.

At lunchtime, Carl was out on a job. He was making cupboards in the kitchen of a house where he had fitted carpets a week before. Most of his work came from people he met while fitting carpets. He would miss the business gleaned from Jennie's customers. Today, Jennie told him there was no hurry to come back. He guessed she didn't want him overhearing her discussion with Joan and Viv Lewis. He was very good at eavesdropping.

He didn't mind. He'd arranged to call for Mair in the cottage near the woods, and have a cup of tea before driving her back to the sports shop. He wouldn't go straight to the shop though, but drop her a few streets away. Best not take risks of their being seen together. He had hinted to her that they needed to keep their friendship a secret for a while. "No wife," he had assured her firmly. "It's just a bit of business I have to sort out before we can be open about the way we feel about each other. Nothing for you to worry about, just trust me for a little while and I'll explain everything." He was pleased with the way his planned seduction was going. Her father working nights was a godsend, he thought irreligiously.

Viv and Joan looked around the small premises and Joan made notes on his muttered comments. Jennie didn't follow them about. She sat at her desk near the phone with her fingers tightly crossed. At the small kitchen unit behind the shop she had offered them tea but they had refused, explaining their need to get back to Westons to open at two o'clock. So she sat and wondered what their decision would be.

The phone rang, startling her. A voice asked if she would send someone to measure up for a new hall and stair carpet. She took the details and wondered whether she would see the job through or hand it over to Westons with the rest of her business. She looked for Carl's notebook to write the address and time, but couldn't find it. She went into the store room where Viv was lifting a rug to see others underneath.

"I'm looking for a red notebook," she explained. "Carl usually leaves it on my desk once he's taken the details from it." To her surprise, Viv took it out of his pocket and handed it to her.

"He left it when he called in on Saturday."

"Oh?"

"He came to ask if we needed a fitter. Didn't he tell you?" Joan asked.

"No, I haven't really spoken to him today." She hesitated, then asked, "Did he tell you I was thinking of closing down?"

"Yes. I thought you must have known. He didn't seem to be secretive about it."

"He offered to buy my stock and I thought—"

"You thought he'd beat you down if he was the only one offering?"

"Yes," Jennie said. "I really hope you will buy it."

"Bit of a sharp one is he, this Carl?"

"Perhaps I'm being unkind, but he's built up a nice little carpentry business by touting for custom when he works for me." She shook her head and waved a hand as though trying to wipe the words from the air. "I'm being spiteful, I know I am."

Viv took the notebook from Joan, did a few calculations and named a price. It was lower than she had hoped, but more than she would have got from Carl, she was sure of that, so she accepted. With a signature and a formal handshake she said goodbye to her hopes of independence.

That evening Jennie was home before Peter. She had steak grilling with mushrooms, tomatoes, and fresh vegetables ready to serve. He walked in, looked at the delicious meal – one of his favourites – and said, "I'm eating out."

"Peter!" She ran up the stairs behind him and watched in dismay as he hurriedly stripped off his suit and changed into more casual clothes. "At least tell me where you're going and why you didn't mention it!"

"I'm eating with Mam and Dad."

"And I'm not invited?"

"Correct." With hardly another word, he left and she went down to stare at the plates of food as they slowly cooled and congealed.

Viv and Joan Lewis went to see Arfon and Gladys Weston when they closed the store that evening.

"Why did you agree to buy the woman out?" Arfon asked. "She was doing her damnedest to close us down not long ago!"

"I don't think there was ever any chance of that, Grandfather." Joan laughed. "She did expand the wallpaper and paint business to sell carpets just before we did, but with a small back-street position she was bound to fail, wasn't she?"

"No way she could win against us," Viv said, reaching over and kissing his wife's cheek affectionately.

Gladys turned away and tutted in disapproval. The Westons were above showing affection in public, but Viv was a Lewis and didn't know any better.

"You still haven't explained why you bought her stock to help her out," Arfon grumbled in his pompous manner. "It seems to me a foolish idea."

"The price was good, very good and, although most of the carpet pieces are room sizes only, I think we can make a reasonable profit. The carpets are excellent, better than some of ours. She obviously went for quality. Besides, I think it's time Westons had a sale. The paints and decorating stuff will go well as people are thinking about spring cleaning, don't you think?"

Gladys groaned. "Spring cleaning, and I don't have anyone to help me. What will I do, Arfon, dear?"

"Ask Victoria's mother," Joan replied.

"I can't. Not now Victoria is married to a Weston!"

"Jack won't mind, his mother-in-law has to live and her piano lessons don't keep them all fed. Mrs Collins still has six children at home, remember."

"As if I could forget! Jack might not worry about what people will think, dear, but I do." Beside the disappointments of her two granddaughters marrying men who, in her opinion, were far beneath them, her only grandson, Jack, had failed her too. He had married a girl who had once been her servant! Where had she gone wrong? "How can I ask Jack's mother-in-law to clean for me?" she wailed.

"I hope you didn't make a mistake, buying Jennie Francis's leftovers," Arfon grumbled, ignoring his wife's worries about housework.

As the young couple were leaving, Joan took Gladys aside and asked, "Shall I ask Victoria whether her mother would like to help you with the cleaning, Grandmother?"

16

"No, dear. I'd be too embarrassed every time I saw dear Jack and Victoria. I can't forget that Victoria worked for me before she married Jack. Who would have imagined it, my dear grandson marrying my servant and running away to Gretna Green, too. It's such a difficult situation. Having her mother here would make everything worse."

"I'll keep my eyes open for a suitable person. Don't worry, it's only January, we don't have to worry for a couple of months, do we?"

Gladys didn't like to admit that the house, with its four bedrooms and three reception rooms and a large garden, was becoming too much for her to cope with, so she smiled and thanked Joan and told her she was a dear.

As they walked home. Viv and Joan discussed their forthcoming sale.

"Best if we plan it for the week after next. No time like now. And, if we sort it quickly, we might also get that order Jennie Francis was taking while we were examining the stock!"

"I'll get onto the printer tomorrow morning," Joan said. "We'll need posters for the window and I think we should put an advertisement in the paper." Chatting excitedly about their plans, they strolled home, arm in arm, calling in for fish and chips on the way. "Too late for cooking," Joan explained, "but don't dare tell Grandmother!"

Jennie told Peter what she had done but he refused to discuss it.

"I should be able to repay the loan to your parents, but there will still be a few debts to clear."

She was hoping he would tell her his parents would wait, that they would agree to her paying off as much as she could afford and then settle the remainer when she could. But he just nodded and said, "As quickly as possible if you please."

He went out again that evening, this time not telling her where he was going, but later there was a telephone call from his parents and she could hear his voice in the background, so she knew he had eaten with them.

It was her father-in-law, goaded no doubt by her mother-in-law, reminding her that they expected the loan to be repaid as

17

soon as the shop closed. "Such a mistake on your part, Jennie, trying to compete with Westons. No room for two in a small town like Pendragon Island, you should have known that."

"Perhaps if I'd opened a gift shop as I originally intended, it would still be open," she argued.

"No. People don't have the money for luxuries."

Jennie knew this wasn't true: that after so many years of shortages, 1956 was exactly the right time to offer luxuries to people bored with surviving on minimal essentials and very little more. No point in arguing though. She put the phone down and poked out her tongue, enjoying the childish response.

It was only eight o'clock. She was too miserable to find herself something to eat. The evening would drag. She had no heart to work on her closing accounts. What was the point? She had a leisurely bath and, choosing a book, went to bed. When Peter came home at ten thirty he ignored her and slept on the very edge of the bed as though touching her would contaminate him. She thought she would never know greater misery.

On Saturday afternoon she decided to go to the pictures. Peter worked on Saturday mornings so she decided to leave before he was due home. If he expected her to prepare lunch he'd be disappointed. Normally she would have stayed in the shop but having agreed to the disposal of her stock she put a notice in the window telling her customers she was closed, sent out a few accounts that were still outstanding and closed the door.

Walking along Sophie Street, she remembered the sweetshop, Temptations, on the corner and stopped to buy some sweets to take to the cinema. The little shop was full. She knew the young woman serving was Rhiannon, Viv Lewis's sister, and stepped back to allow the other customers to be served, and looked at her. Pretty in a shy way, she had long brown hair pinned up high on her head and hanging down her shoulders. Her brown eyes were gentle and friendly, and she chatted to the people she served, obviously knowing them all. When the shop had emptied, Rhiannon turned to her.

"Can I help you?" she asked politely, then she smiled and said, "Oh, you're Miss Francis from the paint shop, aren't you?"

"Mrs Francis, yes. And you're Viv Lewis's sister, I believe."

"That's right." As Rhiannon served Jennie with her selection she wondered whether she had come to ask questions about Viv and Joan. They were sort of rivals, although she had heard that the small shop owned by Jennie was not doing very well. "Shop keeping you busy, is it?" she asked politely.

"Your brother has bought my remaining stock, I no longer have a business."

"Oh. I'm sorry. Starting something new, are you?"

Jennie smiled sadly. "I haven't decided yet." As she turned to leave with her purchases in her hand the door opened and Carl came in closely followed by a plump, dark-haired, rosy-faced girl who said 'whoops' as they all met in the doorway.

"Carl!" Jennie said. "What are you doing here?"

"Same as you I expect, buying sweets."

"I'm sneaking off for five minutes while I'm out buying envelopes for Edward," Mair Gregory explained and it seemed a natural thing to her to introduce herself . . . "I work in the sports shop on High Street. Carl and I know each other," she said. "We met in the shop while he came to buy fishing tackle."

Carl looked very uncomfortable. "Hardly *know* each other," he said, stepping back as though embarrassed.

Mair's normally rosy face became even redder and she laughed and said, "Know each other from the shop, we do. That's all."

Rhiannon was puzzled, both remarks seemed odd. She wondered whether there was more than a brief acquaintence there and, if so, why there was something secretive about it.

When Carl left, Mair hastily followed him. Unable to hide her curiosity, Rhiannon stretched up and watched as they met on the corner and stood for a time apparently arguing, before Mair ran up the street towards the main road. Carl turned in the same direction but made no effort to catch her up.

"I don't think she'll have much luck if she thinks he'll show an interest," Jennie confided. "A loner is Carl Rees and I don't know why."

19

"Married, I bet," Rhiannon said confidently.

Jennie shook her head. "No, I don't think so. He lives in one mean little room in Bella Vista Road and his mother lives near. And that's all I know about the man. Odd, isn't it?"

When she came out of the cinema, Jennie wasn't in a hurry to get home. Why should she rush to cook a meal for a husband who wouldn't eat it? Then she thought that this might be the night when he had calmed down from whatever had caused his anger and would be waiting for her, so she increased her pace as she passed the sweetshop which was now closed, and hurried home. She was breathless when she opened the front door and called, "Peter? Are you there? Dinner won't be long." There was no reply and her shoulders drooped and she wondered how long he was going to sulk this time. It had happened before, this non-communication, but it usually ended after a few days with the explanation that he had been worried about events at work, although she suspected that the discontent, regret, or whatever it was, emanated from his mother, who had protested about her marrying Peter, right up to the day of the wedding.

Slowly she took off her coat and threw it carelessly across the newel post – something Peter hated – and went upstairs to change into slippers. There was a note on the bed.

"I have decided to leave you," it read. No "Dear Jennie", just the bald statement. It went on:

Neither of us is happy and there seems no point in living together when we are so clearly unsuited.

You will be hearing from my solicitor, but in the meantime you can stay in the house and I have returned to live temporarily with my parents.

Peter

She stared at the page for a long time, as though wanting it to be untrue would make it so. What had she done? Why had everything fallen apart? What would she do now?

Two

J ennie had never been in a house alone at night before. Although her parents had died when she was a child, there had always been someone with her. First an aunt, then a series of friends with whom she had shared a flat. Although she was without a family, she had never had to face the ultimate loneliness of sleeping in completely empty house. When she married Peter she had never imagined being alone, and the prospect of sleeping in the house they had shared was frightening. How could he do this to her? Why hadn't he at least discussed it, waited until she could make arrangements, find someone to live in while they sorted out their situation?

She didn't undress, and that made her feel cowardly. The darkness was more than she could bear, so she sat on the bed wrapped in extra blankets with the lights on both in the bedroom and on the landing. She smiled wryly at the thought of Peter's reaction if he found out. Peter hated waste. Remembering this, she went and put on the downstairs lights too.

Sounds alarmed her and brought her out of her light dozing: a cat calling with a pathetic wail, followed by the screeching of a fight when another approached; a creaking floorboard had her sitting up, all her senses alert for danger before she remembered that the old lady next door often got up at night, the footsteps sounding as close as if they were in the next room. She waited, unable to convince herself there was no one in the house, until she heard the flush of a toilet followed by returning footsteps.

It was early morning before she slept and even then she was awake again before seven, fumbling her way out of the excess bedding to go and make a cup of tea. She was thankful the lights were still on. It was bitterly cold and the darkness framed in the windows emphasised the silent emptiness. The place had an alien feel, and the small sounds were somehow distorted by her solitary state. She went down the stairs feeling she were trespassing, that she no longer belonged. As she waited for the kettle to boil she mused sadly over the mystery of how the absence of one person could change the atmosphere of a house so much, so that it felt hollow, unlived-in, lacking in friendliness. She looked at the clock, ticking with exaggerated loudness. Eight fifteen. If this had been a weekday, Peter would be cleaning his shoes as part of his morning ritual. His clothes would be brushed, his tie fixed in an orderly position. He used a napkin while he ate his breakfast to make sure his appearance was immaculate. It was something she had admired: his precise attention to detail. Now she hoped he would drop coffee on his white shirt.

Eight thirty and his mother would be calling, "Peter, will two slices of toast be enough? One egg or two?" Why hadn't he been prepared to leave his parents behind and live his life with her? She had remained an outsider from the first moment she had been introduced to Mr and Mrs Francis. It had been made clear to her even then that Peter was strongly attached to his mother and, as his wife, she would be a poor second. Why had she accepted it? Why had she imagined she would ever be anything else?

When she went to the shop, a little later than usual, both Carl and Viv Lewis were waiting. She had forgotten that Viv had arranged to be there early to collect the goods he had bought. She made half-hearted apologies and opened up. Carl began taking down the shelves and display units he had made such a short time before, while Viv, assisted by two brothers whom he introduced as Frank and Ernie Griffiths, loaded up a rather dilapidated van to take the carpets and tins of paint and the rest of the contents to Westons at the end of High Street. She didn't watch as the van took its final load, busying herself making tea for herself and Carl, pretending she didn't care.

For a while they worked in silence, Carl piling up the shelves and filling in the damage to the walls, and Jennie sweeping and putting the last of the rubbish into sacks. Then she couldn't keep her misery to herself any longer.

"Peter left me yesterday," she said quietly.

"Left you?" Carl asked, spinning round to stare at her. "As in 'gone for good'?"

"It seems that way. He's – he's gone back to mother." She unaccountably saw the funny side of this and began to smile. A bubble of laughter that was based not on humour, but on misery, took her over and she began to laugh. Carl laughed too and the sound increased as the absurdity of the remark caught him afresh.

"She never wanted me to marry her precious son." That too sounded funny. Giggles distorted her voice as she added, "She tried everything to stop him leaving and now – now, she's got him back."

"Serves her right an' all!" Carl said, still unable to stop laughing.

"The worst part is," Jennie sighed, her laughter ceasing as suddenly as it began, "that I don't really know why."

"Why she didn't want you for a daughter-in-law or why he upped and left?" Carl tried to revive the laughter, but failed.

"She didn't want him to marry anyone, and I suppose she eventually convinced him he had made a terrible mistake."

"Mother-in-law jokes are sometimes too close to the truth. Specially the lonely ones who are greedy for a second chance, who try to live again vicariously through their children."

"Personal experience, Carl?" she asked quizzically.

Carl shook his dark head, and smiled. "I'm not cut out for marriage. Too selfish."

"That didn't stop Peter," she said, and this time her laugh was harsh.

The sale at Westons attracted a lot of interest. Joan and Viv Lewis worked all through a weekend, placing posters in the windows as well as displaying some of their best items with prices marked and crossed out and marked again to show the value of the reductions. When the store opened at nine o'clock on Monday morning there was a crowd of hopeful customers waiting.

Dressed against the chill they had formed a ragged queue and were chatting as though they had been waiting for a long time and had become friends.

Surprised, and far from displeased, Joan decided to let them in six at a time. She sent one of the store assistants round to ask Arfon to come and help, although, with so many of the bargains shown in the window, many knew what they wanted before they came in.

Arfon came bustling in, pleased to be asked to help the business that had once been his to manage. His loud, authoritative voice boomed across the showroom as he reminded each customer he served, and others waiting their turn, of the excellent value they were getting for their money.

Victoria and her husband, Jack Weston, Joan's cousin, came and went off well pleased with new carpeting for two bedrooms, placing an order for curtains as well.

"Not buying for a nursery yet then?" Viv teased his friend, and Jack hurriedly changed the subject.

"We going fishing at the weekend?" Jack asked, glancing at his wife and frowning at Viv to warn him not to say any more. Viv guessed from the sad expression on Victoria's face that the lack of children might not be from choice. The exchange hadn't been missed and Victoria said, "My mother had seven and here I am, unable to have one. Odd, isn't it?"

"Plenty of time," Viv said. "Damn me, you need a couple of years to get Jack trained first, mind!"

Janet Griffiths came to stand in the doorway waiting her turn to enter. Behind her stood a very self-conscious Hywel. She looked excitedly around her at the displays that were gradually falling into disarray as item after item found a buyer. Hywel shuffled his feet and wished he was somewhere else, anywhere but in a shop full of chattering women. Viv saw them and whispered to Joan that he would never have imagined the Griffithses needing carpets.

The Griffithses lived in a shabby cottage on the edge of town with their son Frank and their daughter Caroline and her son. The cottage was also home to an assortment of animals including goats, chickens, ducks and, on occasions, a pig or two.

Janet was small and neat, with wiry, untidy hair which started each day in a tight bun which soon defied all efforts at control and flared about her head like seaweed on a subterranean rock. Hywel was not much taller than his wife but he was burly, with a beard almost as unmanageable as Janet's hair. He wore a workman-like, badly stained donkey jacket and a check shirt. His denims were supported by a thick leather belt that was slung under his belly so he looked like a bit-player in a western film. As soon as he entered, trying to hide behind his diminutive wife, Viv, forgetting the other customers, called out, "Bloody 'ell! Hywel Griffiths shopping? Never thought I'd see the day." He pushed aside the assistant who had approached them. "I'll see to Mr and Mrs Griffiths."

"We want something to cover the bedroom floor. Nothing fancy, mind."

"He means a carpet." Janet chuckled. "The first ever, mind."

"What's wrong with them rag rugs you made when we got married?" Hywel grumbled.

"Worn out like you! And that linoleum is bitter cold under my poor feet."

"Good idea, Janet," Viv said, with an unsympathetic face for Hywel. "Time you were spoiling yourself a bit. I'll show you our best bargains."

Dora and Lewis Lewis, Viv's newly reunited parents, bought carpet for a bedroom too, and it seemed to Viv and Joan that half of Pendragon Island had been through the doors of Westons, before they closed at six o'clock on the first day of the sale.

They were leaving the shop at about seven thirty, having stayed to rearrange the diminished stock and tidy the showroom ready for the following day, when Jennie Francis knocked on the window. Joan opened the door and in her forthright manner explained they were just leaving.

"I just wanted to see how it went. Did you have a successful day?"

Relenting, Joan opened the door and invited her in.

"Marvellous," Viv said, then added, "Oh, sorry, I didn't mean to sound so pleased. It's your loss, isn't it?"

25

"You gave me a good price, I'm not complaining. I didn't come for that. I should be able to start again within the year, if I can get a job to pay for my keep, meanwhile."

"Your keep?" Joan asked curiously. "Doesn't your husband do that?"

"Not any more."

"Don't be in too much hurry to start," Viv warned. "I don't worry about competition, mind. But you must see that you wouldn't have much chance trying to compete with us."

"I won't try paint and wallpaper again, and I won't try carpets." She moved towards the door, adding, "Paint and wallpaper weren't my original idea, I was persuaded into that by Peter and his parents. They thought the town wasn't ready for anything as frivolous as a gift shop."

"If we can help—" Viv said, spreading his hands in a vague gesture of offering.

"Come and talk to us when you're thinking of starting again and we'll help if we can," Joan agreed.

Neither of them said 'I', each said 'we' and each knew the other was in agreement, Jennie thought, as she hurried away, preparing herself for entering the empty house.

When she opened the door she knew at once that someone was there. "Peter?" she called and he came out of the living room to stand in the doorway staring at her. "You're back." She tried to hide her relief and pleasure at his return. Then he muttered, "Only briefly," and her heart fell like a broken lift, plummeting to the bottom of her hopes.

"Briefly?"

"There are things we must discuss. Finances for one thing. I'll pay the bills until you get a job then I'll pay half."

"What? You expect me to pay half the expenses of the house? Well, all right, but I'll get a couple of lodgers to help with my half."

"Definitely not!"

They bickered like children for a few moments, each insisting on having their say only for the other to listen without taking anything in, just waiting for their turn to get in a word.

"I've sold the contents of the shop," Jennie said, and that stopped him.

"Good," he said, after a pause, "then you can begin paying your half straight away, can't you?"

"Certainly, as long as your parents don't mind waiting for their money!" she snapped, and they were off again, shouting, arguing, each blaming the other, until Jennie threw down the shopping she carried and pushed him towards the front door. A twist of the latch and she thrust him through. "Speak to me through solicitors in future. Right? Tell your mother that! And," she shouted through the slit of the door, "as of tomorrow, the house is for sale. Right?"

"No! You can't do that! Mam says—"

Jennie slammed the door, then as an idea hit her with sudden and painful shock, she opened it, and said slowly, "There's another woman! You plan to bring her here after you've got rid of me!"

"There's no one else," he replied. They stared at each other for a moment then he asked, "Can I come back in?"

She walked into the kitchen and began preparing her meal, pointedly setting out one plate, one cup and saucer.

Peter shuffled his feet a bit, touching a chair as though about to sit, then changing his mind, and shuffling some more. He was obviously finding it difficult to say what he wanted her to hear. She remained silent.

"You're too independent for me," he said at last. "When we married, I wanted to look after you, I wanted to feel important, needed, in charge of our lives. And there you were, running a business, not being a wife at all. Not needing me for anything, except to keep you while you waited for the shop to provide for you."

"Us," she said quietly. "It was to provide for us." She brought out a couple of rashers of bacon and put them under the grill. The eggs were waiting for the pan to heat. "So we sell the house?"

"It would have been different if we'd had children. You should have had a child."

"Yes, that would have made a difference, wouldn't it? I'd be having to face looking after myself and the child, while earning

27

my living! Your mother would still have persuaded you to leave me. Don't try to tell me different. All this is her doing. Sell the house, Peter. Let's end it thoroughly, shall we?"

"I'll consider it."

"Ask your mother you mean!" When she turned to look at him he was gone.

Rhiannon was closing the shop at lunchtime a week or so later, when Mair Gregory ran in.

"Rhiannon, can you wait while I buy some chocolates? Dairy Box, I think." Smiling, Rhiannon put down the key and prepared to serve her. Mair could easily have bought chocolates on High Street, and she was grateful to her for coming down to buy at Temptations.

"Special occasion?" she asked.

"Only pictures, but in Cardiff and with – guess who?"

"Don't tell me you've finally said yes to poor Frank Griffiths? He's been trying to get a date with you for months."

"No fear. I'm going out with the gorgeous Carl Rees, him that worked in the carpet shop, remember?"

"Then don't buy chocolates, you'll spoil his surprise."

"You mean he's already got some? Great! Perhaps I'll get some peppermints then, in case we get close." She winked and clicked her tongue. "Not a word, mind. We want to keep it a secret for a while."

"What d'you know about him, Mair? He seems to be a bit of a mystery man."

"And all the better for that. Every boy I go out with I've known all my life. I know them all down to their last pimple! It's like going out with one of the family. Been brought up together we have, and with a full knowledge of all the family secrets. Small town stuff. Boring."

"I found Charlie, and I didn't know enough about him to find him boring," Rhiannon said.

"Well that's hardly surprising! Been away in prison hadn't he? He can hardly have – Sorry Rhiannon, I shouldn't have said that. Me and my big mouth. Sorry."

28

"It's all right, Mair. As you say, small town, no secrets."

Rhiannon had learnt a little more about Carl by talking to Jennie, but not enough to satisfy her curiosity. Why should his date with Mair have to be in secret? It was intriguing. Surely she owed it to her friend Mair to find out more, she thought, to ease the guilt of blatant nosiness.

She saw Jennie approaching later that day and, dashing into the back room to put the kettle on, persuaded her to stay for a cup of tea.

"I was sorry to hear that you've closed the shop," she began, "but there wasn't much hope down there out of the main shopping area, was there? Try again, will you? When there's a better spot?"

"This is a long way from the shops too, yet Temptations seems to do well enough. Why is that, d'you think?" Jennie asked.

"Sweets don't take up as much room as carpets and the other stuff you sold. I can carry a great number of lines. And there's the loyalty of customers. They got into the habit of coming here while sweets were rationed and they still make their way here whenever they can. Besides," she added, glancing at Jennie apologetically, "in your case, my brother Viv has got most of the town's business. There wasn't much left for you, was there?"

"I don't intend to sell carpets again, nor paint and wallpaper. What do you think of starting an interior design business?"

"Wrong town! Do it yourself and put the sideboard over the mistakes is more the way of my friends. Frank Griffiths is good at decorating, mind. Really neat with wallpaper, but I doubt whether many people would pay you to let you choose what he puts up."

"Carl Rees is good at those things too. I wonder what he'll do now? Not that he did much work for me, but he did get other work while fitting the few carpets I managed to sell."

"Carpentry, I heard. Any good, is he?"

"Apparently he went to college to do furniture design, but his father died and he had to leave. Money difficulties I suspect. Pity. I think he might have had a successful career. He's still a bit resentful about his lost chances."

29

"He's taking a friend of mine to the pictures tonight."
"Really? I didn't think he bothered with women. Between you
and me, I'd always thought him too mean."

Mair was a bit puzzled by the arrangement to meet Carl on the
six-thirty bus into Cardiff, but she thought it was probably
because of the weather. January wasn't the month to be standing
around waiting for someone, after all. He jumped on several
stops after her and, as she had already paid her fare, bought his
ticket and placed it carefully in his wallet. She handed him hers
and said, "I suppose you might as well keep it. We will be
travelling home together."

"Maybe not," Carl said. "Best if you hold on to it. I have to go
and see someone later, but I'll see you onto the bus."

"Thanks," she said sarcastically. Some date this was turning
out to be. And there was no sign of the chocolates Rhiannon said
he'd bought! He found seats in the back row of the cinema, and
that was encouraging, but he did nothing more than lean over to
take one of the peppermints she offered.

In spite of the disappointments, she agreed to see him again
later that week. The secretive arrangements were rather intriguing and he was good-looking.

"Meet me at the telephone box at the corner of Trap Lane," he
said, as she climbed onto the bus. "Seven on Friday. Okay?"

Once the bus was out of sight Carl stood and waited for the
next one. Better that they didn't travel together more than he
could help. The fewer people who knew, the better. He stamped
his feet against the icy cold coming up from the pavement and
wondered whether Mair had done what he asked and told no one
of their date.

"First on a bus heading out of town, then in a quiet corner on a
dark evening. Is he ashamed of me do you think?" Mair asked
Rhiannon, when she went down to report on her night out.

"A bit shy more like. Perhaps he hasn't been out with many
girls. Anyway, meeting on a bus wasn't exactly hiding you, was
it?"

"No, but he made it look as though we had met by accident. 'Hi,' he said, as though it was a complete surprise. Talk about acting! And sitting in the back row at the pictures wasn't romantic, just another way to avoid being seen."

"No hand holding then?"

"Only to pinch my peppermints." Mair laughed. "I'm meeting him again on Friday, mind. I must be mad."

"Where to this time?"

"Corner of Trap Lane, after dark!"

By the middle of February, Mair and Carl had dated a dozen times and every time, they went to places where no one would recognise them. She was developing a strong attraction for him and their tentative relationship began to grow into something approaching affection or even the beginnings of love, yet she still knew very little about him.

"It isn't that he won't answer questions. He does. But he never seems to tell me anything," she admitted to Rhiannon one lunchtime.

"You do try to get him talking about himself?" Rhiannon asked. "It's easy to ask about family and friends at least, isn't it?"

"Somehow he manages to twist the questions so the words he uses seem like an explanation, but aren't really an answer to what I asked." She sighed. "Then I start to feel embarrassed at my nosiness and shut up."

Sally Weston was one of Gladys and Arfon Weston's twin daughters. Like her twin sister Sian, she no longer had her husband living with her. Ryan lived in a basement flat below the sports shop owned by Edward Jenkins. Both sisters had been supposedly happily married, but a disaster in the firm of Westons Wallpaper and Paint had caused such a furore that the dust had still to settle. Sian's husband, Islwyn, had left her to live with Margaret Jenkins, and Sally's husband, Ryan, had suffered a serious breakdown which had resulted in him hitting his wife. Both men had been directors of the family business until it almost failed for lack of effort on their part.

31

Sally's daughter Joan, was married to Viv Lewis and ran the family business. Her other daughter, Megan, still lived at home with her baby, Rosemary, but would soon be marrying Edward Jenkins and going to live with him in the flat above his sports shop. Then Sally would be completely alone.

The thought frightened her. Keeping a guesthouse meant strangers being there every night and some made her nervous. Jeremy Mullen-Thomas for one.

She told none of her fears to her daughter. Nothing must spoil Megan and Rosemary's chance of a good life and Edward would look after them both, she was certain of that. He adored them and already thought of himself as Rosemary's father. It was Wednesday and half-day closing for the shops in Pendragon Island, so she finished her preparations for the evening meal for the seven house guests and went to the sports shop to talk to her daughter. It was very cold and Sally put on a coat with a fur collar to keep out the chill wind that was blowing in from the sea. The coat was seeing her through the third winter and she thought sadly of how old it was. Until the collapse of the firm, she would never had started a second winter wearing the same coat as the previous one.

"Mummy!" Megan greeted her with obvious relief. "Just in time. Darling Rosemary is very unhappy this morning. Would you walk her for ten minutes while Edward and I complete the order forms?"

"That would be a help, Sally," Edward said. He had decided long ago not to call her mother-in-law. "We're out of skipping ropes and the school children seem to have the skipping craze again. Whip and top too. It's early this year, they usually start those things when it gets warmer, not in cold weather like this."

Sally took the little girl down the road and into the park where the air seemed even colder; with the trees holding down the frost from the previous night. A few children were playing chase and shouting excitedly. On their way back to school and enjoying the last moments of freedom, she guessed, and smiled.

When she returned to the shop, Edward was serving a last customer and the door was already showing the 'closed' notice.

"Come up to the flat and have a bowl of soup and some sandwiches," he said.

"Thanks. I came to discuss the wedding guest list if this is a convenient time," Sally explained.

"Do you agree to Megan's father giving her away?" Edward asked, when they had eaten.

"I don't know," Sally said, glancing down at the floor as though she might see Ryan in the flat two floors below. "Does he want to?"

"Well, not so far," Edward admitted. "But there's time for him to reconsider."

"I see." Sally frowned. "But if he isn't happy about it – might he not be difficult?"

"You are all right about him being there, aren't you? Neither Megan nor I want you to be unhappy on our special day, do we, darling?" Edward smiled at Megan looking for agreement.

"I think he should be there if he wants to be, but we shouldn't try to persuade him." Sally's heart was racing at the thought of the violence her husband had shown her. Could they risk him ruining Megan's wedding day?

Edward thought of his most recent attempt to persuade Ryan to be with his daughter. He had become upset, and had stood, clenching and unclenching his fists in an alarming manner, before announcing angrily that he didn't want to be there to see his daughter display her disgrace to the whole town. Edward decided there was nothing to be gained by him reporting that little scene to either Sally or Megan, so he said nothing.

Sally went home wondering if she would ever be able to trust Ryan again or whether she now had to face living alone for the rest of her life. She thought the latter was the most likely. The last time she had seen Ryan he seemed as resentful as ever, looking at her with such hatred in his eyes that it had chilled her blood.

She stepped into the kitchen and made herself a cup of tea, intending to sit for half an hour and read, to take her mind away from Ryan and the problems he had brought her. A sound startled her and she went through to the hall, wondering if one of her guests had arrived early. Usually they didn't come until evening, but on occasions one of them, Max Powell, who was a stationery salesman, called to pick up stock delivered for him.

"Mr Powell, is that you?" she called. She heard footsteps crossing the landing after a top-floor door closed and her heart sank. It sounded like Jeremy Pullen-Thomas. Where had he got a key? Or had she left the door unlocked?

"I'm glad I caught you," he said, as he ran lightly down the stairs. "I wanted a word before the others return."

"How did you get in, Mr Pullen-Thomas?" she asked stiffly. "You know the house isn't open to guests during the day except by express agreement."

"I got it from old Maxie Powell. He was coming back to collect a delivery, so I asked him to lend it to me. Not a problem, is it?" He was a tall, slim, elegantly dressed forty-year-old and very confident of his appeal to women. Something about him reminded her of Lewis Lewis at his most charming.

"I told him you wouldn't mind," he said, "and promised I'd return it to you as soon as you came in."

"What did you want to see me about that was so urgent?"

"There's going to be a few changes. I thought you'd like to know," he said, casually leaning across the lower banisters and smiling at her.

"Changes?" she asked.

"Yes, Max and I will be changing rooms. I'll be on the second floor instead of the top. Don't worry, we'll deal with it ourselves, you needn't be involved."

Jeremy Pullen-Thomas seemed so certain that everyone would do as he wished, that his presence had begun to frighten her. If she allowed it, he would be taking over completely. He had already persuaded the others to ask for an earlier evening meal, and he had arranged for morning tea to be provided on a rota organised by himself – the occupant of each room taking it in turns to go to her kitchen and attend to the task. She hadn't been consulted until it was too late, and everyone was thanking her for being so thoughtful.

"No, Mr Pullen-Thomas, I don't think that will be convenient. The rooms are different sizes and prices. *I* will decide who uses which one and I thank you to leave the running of the house to me."

"But we both agree," he said, surprise darkening his eyes in a way that reminded Sally of the approach of one of Ryan's rages. Afraid but determined, she said firmly, "And I disagree. And while we're on the subject of who uses which room, I would like you to vacate yours by the morning. I don't want you here after tonight."

"But I usually stay two nights every week. It's a regular arrangement. Look here, if any of the others have complained –"

"I'll have your account ready for you at breakfast time," Sally said, as she returned to the kitchen. She had to face the fact that she would be doing this for many years and she would be on her own. She had to be strong, and only have people staying about whom she was completely happy. Max Powell was no trouble and no threat. She would tell him tonight that if he wanted the smaller, less expensive room in future he only had to ask. With a sigh of relief, feeling ridiculously pleased with herself, she began to think about the meal.

Megan would be pleased that Pullen-Thomas would not be back, she hadn't liked the man either. Feeling stronger and more in control, she began to hum a tune as she worked.

Sally went out again later that day, this time to see her sister, Sian.

"The wedding," she explained. "What are we doing about food?"

"Mother wants Montague Court. Can you imagine the fun there'd be with Edward's sister Margaret, like a wicked fairy at the feast? No, I think both Edward and Megan want a quiet affair and it will probably be Gomer Hall again."

"Poor Mummy," Sally said. "She'll probably cry." They both laughed at the thought of telling Gladys that her last hope of a grand wedding was going to be quashed.

"I'm glad Megan and Edward are getting married," Sally said. "Plans for a new one helps to take my mind off the remnants of mine."

"And mine." Sian sighed. "Thank goodness we won't be celebrating at Montague Court! Talk about a pantomime! Besides Edward's ugly sister, my one-time husband would be there, as Buttons, playing a waiter."

"Sorry, Sian, for the moment I was so wrapped up in my own mess, I'd forgotten yours."

"At least the youngsters seem happy."

"I thought we were," Sally reminded her with another deep sigh.

"Habit, that's what it had become. And enough money to help us pretend. It was little more than that," Sian said with a sigh that matched her sister's.

Gladys Weston told her husband that she would have to swallow her pride and ask Victoria's mother to come and help in the house.

"I can't do it all, Arfon, dear. Not after being used to having a servant."

"No, Gladys. You mustn't ask Mrs Collins to clean for you, it wouldn't be right. Jack would be furious if we had his wife's mother working for us. Good heavens, woman, can't you see that?"

"I do see that, but I've been trying for weeks to find someone, and all the young girls want better pay and not much work. I don't know whether you realise it, Arfon Weston, but running a house is hard work!"

"I'll ask Viv. See if he knows someone." He knew it wouldn't be easy, Gladys had a reputation for squeezing the last ounce of effort from anyone she employed.

"Why bother to ask Viv, dear? He's one of the Lewises and they'd hardly be experts in employing help in the house."

"Viv and our Joan know a lot of people. It's worth a try."

"If you say so, dear, but I do so hate mixing with the Lewises."

Arfon didn't reply as he tried to disguise a smile. He knew it was hopeless to argue. Gladys would never think of the Lewises as more than peasants. Since Joan had married Viv Lewis and undertaken to help him run the family business, Gladys had been waking each morning hoping the whole thing had been nothing but a cruel dream.

Gladys and Arfon had spoilt Joan and Megan who had been used to getting their own way about everything and had been taught to accept nothing but the best. Gladys had thought this a certain way of making sure the girls married well, avoiding the mistakes that Sally and Sian had made. Lazy, useless men her sons-in-law had turned out to be: Ryan, suffering what was euphemistically called a breakdown, which Gladys considered to have been brought on by remorse and shame; Islwyn, leaving Sian and going to live with Margaret Jenkins. Now she was facing another wedding. It was her last chance of showing everyone how it ought to be done but Megan was insisting that, again, it wouldn't be the town-stopping wedding for which she had hoped.

Their one grandson, Jack, taught at the local school. Jack had also offended Gladys's standards of social niceties by marrying Victoria Collins who had been her servant. She sighed. She'd had such high hopes of her grandchildren, dreaming of them marrying the rich and powerful, but both Joan and Jack had married employees, and she still couldn't accept it. At least Megan was marrying one of the Jenkinses of Montague Court, a family with an ancient tradition even if they were impoverished. She mulled over the word 'impoverished', it had a rather elegant ring, far better than 'poor'.

Edward Jenkins and his sister Margaret had run their home as a hotel until financial problems after the death of their parents had forced them to sell. Now Edward had a sports shop in the town, and his sister worked in Montague Court with Islwyn, Sian's husband. Even thinking about that woman made Gladys's anger rise. Not content with stealing her son-in-law away from his wife and son, she was living with him here, right in the town, for Gladys's friends to see. No shame, no embarrassment, she and 'Issy', as she called him, were to be seen walking through the town as bold as you like and even calling to see Islwyn's son, Jack. She lowered her head so Arfon wouldn't see her eyes filling with tears. What had she done to cause such a mess?

Arfon did see that she was upset, and said gruffly, "Don't worry Gladys, I'll find you someone to help in the house."

"Thank you dear," she said, glad to use the excuse for her tears he offered.

During the cold months of January and February, Mair and Carl had met a number of times, mostly to go into Cardiff, meeting on the bus, to go to a cinema or just to walk around before finding a cafe to warm themselves and have something to eat. Mair wondered whether he would fade out of her life as the nights opened out into spring and the darkness was no longer available as a place to hide.

One Saturday evening, when she had not arranged to go out, she became restless, thinking about the ridiculous situation and wondering whether she could demand an explanation, a better one than the futile excuses he had so far given. There was no way of getting in touch with him and, suddenly, Saturday night was not a night to stay home alone. Her father was on duty from ten o'clock and, when he left their cottage at the edge of the wood to cycle into the town, she went with him.

"Where are you going at this time of night?" he asked in surprise when she reached for a coat, pulled on fur-lined boots and stood at the door. "Gone nine o'clock it is."

"I'm going to the Railwayman's," she said, glaring at him, daring him to disapprove.

"Meeting anyone?"

"I hope so! Someone who'll make me laugh, tell me I'm wonderful, help me to forget this boring Saturday evening!"

"That Frank Griffiths'll be there, mind," he warned.

"I'll even settle for Frank. I was up at six, working in the shop from nine till half-past five and I come home to an evening sitting on my own, staring at the walls. What a life!"

"No Carl?"

"Carl?" she asked, startled. "What d'you know about Carl?"

"Carl Rees, who worked for Jennie Francis and now does a few carpet-fitting jobs for Westons and any other job he can find."

"I didn't think you knew," she said lamely. "We haven't told anyone. Except Rhiannon. I bet Frank knows too," she added.

"Of course I know. D'you think I wouldn't find out something about a fellow you were seeing, Mair? What sort of a father d'you think I am, eh? Specially someone who you don't tell me about. Got curious, didn't I?"

"He's a bit shy, that's all. Nothing sinister. He'll be working all the weekend, or so he says. Fixing shelves and cupboards and decorating a kitchen for someone."

"Like Frank? He does painting and papering and a bit of carpentry, doesn't he?"

"Yeh, but when Carl fits shelves they don't fall down!"

"Be fair, Frank does a good job, when he can be persuaded to work."

"Carl is a craftsman, Dad," she argued.

"Frank is cheaper! Come on then," he urged, "you'll be cold on your bike, mind."

"My bad temper will keep me warm!"

In spite of her bravado, Mair didn't like walking into the public house alone. Women rarely did and, even though she would know most of the customers already there, she had to force herself to go in, and not turn and cycle back home. There was a gale of laughter as she opened the swing doors and stepped gratefully into the steamy warmth. The fire burned brightly at the end of the bar and round the room there was a sea of faces, most of them red with sweat and over-indulgence.

She saw Basil and Frank Griffiths straight away; With Viv and his wife, Joan, they had formed a group in the corner behind the entrance, their usual place. Frank saw her at once and stood up to greet her, his long gangly legs stepping over knees and tripping over feet in his haste.

"Mair. Nice surprise." He looked expectantly at the door. "You with someone then?"

"Not unless he's invisible!"

"What you havin' then? Port an' lemon, is it?"

She thanked him and went to where the others were making room for her next to Joan. "Who we talking about tonight?" she asked in a hoarse whisper.

"You'll do for a start," Basil said. "What's this about you

39

going out with that Carl Rees and him trying to keep it a secret?"

"Keeping it a secret? In Pendragon Island? There's more hope of two Christmases in a year!"

"Keeps you out of sight though, doesn't he?" Frank said. "That's not natural."

"That's not your business either, Frank Griffiths!" she retorted.

Someone entered the pub but stood in the doorway, out of sight of the group in the corner, and Viv shouted, "Shut that flamin' door!"

"Sorry," a voice said, and both Mair and Frank recognised Carl's voice from the single word. He came round the doorway and was clearly shocked when Mair stood up, glass in hand and waved to him. "Mair! I didn't expect to see you here."

"Nor me you. Been working, have you?" she asked, although she already knew that he had.

"Yes, putting up kitchen cupboards, but I ran out of wall plugs and it didn't seem worth starting on something else so late."

He went to the bar and ordered a pint and came back to stand near the group, but away from Mair, who tried in vain to appear indifferent. No one offered to find him a seat and he was reluctant to push in without being invited to do so. So he stood, sipped his drink and looked around the room at the groups involved in their various discussions, some producing laughter and others frowns of disapproval. He wished he hadn't come.

Viv turned to Frank and said, "Got a job for you, if you want it."

Frank groaned. "Not more decorating?"

"Afraid so. Jack and Victoria want a bedroom smartened up. They've bought new carpet an' all, they have."

"Not a nursery?" Joan asked.

"Jack didn't say," he said evasively. "But if Frank goes to see them, he can report back, eh?"

"Don't be ridiculous, Viv. Jack's my cousin, I can ask him!"

Remembering Victoria's sad face, Viv hoped she wouldn't.

Carl was obviously listening but didn't join in as Jack and

Victoria were discussed. When there was a lull, he leant over and asked Viv, "Any chance of a bit of fishing next weekend? I might be able to borrow Jennie Francis's van now she doesn't have a use for it. We could go down west and try a bit of sea fishing, the tides are suitable for an evening session."

Viv agreed to ask Jack. Basil thought he might join them, but Frank said nothing. If Carl was fishing, it might be an ideal time to call on Mair.

There was a shuffling of feet as Viv and Basil went to buy more drinks. This time they asked Carl for his choice but he shook his head. He looked at Mair when the opportunity came and gestured with a slight movement of an eyebrow for her to leave. He made his excuses and left and, within a few minutes, Mair followed. She didn't get up at once, but relaxed as though settled for the rest of the evening. She waited until Frank was at the bar. She didn't want him spoiling things by following them. Carl was waiting for her outside.

"I wanted to come and see you but it was a bit late and your father wouldn't have been pleased if I suggested a walk, would he?"

"Dad isn't there," she said, as she began to walk beside him pushing her bicycle. "He's on nights this week."

"In that case I'll see you safely home. But, love, can't we dump this bike? It's like a mobile chastity belt and its digging into my hip something awful."

Laughing, she pushed it into some bushes, where she guessed it would be safe until morning and they strolled on, arm in arm along the crisply cold country lane. Opening the cottage door the warmth that met them was not as welcoming as that of the Railwayman's.

"I bet the fire's out." she sighed. "Hardly worth lighting it."

"Oh, I don't know. You shouldn't go to bed cold, you won't sleep for ages if you do."

Gathering some sticks from the pile in the hearth, Carl soon had the fire burning and at once the room had a more friendly feel. The living room was small, over-full of furniture, with shelves of knick-knacks in every available space. It had the

41

clutter of years displayed and, for the first time, Mair recognised its unworldliness and felt embarrassed. She had changed very little in the house in the years she had been looking after it. Conscious that its carelessly arranged, old-fashioned muddle was her mother's and father's choices, she had been hesitant to suggest modernising. Now she wished she had.

"I love this room," Carl surprised her by saying. "It's warm, and friendly and it makes me realise what I've missed not having a family. It's the centre of people's lives, just like a home should be."

"There's only me and our dad," she said. "He likes it this way. The clutter is to hide the emptiness, I think."

Carl stood up from the grate, where he had brushed the hearth clean, and waved his coal-blackened hands in front of her playfully. "Take me to the kitchen or I'll clean them off on your pretty face." He washed his hands then put the kettle on to heat, taking out cups and adding tea to the teapot as though he had been there before.

Looking through a slit in the carelessly closed curtains, Frank had the same thought and was saddened. He left and went back to where he had seen Mair leave her bicycle. Perhaps he'd collect it and deliver it to her tomorrow morning. He tried never to miss an opportunity to call. Surely that showed her how much he cared? A Griffiths, visiting a copper?

When he had made the tea Carl sat on the couch and pulled Mair onto his lap. Slowly, his hands caressing her body and, he turned her to face him. He wrapped his arms around her and held her close, sliding down on the worn old couch with a sigh that made her tremble. Then he kissed her. It was the first time and, being nervous, she had to make a joke of it.

"Better than the pictures, eh?"

He kissed her again and soon it was no longer funny, it was the most wonderful sensation and she didn't want him to stop, ever. She had kissed any number of boys but the feelings Carl evoked were new to her. The kiss didn't stop with her lips but spread in

42

waves of urgent excitement throughout her body. Desire was strong and demanding, the need for fulfilment reaching through her nerve ends to the tips of her toes and she knew she was too weak to refuse him.

He lifted her up, his lips still firing her body with longing, and carried her to the foot of the stairs where he raised his face slightly above hers, staring deeply into her eyes, and tilted his head, a query for which there was only one answer.

Frank watched as the lights in the small cottage went on and then off; downstairs and then up, telling him a story he didn't want to be told. It was freezing. The ground crackled beneath his feet. The cold air penetrated through his clothes but he still didn't move. Surely Mair wasn't in her bed with Carl? It couldn't be happening. It couldn't, he kept telling himself.

It would be a good night to get a couple of pheasants, Farmer Booker would be in his warm bed if he had any sense. But he didn't have the heart for it. Not tonight when he had to accept that Mair would never belong to him.

He went home and tried to sleep, but his imagination kept wandering back to Mair, and to the lights on and then off, in the Gregorys' cottage. At five o'clock he took a shotgun and called to a rather reluctant dog, thinking that he might get a couple of birds after all, and went silently back through the trees to watch outside the cottage. The night was quiet and still. Frost glistened on the ground and on the gates. He stood just within the trees, guessing that with Constable Gregory due home in little less than an hour, Carl would have to leave soon. In his patient way, he stood against a tree, hunched his shoulders within his coat and watched. At his feet the dog curled up and leant against his skinny legs, trying to find a little warmth.

It was five thirty when the light went on in the bedroom. It was so quiet that Frank heard the tinny sound of an alarm clock ringing. Cautious bloke, this Carl Rees, he thought. Not a man to take risks. He wondered where the risk was in letting people know he and Mair were courting? Did Carl have a wife somewhere? Perhaps if I can find out, he mused, I could warn Mair and comfort her when she was confronted with the fact. Then he shook away the stupid daydream of Mair falling into his arms. *If I were the one to tell her, she'd hate me more than she'd hate Carl.*

He saw lights go on downstairs and within a few minutes the back door opened and Carl came out. At the corner of the building, he saw Mair. She waved, but the man didn't turn and acknowledge her salute. He put his head down and hurried off down the lane.

Frank followed.

Carl lived in a row of seven houses called Bella Vista. Large properties with three rows of windows, the topmost jutting out of the roof in a gable, they had once been homes for the middle-class wealthy. Now they were run down and sadly in need of repair. Paint had peeled, showing the effect of weather damage; wet winters and dry summers had each done their worst. The exposed wood had softened into an ugly drabness.

The once-splendid houses had been divided into separate dwellings: mostly bedsits, a few two-roomed apartments with a shared kitchen and a bathroom, and one or two flats. Frank watched as Carl went into number four. No lights came on, the front door closed softly behind him and there was no other sign or sound of his entering. After waiting for half an hour, without knowing what he was waiting for, Frank turned and went home. The next day he didn't wake until eleven and he then went straight down to Bella Vista and chatted to neighbours and to the woman in the corner shop, gathering as much information about Carl as he could. It wasn't much.

"The man's a mystery," he said to his father when he went home to eat. "I think Mair ought to be warned that if someone is secretive it's usually because he's got something nasty to hide."

"Mair's a sensible girl, Frank. She wouldn't be taken in by someone like that." Hywel said.

Hywel was uncomfortable with this sort of conversation. If he told the truth and said he thought Mair was a tart, Frank would start a fight. and if he said she was gullible, then that would be wrong too. "Go an' talk to your mam," he said.

Three

T he Griffiths family lived in an almost self-sufficient way, growing food, poaching fish, rabbits and wildfowl, bartering for the rest of their needs and working when absolutely necessary. Janet and Hywel had three sons, although one of them, Ernie, was in fact a nephew who Janet and Hywel had adopted when he was a baby. Basil and Ernie were married: Basil happily, to Eleri who had once been the wife of Dora and Lewis's son, Lewis-boy, who had died in an accident; Ernie less contentedly, to Helen, whose parents were trying to educate him into the proper way to behave. Frank was unmarried and his dream was to be wed to Mair Gregory although he had very little hope of that ever happening.

Janet and Hywel had one daughter and for her, married bliss seemed an impossible dream. She had been expecting a child, when her future husband Joseph Williams, had been killed and her marriage to Joseph's brother Barry hadn't worked out. Caroline now lived at home with her parents and worked in a wool shop in town. Her son, Joseph-Hywel was looked after by her mother during the day and Janet sadly thought that the arrangement wouldn't change.

Hywel and his sons were well known to the police due to their persistent poaching. Taught by their father, the boys were experts and, although often caught, their efficiency at gathering fish, fowl and game to sell was legendary. Basil, now married and with two small sons, went out only rarely and Ernie, too, was caught up in the attentions of his new wife.

Frank still roamed the fields at night mostly to satisfy himself that he still had the skills, and to take home one or two items for the family pantry. Sometimes with Hywel but more often alone, he wandered the fields and woods and river banks, knowing every path and short cut, unerringly finding his way on the blackest of nights. He boasted that he could find his way home blindfold.

Frank followed Mair again the following night. She again left at the same time as her father, and again entered the Railwayman's to sit with Viv, Basil and Jack. This time she didn't stay long and left before Carl, without exchanging a glance with him.

Frank guessed their plans. So devious he thinks he is, he said to himself as he rose to follow: pretending not to know her, and then staying the night. Why can't she see how he's using her?

Pushing Mair's bicycle into a gap in the hedge as they had done on the previous night, Carl and Mair walked along the dark lane hand in hand. Frank followed like a cartoon character, slipping from cover to cover, lost in shadow, and not making a sound on the crisp cold ground.

He watched as the bedroom light flicked on then off, ending all hope of Carl being turned away. The darkness was a comfort to him. Frank didn't go home, just wandered around his regular haunts, making small circuitous forays through the trees returning regularly to see whether there was a light showing or any other sign that Carl was leaving. Imagining him there with Mair was painful, but he knew that even if Carl hadn't been the one there would have been someone other than himself. Mair considered him a fool – if she considered him at all.

Although there was no moon and few houses offering even the slightest light, Frank moved around the wood as though it was daytime, listening to the small rustling sounds as the denizens of the woodland went about their night's activities. But instead of seeing the creatures in his mind's eye and imagining their perambulations in search of food, he could only see the bedroom of the Gregory's cottage, and two people there making love.

At three a.m. he stopped his aimless roaming through the narrow, almost invisible paths made by the animal population of the wood. An expert at keeping still he stood, unmoving, leaning against a tree and watching Mair's house. He wasn't tired. He was used to being out most of the night, but he felt a weariness that was due solely to the realisation that Mair was lost to him. He spent the next two hours motionless, listening to the sounds of the night and planning ways to annoy Carl.

Carl left at five thirty, allowing plenty of time before Mair's father was likely to return. Always secretive, Frank thought with a sneer, although, this time he had good reason. Big Carl might be, but Constable Gregory wouldn't be an easy man to manage if he caught him with his daughter. The Griffithses were frequently in trouble for fighting and Frank felt rage growing and swelling inside him; he allowed it to develop, enjoying it, until he was actually moving towards the tall figure hurrying away from the cottage. But he held back. What good would it do? It would only alienate Mair even further. Slowly, anger subsided leaving a dull, aching sadness in its wake.

He waited until the bedroom light was extinguished, then quietly went to collect her bicycle and placed it outside the back door where Mair was certain to see it. She would guess who put it there, and perhaps experience a couple of guilty moments.

For no reason, Frank watched the house until the wavering light of Constable Gregory's bike appeared. House lights told of his movements as he went into the kitchen to make tea before going upstairs where a light appeared in the bedroom as he apparently changed out of his uniform before coming down again. Creeping closer, Frank heard him scraping together the ashes of the fire, and he stepped back as the door opened and the constable came out to collect wood and coals to relight it. There was a yell, a stream of invective and Frank saw that Mair's father had tripped over the bike. Chuckling, he loped off on his long legs, through the wood and home.

In the continuing absence of Peter, Jennie was still uneasy in the house at night. Sometimes she dozed fully dressed on the bed, at other times she fought her fears and half undressed, before giving in to her nervousness and adding a dressing gown and extra blankets and sitting propped up with pillows, waiting for dawn.

She became expert at recognising the various sounds, listening and becoming attuned to the very different world of the darkness hours. She learnt to know every noise and when to expect that wonderful moment when the light changed and dawn crept around the curtains. She was surprised at how early the day began. Even in the winter, there were sounds long before she had expected them. Birds began to stir and neighbours rose, to visit the bathroom, or open the door for a dog, or sometimes to stoke a fire, hopeful of reviving it. Men's feet passed as they set off for work, with murmured conversations.

The milkman was often the first to relieve her feeling of isolation, whistling as his chinking bottles were left, one beside each front door, his van purring away to his next stop. No matter how she pretended, Jennie always welcomed these sounds, grateful for the end of the worst of her loneliness.

Windy nights were most unsettling, with unexplained sounds frightening her by their suddenness, encouraging fanciful thoughts of damage or of someone breaking in. On these nights she didn't go to bed at all, but sat near the fire drowsily waiting for the hours to pass. She kept the fire alight, its occasional flickering a comfort and the snap of a piece of wood or a fall of coals friendly sounds.

In her angriest moments she blamed Peter's mother. In her saddest she blamed herself. In her weakest she wished Peter's mother were dead.

She needed to contact Peter and speak to him without the presence of his mother. She thought that if they met they might start talking and come to see their present separation as a mistake. She searched her mind for an excuse. Any bills that came, she re-addressed and posted to him at his parents' home. There seemed no excuse for her to go and see him, and she was too proud to go without one. She remembered that the front window was rattling and needed fresh putty. Was that a reason to call? To warn him of the extra expense if the window fell out in a strong wind? March was always a wild month.

That evening, when she knew Peter was home from work and would have eaten his meal, she knocked on a door through which, in normal circumstances, she would have walked. Peter answered and at once he glanced behind him clearly not wanting his mother to see her there.

"What d'you want?" he asked coldly.

"There's work needed on the house and I thought you should know," she answered, equally indifferent.

He reached up and snatched a coat from the row of hooks and checked his pockets for a torch, as he called to tell his parents he was going for a walk. Slamming the door behind him he began to stride off down the road. Mulishly she stood beside the door and waited until he turned, waited for her, then walked back.

"Aren't you coming?"

"Why wasn't I allowed in? Am I likely to soil the carpets with my shoes? Or poison the air?"

He had the grace to mutter, "Sorry." She waited and he added, "It's just that I didn't want to start Mam off again."

"That I can understand. All this is because your mam won't allow you to think for yourself, isn't it?

"Why haven't you found a job?"

"There isn't anything available at present, at least, nothing I'd enjoy. I want to work for myself." Why should she get a job she thought as she walked beside him watching his face, curled up with – what? Anger? Frustration? As soon as she had a wage coming in he would only pay half of her outgoings on the house. Some incentive for getting work!

"You're being difficult."

"Yes, I am. I'm following your mother's teachings."

"Don't keep on about Mam, the decision that our marriage was ended was mine not hers."

"There is a job going that I'm pretty sure I would get," she said. "Old Gladys Weston wants a cleaner. How about that?"

"Don't be ridiculous!" He snorted. "Mam would – I mean – I would be embarrassed."

"I heard you the first time," she said sadly.

Peter saw her home but didn't stay to make sure she was safely inside. Standing for a moment outside the house where they had begun their married life he was filled with disappointment. He

49

hadn't wanted to buy a house. They should have lived with his parents for a year or two and saved properly so they could have afforded something better. But no, Jennie had to have her own way, as usual.

He didn't return to his parents' house straight away. He walked around the empty streets of the town, fumingly angry at life, and how badly it had treated him. Mam had been right about Jennie, he admitted. She was selfish, greedy for her own success instead of supporting him in his career. She was constantly letting him down. He remembered the leaving do for Freddy Parker. He had been asked to give a speech and she hadn't bothered to remember.

Mam had warned him she wasn't a loving, caring woman. Jennie was too thin she had told him, and vain. A wife needed to be plump and affectionate; Jennie was neither. She had said the same about any girl he had brought home. Fat girls are happy, and not constantly worrying about their appearance and whether they can attract other men, she had said. He had often laughed at her insistence that his girlfriends needed to be plump, but perhaps she had been right about that, too? Perhaps Jennie was too attractive? He remembered taking her arm and being aware of its thinness. It had been repulsive then, in his anger and hurt, but now he remembered it as vulnerable and wished she needed him and hadn't caused everything to fall apart.

Most of the shops in Pendragon Island closed for the half day on Wednesdays. Rhiannon often went back to Temptations to clean the top shelves and do other tasks while the shop was closed. This had become a little difficult as Barry Williams, who owned Temptations met his estranged wife in his flat above the shop each Wednesday in an attempt to give their marriage one more try. Hearing them arriving, and moving about as they made tea and settled to talk was rather embarrassing. These days, if she did go back after lunch, she no longer stayed more than an hour. Caroline and Barry's marriage had been on and off more times than Rhiannon could remember. She wondered whether they would ever be content, or if the ghost of Barry's brother, who had died in the same crash that killed her own brother, Lewis-boy, would always be there, between them.

One Wednesday at the beginning of March she decided to take Gwyn's dog, Polly, and go for a walk instead of trying to work in the closed shop. She had a lot to think about. She was almost certain she was pregnant again. Having lost a baby the previous September she was in no hurry to tell people. Too many told meant too many explanations if it went wrong again. Charlie knew, of course, and he was thrilled and so was Gwyn. But fear of a repeat disaster made her hesitate to make the news generally known, although, she knew it was time to tell her mother.

Rhiannon's feet took her to Dora and Sian's cafe that cold but sunny afternoon. The wind that had tormented the town for several days had stopped and the debris of a few fallen tree branches were littering the streets. The steamy windows of the cafe told her it was full. For years it had been a place for women to meet for a cup of tea and a gossip, and the service provided by her mother and Sian Weston had increased its popularity.

Stepping inside, engulfed by the warmth, she wondered how to begin her announcement. She looked at Dora, searching for the words, unable to hide her smile and didn't need to explain.

"A new baby on the way, Rhiannon, love?" Dora whispered, as she found a table for her daughter and promised tea and lemon pancakes.

"Mam! How did you guess?"

"Don't really know, something about the shape of your face, and the look in your eyes I think. Hang on while I see to these customers and I'll be back." She busied herself dealing with the requests at two newly occupied tables then told Sian that she was going to talk to Rhiannon.

"Take your time, I'll manage for ten minutes or so," Sian replied.

"So, when's it due?" Dora asked. "Oh, I should say congratulations or something first, shouldn't I? I'm very pleased for you both, love, and so will your dad be, you know that."

"I am pleased of course, but I don't feel able to talk about it yet. You and Charlie and Gwyn are the only ones to know."

"Losing a baby like you did is bound to make you anxious, but there's no reason to suppose the same thing will happen. When's it due?" she repeated, patting her daughter's hand.

"September. The same month I lost the last one."

"What a perfect time to have a baby! He'll be sitting up and taking notice in time for the spring. Wonderful. Now, how long will you go on working at Temptations?"

"Charlie wants me to leave straight away."

Dora took her lead from the doubtful look on her daughter's face. "But you'd rather continue for a while?"

"I'd worry more sitting in the house with nothing to do, wouldn't I? Sit there panicking at every twinge and waiting for a repeat disaster."

"Come on, Rhiannon! This isn't like you, worrying about nothing at all."

"I couldn't bear the disappointment of losing another child."

"For lots of women, a first pregnancy ends in disappointment. Some don't realise it's anything more than a late period." She mentioned her own experience, although it was something she still had difficulty discussing. "Your dad and me, we still think about the baby we lost, you know. Before we had Lewis-boy and our Viv and you. Full term he was and we lost him. So, if anyone understands how you're feeling it's me and your dad." She watched her daughter's face sadden even more, regretted mentioning it, and said brightly, "Come to supper tonight, you and Charlie and young Gwyn. We'll celebrate the news and decide who to tell next."

"Viv, of course, and Eleri and Basil."

"Of course our Eleri. Lewis-boy's lovely wife. That was another loss of a child," Dora couldn't help saying. "Our Lewis-boy was a grown man, but his death in that stupid accident was just as hard. Harder really, we'd had him for so long we believed him to be a permanency." What a lot of other troubles his death had revealed, she remembered with sadness. Revelations that had split herself and Lewis up and had her life tumbling about her ears.

Dora and Lewis still thought of Eleri as their daughter-in-law, even though Lewis-boy was dead and she was now happily married to Basil Griffiths and had two small sons. For Rhiannon too, Eleri was still the sister she had always wanted.

"Eleri will be pleased, won't she? Charlie and I want her and Basil to be the baby's godparents."

This was more positive thinking, Dora was pleased to notice, and when Rhiannon left half an hour later she relaxed, believing that Rhiannon's fears had been soothed away.

Charlie was home when Rhiannon dragged a tired Polly through the back garden gate and opened the back door.

"Charlie! This is a surprise. Mr Windsor let you off early, did he?"

"I thought we'd go out tonight, to the pictures, there are one or two Gwyn might like to see."

"Oh, but Mam's invited us all to supper," she interrupted. "If that all right with you?"

"You've told her then?"

"Thrilled she is. I expect she'll be looking out knitting patterns the minute she gets home."

"Good on 'er!" Seeing that his mother-in-law had succeeded in lifting Rhiannon out of her apprehensive mood, he added, "I'll slip up to High Street and buy her some gorgeous flowers, shall I?"

"Good on you, too," she teased, with a smile.

"I asked Mr Windsor for more work today but he refused," Charlie told them as they ate supper in 7 Sophie Street. "I want Rhiannon to pack up work and stay home. We three have to enjoy these next few months. The build up to the new arrival should be special, don't you think so, Dora?"

"Yes, and no. These next few months will be specially sweet, but I don't think Rhiannon is ready to give up her job yet."

"Mr Windsor said he doesn't want our Dad to do more work because he needs him to be efficient and hardworking but not tired," Gwyn explained. "He said a car mechanic is a very important person, didn't he, Dad?"

"He told me that once, a long time ago, he heard someone refer to him as, 'only a mechanic'," Charlie explained, "and he realised then that his job, his skills, were far more important than some believed. We put cars on the road knowing they are as safe as we can make them, he reminded us. People depend on us, people like me and Gwyn, for their safety."

"And that's big responsibility," Gwyn added proudly. He loved his work.

"So, no overtime for Charlie," Rhiannon said, "and, as I want to carry on working, we'll have a chance to put a bit by for the new baby. There's a lot it will need."

"I wish we knew whether it was a boy or a girl," Gwyn sighed "I hate saying 'it'."

"Let's call it he-she, and cover the choices," Lewis smiled.

"Now, Rhiannon, come and look at these knitting patterns and tell me what you think we'll need," Dora said. She was surprised when Charlie, Rhiannon and Gwyn looked at each other and laughed.

Baby talk was an occasional subject for discussion in 19 Philips Street, where Sian Weston's son, Jack, lived with his wife, Victoria. They both wanted a child and having no luck was beginning to worry them. "It's so odd, with my mother producing seven, that I can't manage one," was Victoria's oft repeated statement. "Perhaps I should get a job," she said. Word had reached them, via Viv and Joan, of Rhiannon's happy news and for Victoria it was an added reminder of her own failure.

"Do you want a job?" Jack asked curiously. "What would you do?"

"Work in a shop? I don't know. Perhaps I should look for some voluntary work. Or work in a nursery. I'm used to children after all – even though I don't have one of my own."

"Leave it for a while. You seem to find plenty to do, both here and helping your mother from time to time."

"I saw Eleri and Basil last week with their two boys. Eleri is thinking of going back to work in the cinema and she wants someone to look after the children occasionally, on the days

when there's a matinee performance and Basil isn't there. What
d'you think?"

Jack hugged her and said, "Whatever you want to do is fine by
me, you know that, love."

Victoria's mother, Mrs Collins, was a widow who lived in
Goldings Street, with six of her seven children. She taught piano,
but only to third grade. Her pupils then went to another, more
confident, teacher. So, needing to earn more money, she had
taken two cleaning jobs, depending on Victoria to stay with the
youngest children sometimes.

One job was at the house on Chestnut Road which had been
the home of Nia Williams and her son Barry and which she had
also shared with Lewis Lewis, when Dora had discovered their
affair. She had died in the garden. After his mother's death,
Barry had lived there for a while with his wife, Caroline. But
when Caroline had gone home to live with her parents Barry had
eventually sold the place, glad to be rid of its memories.

It had been bought by a brother and sister Martha Adams, a
war widow, and her brother, Sam Lilly. Originally Mrs Collins
had gone daily for two weeks to help them clean up and settle in,
now they needed her one day each week to clean floors and dust
and polish furniture.

She quite enjoyed the work, the couple had some beautiful old
furniture which was a pleasure to polish and leave glowing with
the patina of years, and the work wasn't hard. Mrs Adams was
rather critical, but her brother compensated by helping Mrs
Collins move heavy furniture and even doing some of the more
unpleasant chores, like carrying coal and logs.

One afternoon while she was in the park with two of her small
children, pushing one on a swing and watching the other crawl-
ing around on the grass, Mr Lilly saw them and came over.

"Are these your children, Mrs Collins?" he asked, doffing his
trilby politely.

"Only some of them," she smiled. "There are more at home!"

"You have more?"

"There are seven but my eldest daughter is married and living

55

in a house of her own. She married Jack Weston, a school teacher," she said proudly.

"If you'll excuse my impertinence, you don't look old enough to have a married daughter."

"I'm forty-three," she replied, never having had a problem admitting to her years. "My daughter was married last summer and, would you believe it, she and Jack – who is a grandson of the grand and important Gladys and Arfon Weston no less – couldn't face the big wedding the Weston family wanted, so they ran off, telling no one but me, and were married in Gretna Green."

"How splendid! Tell me more," he begged.

She wondered afterwards why she had relaxed so easily with a man she hardly knew. They had talked for a while, exchanging details of their lives, Sam taking his turn at playing with the children, pushing the swing and playing chase round the shrubs. When the town hall clock struck four, they both seemed suddenly aware of how much time they had spent there, and parted with reluctance.

In 1956, March was a month that wouldn't make up its mind whether spring was on the way or winter was hanging on. Some days had the air of excitement that the promise of spring sometimes brings but there were other days when winter seemed set firmly in place for several more weeks. One dark night when there was no moon but when the sky was full of stars and the ground was stiff with frost, Mair stood waiting for Carl. She stamped her feet in her fur-lined boots and jigged on the spot. She even tilted one foot back and rested her toe, in the way horses did, in the hope they had something to teach her.

Soon the icy air penetrated her thick dufflecoat, and she began to shiver. Not for the first time, she questioned her behaviour. What was she doing meeting a man who cared so little for her comfort? Carl had made it quite plain that he didn't want it known that they sometimes met, he had practically ignored her on the few occasions when they saw each other and there were others present. Where was her pride? Why couldn't she take the hint and find someone who would show some pleasure in being seen with her? The truth was, she admitted sadly, the excitement had taken away her senses.

It was ten more minutes before he came running along the lane to the telephone box, which was one of their meeting places. At once she turned away from their regular walk along the path to the wood. He was arriving later and later because the nights were getting lighter and lighter she admitted to herself. What a fool she was.

He chased after her, apologising for being late. Putting his arms around her he held her and she could feel his beating heart. "I ran all the way," he said and for a moment she believed him. "I had a tricky job, fixing a carpet in a room that wasn't square. Every wall was out of true. Damned pattern was a nightmare to fit and it took twice as long as I thought it would."

"Nothing to do with the evening being so light someone might see us?"

"No. Well, all right, I do want to keep quiet about us a while longer," he admitted.

"Well it's too late to go for a walk," she said angrily. "Frozen stiff I am and I'm going home to a warm fire and a cup of something hot." She looked at his hands to see whether they held a box of chocolates. Rhiannon reported that he called in to Temptations regularly for a small box of either Dairy Box or Milk Tray. They were never for her, she thought with disappointment. Cold, stiff, and feeling more than a little foolish for allowing herself to be treated so badly, she asked, "Brought any sweets, have you?"

"No, I didn't think, sorry. Besides, the shops were shut by the time I'd finished wrestling with that carpet." She wondered who had been the recipient. Some other girl he met well out of sight? Humiliation swelled up inside her and, giving him a push, she shouted, "Clear off, Carl Rees! I've got better things to do with my evenings that wait for you in the freezing cold."

"Don't, Mair, love. I've been waiting all day for these hours with you."

She stopped and looked at him, her heart pounding. His face

was hardly visible in the darkness but it was a handsome face, a tempting face. "You can come with me, if you like," she said, and the words were a challenge. She was saying, 'meet my father', and the answer, given with a silent shake of his head, was, 'no'.

Running along the dark and narrow lane to the cottage on the edge of the wood, she ignored his calls, his pleadings, and didn't stop until she reached her gate. She stopped to regain her breath. Dad would wonder what was up if she went in in this state. As she stood there, building herself up to the decision to break off the romance that wasn't, the courtship that was nothing more than a joke, she heard a faint sound, hardly more than a movement of the trees but in the almost silent night it came to her ears clearly. She at once presumed it was Carl, although she knew with that second thought that she would have heard him coming. The country lane and the wood on either side were not places to walk silently unless you were an expert. But she had been running, crying. It must be Carl. He would have made sure she was safely home wouldn't he?

"Go away. I never want to see you again. D'you hear me? Never!"

"Mair?" a voice called hesitantly. "It's me, Frank. Are you all right?"

"No I'm not!" she shouted, "so what d'you think you can do about it, Frank Griffiths, eh?"

"Walk with you while you calm down?" he suggested. He appeared out of the darkness then and, taking her arm, led her away from the gate and towards his cottage. "Come an' talk to our Mam, have a cup of tea."

She went without argument and he talked in whispers telling her where he'd seen an owl nesting and pointing out the path, marked on a low stretch of barbed wire with small bunches of hair, where the badger strolled on his nightly search for food.

"You can see so much in the dark," she said. "Walking with you is like one of those Romany stories we used to listen to on the wireless."

"It's partly experience, I suppose. I recognise things because I've seen or heard them many times before. And pupils widen and take in the light, according to the doctor. Have a look," he said and he pulled her round and bent his long skinny frame down until they were face to face.

"Daft 'apporth! As if I can see anything in this light!"

"You can if you give your eyes a chance," he insisted. He brought his face closer and she smelled the honest, earthy smell of him, the clean night air created a special scent, leaving his skin excitingly perfumed with a hint of pine trees. So different from Carl with the rubbery smell of carpets which never seemed to leave him. They were close, very close. He didn't kiss her, but she knew he wanted to.

Perhaps she wanted it too. Wanted to be held, flattered, admired.

"A cup of tea?" she said breaking away from him in confusion. Frank Griffiths attracting her? She must be madder than she thought!

But she didn't release his arm as he led them unerringly through the trees, moving aside low branches she couldn't even see, taking them on a short cut to his parents' home. They stopped for a while and he showed her where foxes lived, and made her promise not to tell Farmer Booker or his father. "Some people hate foxes and kill them without reason," he explained softly. "I can kill for the pot, but for no other reason."

"Farmer Booker has an excuse to kill foxes, he's lost dozens of rabbits from his warren," she replied.

"I've killed more of his rabbits than the foxes," he chuckled. "And I've walked past him and given him a 'goodnight' with a ferret up my jumper, a pocketful of nets, and a sackful of his rabbits hidden only yards from where he stood."

Janet and Hywel welcomed her without comment except to move up and make room for her near the roaring fire. Caroline came down from putting Joseph-Hywel to bed and made tea, while Janet set out a tray of sandwiches and cakes.

"I had a date and was stood up," she said as soon as she was settled. She didn't want anyone to get the idea that she was going out with Frank Griffiths, did she?

"Anyone we know?" Caroline asked, handing her a hot drink.

"No, no one you'd know. Just someone I met in the shop. He wasn't important."

"Best you take care who you meet these dark nights, girl," Hywel said. "You never know who's about these days."

"Poachers, d'you mean?" she asked innocently and Hywel smiled delightedly and nodded at Frank.

"She'll do this one," he said.

Frank walked her home and stood looking up at the cottage for a long time. If only things were different, if only he was good-looking, or rich or something. He strolled home unhurriedly, calling a goodnight, to the still figure of Farmer Booker standing in a hedgerow not far from his farm.

"Hawkeye you are and no mistake," Booker retorted.

"I don't need to see you. Stink of that filthy ol' pipe, you do. I could smell you at the other end of the field."

"Clever bugger."

"If only I was clever at something else. Sniffing out suspicious farmers won't help me with Mair, will it?" Frank sighed, but the farmer didn't hear.

Carl called at the sports shop to see Mair the following morning, but she told him to go away. Although she couldn't imagine ever being serious about someone as daft as Frank, she knew she could do better than secret meetings with Carl. She had begun to feel guilty about them, without knowing the reason. Putting shame on me, he is, she told herself angrily.

The next few days were miserable. There were moments when she weakened and knew that if Carl appeared she would agree to meet him. Fortunately, when she did see him, her anger was stronger than her regrets.

Frank knocked at her door late one evening and asked if she fancied a walk. He had been planning what he'd say all that day but when he plucked up the courage to ask her, he chose the wrong moment.

"What makes everyone want to take me out in the dark?" she demanded. "Am I such an embarrassment to be seen with, then?"

"No," Frank said. "You're nice." He wished he could think of a better word but his mind didn't work very quickly at the best of times, and talking to Mair was one of the worst of times for him, because he liked her so much. "I know I'm no great shakes, and I thought *you'd* be ashamed to be seen out with *me*." He shuffled his feet in an embarrassed way, wondering if she understood what he was trying to say. "I'd love to take you out in the day. Smashing that'd be."

"Sorry I snapped. Come on in. Dad and I are just going to have a sandwich and a cup of tea."

"Don't encourage him," her father warned, when Frank had gone happily on his way. "You'll never get rid of him if you do."

Her father's words worried her. Frank was not what she wanted. When she saw Carl a few days later she made it clear that she wanted him back in her life – secrets and all.

Sally had rearranged her house to accommodate more guests. Planning for the time when Megan and her baby were no longer living there, she decided to move into a smaller room on the ground floor. It would be separate from the strangers who filled her rooms on most night and somehow she would feel safer. She didn't admit to her daughters that she was occasionally afraid, or tell them about the rather forceful man she had asked to leave. She didn't want them to worry unnecessarily about her. Jeremy Pullen-Thomas, with his attempted organisation of her had been frightening and had reminded her how vulnerable she was without Ryan. When she had begun taking in guests Ryan had been living with her and the idea of trouble hadn't even been a passing thought. Now, facing the situation of being alone here while strangers wandered about the house was very different.

She thought of her strong-minded daughters and smiled as she imagined their disparaging response to her admitting being afraid. Yet her own husband had attacked her and if Ryan could frighten her so much, what could a stranger like Jeremy Pullen-Thomas do?

Max Powell was helpful, but at six thirty one morning, he had knocked on her bedroom door and offered her an early cup of tea. Her nervousness had crept up a notch as she realised she had made the serious mistake of fuzzing the line between business and friendliness. Perhaps it was because some of the men had become regulars, calling once or twice each week and beginning to relax in the homely atmosphere she provided. Better if she could attract once-only visitors who would remain strangers, but that was impossible to arrange. No, she would have to withdraw from any overtures towards friendliness and keep everything formal. She might even make the excuse that she was fully booked the next time Max Powell rang. Seeing him behave like a close friend might encourage the others to do the same. Offering her early morning tea! Really! Better if he stayed away for a while to allow her to practice her new role.

The room she intended to make her own had been used only as a small sitting room for those guests who didn't want to watch the television. It would need shelves, cupboards and a small wardrobe before she could sleep there. The other room, which Megan now used for baby Rosemary would have to be dealt with later, after Easter, when Megan and Edward would be married.

Megan had recommended Frank Griffiths to do the work, but Sally thought Carl Rees, who had worked for Jennie Francis, might be a more suitable character to have in the house while she was busy. The Griffithses were not to be trusted, everyone knew that. She wondered how her daughter could ever pretend they were her friends. Leaving a note for Megan to pass on to Carl when he went into the shop, she waited for him to call.

As she considered her plans to move to the smaller room, she thought of the other spare room in which Ryan had sat sometimes and which, with some self-deception he called his study. It was small but it would hold a single bed and a dressing table and perhaps Carl could fix a rail of some sort where clothes could be hung? She began to make a list to discuss with him.

Since Christmas, when Rhiannon's parents had ended their long-running row and settled down together again, Rhiannon and Charlie had lived in silent dread of the fiery Dora throwing Lewis out again and having him return to sleep in their back bedroom.

So one night when they woke about midnight to the sounds of shouts and yells coming from her parent's house, they looked at each other in alarm.

"I knew it! Our Mam's lost her temper with him again!"

"Oh no." Charlie groaned. "Get the spare bed aired. He'll be back."

"Why can't she stay calm and discuss their differences?" Rhiannon complained.

"Because she's Dora and reasonable discussion is something she wouldn't understand."

They crept out of bed and Charlie wrapped a blanket around Rhiannon's shoulders. Kneeling down by the window they looked across the street to number seven, where the bedroom light was on. Even in the winter, Dora liked to sleep with the window open and the sound of what was apparently a heated argument, greeted them as they opened theirs. The two voices were like a comic opera with the almost soprano shrieks of her mother and the lower, more reasonable, baritone of her father. Rhiannon began to giggle. "Did you ever know such a pair?"

"They are unique," Charlie said, sharing her laughter.

Other lights came on in the Lewis's house and the front door burst open. Lewis, wearing pyjamas, with a dressing gown across one arm which, dragged on the floor behind him, ran across the road.

"This is it, then," Rhiannon said, all laughter gone. "She's kicked him out and he's coming back to live with us. Oh Charlie, why can't they behave?"

"Wait a minute," he said, as Lewis began to bang on the door. "He's laughing!"

All thought of sleep had gone as they went down to open the door to see that Lewis was indeed laughing.

"You'll never guess what's happened," he said, and they waited in silence for him to continue. "Next door's cat came through the window with a mouse in its mouth. He let it go and me and your mam have been trying to catch it. At least, *I've* been trying to catch the wily thing. Dora's standing on a chair trying

to get up on top of the wardrobe! You'll have to have her here
while I get the poor thing out.''

Gwyn had been woken with the midnight activities and said,
''I'll come as well. Three of us and a cat should be able to catch a
mouse, eh, Grandad?''

Dora was carried over holding her night dress tight around her
and, as Lewis waited for Charlie and Gwyn to go with him,
Rhiannon smiled at Charlie. ''Better a mouse than a lodger,'' she
whispered.

From the bedroom window, Rhiannon and Dora looked across
the road and watched the antics of three men versus one mouse. If
they hadn't known better they might have thought they were
witnesses to a blood-curdling drama: there were sounds of furniture being moved and the banging of a stick on the floor, presumably to persuade the poor little thing to run across an open
space where they might stand a chance of capturing it; there were
silhouettes of figures passing to and fro behind the still-closed
curtains, this way, then that, but it was almost fifteen minutes
before everything went quiet and Lewis's face appeared.

''It's all right, love, Gwyn got him and he's putting him out in
the garden.''

''Where's that cat?'' Dora shouted back.

''Locked in the bathroom. And for heaven's sake Dora, shut
up! You're waking the neighbourhood,'' Lewis shouted back.

''Danmed cheek, I—''

''I think it's time to put the kettle on, Mam.'' Rhiannon
laughed.

After telling Sian Weston about the adventure the following day,
Dora was asked, ''How are things between you and Lewis now?
Happy, are you?''

''Ye-e-s,'' Dora said hesitantly.

''But?'' coaxed Sian.

''I don't know. Yes, we are happy. But I have the feeling that
I'm waiting for something else, that Lewis coming back home
was only a first stage of this new life. There's something missing,
but I don't know what it is. Daft, eh?''

"I think I know what you mean. To have him back was something you'd wanted for a very long time, even if you'd never admit it, and now he is there, you're left with a feeling of anti-climax."

"That's it. But I don't regret having him back. I couldn't cope with losing him again. And Rhiannon and Charlie's prayers were answered as well as mine, when Lewis came back to number seven. Lewis said their faces were a picture of unadulterated horror last night, when they thought I'd thrown him out again!"

With the approach of spring, the Griffithses' cottage was in chaos. Janet was spring-cleaning and the whole family was suffering. Frank and Hywel were given instructions about painting the rough stone walls made smooth by years and years of painting, the layers filling in the gaps, disguising the uneven surface so it looked almost like plaster.

"White again?" Hywel said rhetorically.

"Except the bedrooms," Janet surprised him by saying. "Caroline wants pink and we'll have a cheerful yellow in Frank's room."

"Yellow? What the 'ell sort of colour's that to sleep in? No, white's best," he argued. He was still arguing as they went to Westons and carried home pink and yellow emulsion and white gloss, plus packets of sandpaper.

"You're never going to ask me to paint doors and skirting-boards white, woman? Brown it's been for as long as we've lived here and brown it stays." He was still arguing as he handed the sandpaper and white undercoat to Frank. "Go on, son, you get on with this and I'll get my potatoes in the ground, before she wants me to grow flowers instead. I don't know what's got into your mother these days, and that's a fact." He rubbed his beard up the wrong way which was a sign that he was seriously upset.

Hywel went to the top of the garden and dug furiously for the rest of the day. Janet wasn't getting restless, was she? Wanting carpets? And yellow bedrooms? It wasn't natural.

During the next few weeks the preparations were done for

65

planting the vegetables. Two long lines of bean sticks were arranged. "North to south," Hywel told Frank, who was unwillingly helping him, "so they all get a bit of sun either in the morning or the afternoon, see." Frank tried to escape this annual torment, but Hywel insisted he helped. "This is what you do to earn your keep, boy. You eat here, you work here, right?"

"Right." Frank began clearing out the greenhouses ready to grow the tomatoes and cucumbers which Hywel and he sold from the van. Why argue? He had nothing better to do. Mair wouldn't speak to him except to tell him to 'get lost'. Basil and Ernie were both involved with their wives. He was on his own, so he might as well give in and do what his dad wanted without argument. Dad could still land him one, and thought he had the right to do so if he didn't do what he was told. What a life! And a future containing more of the same. What a prospect! If only Carl Rees would drop dead.

Carl found temporary work on a building site where three houses were nearing completion. Finishing off the kitchens when the regular carpenter was off sick suited him admirably. Short-term jobs with several other offers of work coming in almost daily. He was able to charge a good price and work for as many hours as he could stand up. He only had to work like this for a few more years and he would be clear of the debt.

The houses were in Twill Lane, the other side of the town from Bella Vista, but by using the van he had bought cheaply from Jennie, he had no difficulty in working any reasonable distance from home.

One of the labourers offered friendship and they sat sometimes sharing their snack during the half-hour break at midday.

"In lodgin's, are you?" the man asked. "Or still home with Mam?"

"Lodgin's," Carl replied. "And you?"

"Home with Mam at present, but I'm hoping to get my feet under the table at a very nice widow lady's posh house soon. Softening her up I am. Pretending to have a better job than this. I stay there sometimes, as boarder, mind, nothing more. But I know she likes me and I think I'll give it a few more weeks, then invite her out."

"Expensive hobby, courting," Carl warned. "And if she's a wealthy widow, she'll expect more than a picture show and a bag of toffees, won't she?"

"I think she needs someone. Livin' alone has its drawbacks for a woman."

"Dream on! You'll need to offer more than companionship if she's wealthy!"

"Runs a guesthouse she does and she needs a man about the place."

"I'm Carl Rees," Carl held out a hand. "I'll be intrigued to know how you get on," he smiled.

"I'll keep in touch, Carl," said Maxie Powell.

Four

S ally was determined to change the attitude of her guests and keep herself distant from them. A few pleasantries was all she would allow herself. She began this new regime by talking to the four people staying there that evening, including Maxie Powell.

"I would like to thank you for your kind thought in offering to help in some of the small tasks I perform for you, but I would prefer you to accept that my kitchen is out of bounds, except when I have given permission," she said, smiling and hoping her words were not too harsh.

Maxie stood up, throwing his napkin across the table dramatically. "No," he said kindly. "No, Mrs Fowler-Weston, we don't want you to think we mind helping. We don't, do we?" He looked at the other three for agreement and went on, "You work very hard here and your day is a long one, waiting up to give us a late-night snack as well as serving breakfast from eight o'clock. We love helping by starting your day with a cup of tea and if there's any other way we can spoil you a little, you only have to say. So, please, not another word about it."

Wrong-footed, Sally could only retire to her kitchen.

Carl Rees arrived before she had finished serving breakfast and when he saw Maxie, carrying out the cereal dishes to an obviously flustered Sally, he was surprised, then amused. So this was the widow Maxie thought he would cultivate. Mrs Fowler-Weston, who was married to Ryan who was very much alive.

"Hello, Maxie," he said, when Sally had offered him tea and asked him to wait until she was finished. "Don't tell me this is your fancy woman who's about to fall into your arms?"

"Carl! What are you doing here? Not a word about where I work, please, she thinks I'm a stationery salesman."

"Surprise surprise, and you think she's a widow. Sorry to disappoint you, mate, but her husband is still with us – even if not with her at present."

Subdued, Maxie went back to the dining room to continue his breakfast.

Sally had very little help, but twice a week she employed a young girl, Anne Davies, to change and wash bedding, vacuum floors and do the dusting. She arrived as Carl was starting to measure up for the work Sally wanted done and throughout the day in odd moments, they talked. When he finished at five thirty, he gave her a lift home.

Anne lived in a run-down street only a few doors away from Molly Bondo, a well-known prostitute.

"See all sorts coming and going at that house," she told Carl. "People you'd never expect would stoop so low. And that brazen you'd never believe! Walk in as though they're calling to buy a newspaper they do. I ought to have kept a diary. There'd be a few upset families if I had and that's a fact. Respectable ones too, mind."

Carl said very little at the revelation. He'd often seen Molly at the Railwayman's, and had bought her a drink once or twice. He would have to be more careful. There were watching eyes everywhere.

He didn't go straight home after leaving Anne. He went to the back lane behind Edward's shop and knocked on the door of the basement flat. Ryan opened it and asked what he wanted. The man looked surprised, Carl thought, and wondered if he ever had any visitors. From what he had learnt, his family didn't bother with him; nor had he been the sort to make many friends.

"I'm doing some work for your wife," Carl said.

"So what? I'm not responsible for her debts," Ryan said irritably.

"This isn't about a debt, Mr Fowler-Weston."

"Fowler. The name's Fowler."

Embarrassed and wishing he hadn't come, Carl said, "It's just that your wife has a lodger, who I think might be a nuisance. Maxie Powell he's called, and he—"

"What d'you expect me to do about it?" Ryan demanded.

"Nothing." Carl began to move away. "Nothing at all. Sorry I bothered you." Perhaps Maxie had a chance after all, if the Ryan Fowler's attitude was one of such indifference?

After Carl had gone, Ryan grabbed a coat and went out. White-faced with rage, believing that Sally had sent the man to plead for his help, he headed towards Glebe Lane, once his home. The closer he got to his destination, the slower his footsteps got until, at the end of the lane on which several expensive houses stood, isolated from each other by large gardens, he stopped. He knew he would only lose his temper again, which would make him feel ill and then he might not be well enough to go to work the following day. He turned and retraced his steps back to the basement flat, where he felt safe.

Jennie and Peter both felt their lives were in a strange sort of limbo waiting for the next stage but unable to do anything to set it in motion. There had been no serious discussion about divorce, yet Peter continued to live with his parents and only occasionally contacted Jennie, usually to argue about the bills she posted on to him.

Jennie had made no effort to find a job, it seemed like defeat to be independent now: it was what Peter wanted. If he blamed the breakdown of their marriage on her attempts to be a modern woman earning money by running her own business, well, he'd have a taste of keeping her, while at the same time paying for a house he didn't use. Peter was always careful about money and it would worry him. There was childish satisfaction in that. She went through the post, gathered together the few bills that had arrived, including one from Carl for replacing the putty in a window, and addressed them in her large scrawling writing to her husband, care of Mr and Mrs Rodney Francis.

He called that evening on the way home from work. She opened the door, but didn't step back and invite him in. "I'm sorry I can't be sociable, Peter, but I'm going out."

He was breathless, as though he had been running. "It's Mam," he said. "She's ill."

"Oh? Got the usual cold, has she?"

"No, I wish it was that simple. She can't get out of bed. She couldn't even get tea for me and Dad," he said, in mild outrage.

Jennie laughed. "Poor Peter, that must be worse than having an ambitious wife."

"It isn't a joke, she really is ill this time."

That was the closest he had come to admitting that there were times when his mother was a bit of a hypochondriac. "I'm sorry. Is there anything I can do?" She felt ashamed.

"No, unless you could do a bit of washing for us and—"

"No, Peter, I couldn't do that. You left me, remember?"

"She's in a bit of pain," he said.

She was tempted to help, urged on by guilt at her immediate reaction, but she hardened herself and shook her head. Peter's mother had caused her more distress and pain than anyone else in her whole life, and had made sure their marriage had failed. She owed the woman no favours whether she was genuinely ill or not.

"I'm sorry she's ill and I hope she's well soon. But I really don't think I can help. She doesn't like me, and seeing me in her kitchen would probably make her feel worse."

Peter went home still carrying the bills and the cheques he had intended to return to Jennie. If Mam were ill for more than a few days, what would they do? He knew that making a meal was beyond him, and his father was no better. Mam had always looked after them and there had never been a need to learn.

What was wrong with Jennie that she didn't want to be a proper wife like Mam? All this mess was her fault, leaving him to fend for himself while she played at running a business. Women's work was women's work and men should have no part of it. He called in to the fish and chip shop and carried home the steamy package with something approaching despair.

The reason he had left Jennie was because he couldn't cope with her casual approach to looking after him. Mam had promised a meal on the table when he got in from work every day, a cooked breakfast every morning, washing taken away and returned to his bedroom drawers without fuss by the following day. It was what he'd been used to. With Mam out of action he was more than a little anxious. What if she was ill for a long time? Who'd look after him then? The fish and chips in their newspaper-wrapped parcel issued an appetizing smell and he began to run, wanting to be home, wanting to be reassured that everything would soon be back the way it should be. The door was open when he reached the front gate and the hall light was on. Voices from upstairs murmured and he ran, still carrying the fish and chips, up to his parents' bedroom.

"Mam's got to go to hospital," his father said stiffly. "The ambulance is on its way."

When the ambulance had taken his parents, Peter threw the supper into the dustbin and stood for a moment wondering what to do. Closing the door, he went back to tell Jennie. Surely she'd help now? The house was in darkness. She was obviously out. He sat down on the front step and stared into the night. He'd have to come back home. Irregular meals were better than none. Pouting like a small boy, he muttered, "Dad will have to shift for himself."

For Basil, Frank and Ernie Griffiths, poaching was a way of life. They had kept their family – and several others beside – well fed during the long years of food rationing and, Janet thought, they had been rather disappointed when their illegal talents were no longer needed. They still used their expertise to get meat though, and although not as frequently as before, every now and again one of them would appear in court. If it wasn't for poaching or tresspassing with intent, it was for fighting.

The routine was well practised. Best suit on, a freshly ironed white shirt, the one kept for all of them to use for these, 'special occasions'. A trip in the van, usually driven by Hywel, an appearance in court and a plea of guilty, then a fine and a countdown to the next outing for the white shirt and best suit.

With Basil and Ernie now married it was only Frank, and on

occasions, Hywel, who went out at night and returned with something for Janet to cook. Now, Frank needed the expert skills of his brother, Basil. He wanted a salmon and he didn't want to pay for it.

Frank met Basil one morning when he was on his way to work at the plastics factory.

"Help me net a salmon, will you?"

"What for, our Mam planning a party is she?"

"No, its not for Mam, it's—" He hesitated and Basil stopped his long striding walk and waited. "It's for a bit of owns back. That Carl Rees is messing Mair about."

"How will giving him a salmon help?"

"If it's illegal, and he's caught with it, it'll cost him money, that's a start. Too mean he is, only takes Mair on long walks on dark nights. Never gives her a real treat. Never a box of chocolates. He should be taught a lesson."

Basil scratched his head and frowned. "I'm mystified, Frank, and that's the truth. And," he added as he moved on, "I'm going to be late for my shift."

"Meet me tonight?" Frank pleaded.

"About ten?" Basil replied as he hurried on to the factory work he hated but tolerated because he loved Eleri more than he loved the freedom of the fields.

None of the Griffithses had worked regularly until recently. Living off their wits and the occasional casual work like gardening, or repairing fences, they survived in reasonable comfort. When they were younger and needed more money to keep up with friends in regular employment, they had earned a reputation for seasonal work on farms, dealing with hedging and ditching, pruning fruit trees, hay-making, all the work for which farmers traditionally needed extra hands.

They had to travel to farms further away than Farmer Booker, who knew they visited him only after dark and with illegal intent. Respectability had only come with marriage and, for Frank, that longed-for moment had yet to arrive.

He was attracted to Mair Gregory and he often wondered whether her acceptance of him as a life partner would be enough to persuade him into regular employment. In his more honest moments he was doubtful. But then, he reasoned sadly, the chances of her looking at him with something other than mild amusement was so slight, he might never have to decide. Her father being a policeman was a serious problem too. Perhaps he should forget her and look elsewhere? But there was still Carl. He wasn't the right one for Mair and had to be discouraged. It would be fun tormenting him for a while.

Entering the river and finding one of the deep holes where salmon rested, was easy. Basil had done this so often he knew every part of it. Deep in one of the holes, his hands and feet confidently found every depression and every rock. For a long time several of the local families had had a syndicate: one had a second-hand freezer bought from a retiring fishmonger; one had access to the river where they could reach the spot with little chance of being seen; one had a daughter who knew the river warden rather intimately; and then there was Basil Giffiths who could fish with the aid of only the most basic of equipment.

For one salmon they didn't need the rest of the team. In fact Basil and Frank took two. Walking back across the fields each of them swollen with a salmon in place of a waistcoat, taking the small paths where they were unlikely to be seen, they were grinning like the experts they were.

Salmon fishing was a good way of earning extra cash. Selling to hotels who asked no questions was the best way and, to achieve greater success when using a rod and line, an illegal bait was used. A paste, which the locals called jam, contained roe and attracted the fish so readily it was frowned upon by purists and punishable by law. Basil didn't need this to take the two fish he captured that night, but when Frank placed the fish in Carl's van, he added a small supply of the paste as well. Telling the police was fun: disguising his voice with a handkerchief across his mouth, pretending to be a woman. He watched as two men came to investigate the contents of the van and saw them take the newspaper parcel and examine it, before knocking on the door of 4 Bella Vista, where Carl had his lodgings. Frank was grinning widely as the policemen took Carl and the parcel away. Then he ran through the lanes and woods to tell Mair what he had seen. "Arrested he was, that Carl Rees. Never did like 'im, mind. What's he been up to d'you think?"

He gave Mair a bar of chocolate that he'd had in his pocket for days, while trying to find an excuse to call on her, and went home, whistling, convinced that Carl would keep away from the policeman's daughter after his embarrassing brush with the law.

While he walked home, pausing a while to watch a barn owl gliding along a hedgerow, marvelling at its ghostly beauty, the police were talking to his father, demanding to know how the fish and illegal bait had been found in Carl Rees's van, wrapped in that day's newspaper on which the newsagent had pencilled the address of the Griffithses' cottage.

Mair guessed the truth of it when her father laughingly explained what had happened.

"Can't you leave it, Dad? It has to be Frank and he was only trying to be clever and get Carl into trouble."

"Oh yes, Carl Rees. The man you've been seeing – er – in secret."

"Hardly secret," she protested. "You've known long enough! So have most of Pendragon Island! He's a bit shy, that's all."

"If it's only shyness that's the trouble, why didn't *you* tell me?" her father asked. "And why haven't I met him?"

"He's a bit older than me, and he doesn't want people to know just yet."

"Bring him in for supper. I've heard a bit about him and there isn't a satisfactory explanation of that fish. I want to meet him. Right?"

"I'll try, Dad."

"You'll do more than try. I want him here tomorrow night. Seven o'clock sharp. Right?" He spoke with emphasis and Mair knew that, easy-going as he was, this was one time when she couldn't argue.

Basil was unsympathetic when Frank told him the disappointing result of his enterprising attempt to get Carl in trouble with the police.

"You wrapped it in a newspaper from the house? Barmy you are. No wonder Mair can't take you seriously. God 'elp, Frank! Neither can I!"

Frank played with his nephews for a while, Ronnie aged four and Thomas, who was fourteen months old. He envied his brother. Basil was so happy with his life. Eleri and the children adored him. He left their flat in Trellis Street wishing he could find a way of showing Mair that he'd be as good a husband as Basil.

Walking home via the woods as usual, he couldn't resist passing her cottage. There was a light on and, stepping with ease over the low fence, he crept forward to look through the uncurtained window into the living room and there, in front of a fire, sat Mair and Carl. He watched for an hour and was sick when the light snapped out and the bedroom light snapped on. What was the use? He was a failure with women, he might as well face it.

Once home Frank stood for a long time leaning over the goats' pen, then opened the door of their shed and went in to talk to them. The curious and friendly little creatures came to nuzzle against his hand in the hope of a tidbit. He took down a clean bale of hay and sat, nursing their heads as they dozed. Janet found him there, fast asleep, when she went to unlock the goats the next morning.

Peter's mother was home from hospital but still spending most of the day in bed. She would get up at midday and attend to the most urgent tasks, preparing food, dealing with washing and ironing and making sure the house was running smoothly, before returning to bed to read one of her favourite Agatha Christie mysteries. Peter and his father dealt with dishes and some of the routine cleaning but, although his father seemed happy to help his wife, for Peter the menial jobs were degrading.

"Can't we pay someone to come in and do all this?" he asked, on the third day of his misery.

"Pity is you quarrelled with Jennie just when we needed her," his father said sadly.

"I did ask her to help," Peter said, "but as usual she found reasons not to do what she didn't want to do."

"There aren't many women like your mam any more. She's getting out of her sick bed to cook for us."

"Can you manage the rest, Dad?" Peter asked. "I think I'll go and see Jennie again."

"Waste of time, but I suppose it's worth a try, son."

Peter cleaned his already mirror-like shoes, put on a fresh shirt and his best suit, and went out. He knocked on Jennie's door. The place was in darkness and there was no reply. "Out again," he reported to his father on his return.

Carl went into the sports shop the following day and when she had finished serving a customer, Mair invited him to supper that night. "It's our Dad's day off and he's promised to cook something for us. Not a bad cook, mind, my father. We share that chore, I cook at weekends and when he's on the wrong shift and he does the rest. So, you'll come?"

He thanked her, but hesitantly. "I'd love to, but I might be working."

"Can't you change your plans? I don't mind as a rule, you know I never push for anything you don't want to do, but this is a bit of a royal command. He wants to meet you."

"We've met! I was taken in for questioning when someone mistook my van for someone else's and left an illegally caught salmon in it!"

"Yes." She laughed. "I'd heard!"

"Who d'you think it was?"

"How would I know?" Her eyes widened innocently. "My dad knows all the local villains, though. So why don't you ask him when you come to supper tonight?"

He again promised to try, and when the shop was empty and Edward had gone upstairs to his flat, she kissed him with a promise of better things to come.

"I'll be there," he whispered, before leaving the shop.

He hurried away angry with himself for allowing the situation to develop so far and so fast. He should never have started it. Now everyone knew; Edward leaving them alone, obviously under-standing their need for privacy. Rhiannon in the sweetshop saying coyly that the chocolates he was buying must be for Mair. Even Jennie Francis was teasing him. It should never have been allowed to become general knowledge. Why couldn't Mair have enjoyed the secret? It had to stop. Meeting her father was one step too far.

In the basement flat below the sports shop, Sally's estranged husband, Ryan, was staring out at the garden. It was overgrown and badly in need of tidying. He wasn't going to start doing that or Edward would expect him to make it a part of his tenancy. Pity he'd missed work today, but he'd had a sleepless night, angry with Sally for sending that man to talk to him.

The day was dull but he looked out at the rain-soaked trees and shrubs and at the strong spears of daffodils boldly declaring the arrival of spring. Buds were breaking and showing the cheerful yellow that would fill the corner where Frank had planted bulbs he had found when he had cleared the neglected garden before Christmas. Late they'd be, but better for that.

He was content, he realised. If only he could get Sally and the rest of the Westons out of his mind, life would be perfect. He went to work, doing an undemanding job just well enough to keep it. He went for a walk after work each evening, then home for supper. The rest of the evening was spent listening to the radio or reading. Peaceful, no interruptions.

Above him, the shop was closed and there was very little noise from Edward's flat on the top floor. Edward was a fool to think of marrying Megan. Megan, his daughter, who had been given everything she wanted. How well she had turned out! There she was, promising to marry Edward, to love honour and obey, with another man's child in her arms. Women were not to be trusted. That Molly Bondo had been someone's loved child once and look at her now, sitting in the Railwayman's looking for a man she could cheat out of his money. Another example of how weak most men were. Couldn't manage without a woman. He didn't need a woman. He was happier without them.

Besides Mair and her father inviting a reluctant Carl for supper, Dora issued an invitation that evening too.

When Lewis called at the Rose Tree cafe and had a snack there at lunchtime, he said, "We've been given a piece of salmon, Dora, from Hywel Griffiths, what d'you think of that, eh?"

"Probably pinched!"

"Tasty though."

"Enough for five?" Dora asked.

"Yes, with a bit of salad and some new potatoes. Thinking of inviting our Rhiannon and co are you?" When she nodded he said had call in to the sweetshop and ask their daughter.

"No," Dora said, in her sharp voice. "Better than that. Why don't you go to the garage and ask Charlie and Gwyn?"

Lewis was still a little unhappy about Rhiannon having married Charlie Bevan, who had spent several years in prison, and taking on his son, so he understood why Dora had made the request. "Give me another cup of tea, love and I'll go straight away. Gwyn'll be pleased, won't he?"

Frank was wandering aimlessly through the wood that evening. At seven it was still just light and he had been to see someone who wanted a coal house built. He'd refused the job. No particular reason except that he had no urgent need of money. He only worked when his wallet was looking a bit thin, and at present he had enough cash to last another month including, paying Mam and buying a few pints for his friends.

Without really planning it, his feet took him to Mair's cottage. To his delight she was standing at the gate.

"Waiting for someone are you?" he called, as he stepped out of the trees opposite the house.

"None of your business Frank Griffiths."

"Oh, I see. It's that Carl is it?"

"What if it is?" she snapped.

Guessing that Carl was either late or had forgotten, he sidled across the lane and asked, "Come for a walk if he doesn't turn up? I saw the barn owl again last night and I'll show you where she nests . . ."

"He'll come."

Desperately trying to think of a subject that would persuade her to enter into a discussion and take her mind off Carl, he said, "I've been to look at a job, building a coal house." No response. What a stupid idiot I am to think she'd be interested in a coal house, he berated himself. Only slightly better, he said, "This gate's a bit wobbly, want me to fix it?"

"Shut up, Frank."

"He won't come. He can't face your father. Not after being found with a salmon he can't."

"What d'you know about that salmon?" she asked suspiciously.

"You know me, I wander about picking up odd bits of conversations, get to know a lot of what's going on, just wandering about. Like I told you, I saw your father taking him away for questioning while someone searched his room. Found a lot of fishing tackle they did."

"You put the salmon there, didn't you? Leaving your name and address on it. Real clever, that was!"

"No, that wasn't me, that was someone trying to incriminate me," he said, having been primed in his answer by Hywel. "No, Carl won't face your father. Not now."

"And you can?"

"No problem for me."

She opened the gate and hauled him through. "Come on then! *You* can come for supper!"

When she opened the living-room door, her father was sitting in a fireside chair. On the table stood a dish of new potatoes, over which butter slowly melted, a bowl of salad and, on a platter, decorated with wedges of lemon and slices of cucumber, sat a whole salmon.

"Pity to waste it, don't you think?" Mair's father said, studying Frank's startled face suspiciously.

At 7 Sophie Street, the Lewises sat down for supper at the same time as Frank and the Gregorys. Dora had scraped the potatoes in between attending to customers at the cafe, putting them on to boil as soon as she reached home. With the salmon – ironically – poached the meal was easily prepared, but tasted like a feast.

When Rhiannon and Charlie and Gwyn left to return to their home across the road, Dora sighed. "Nice having a crowd here, isn't it, Lewis?"

"You still miss Rhiannon and our Viv living here, don't you? What about a lodger then? A pretty young girl. Someone to keep me amused while you're at the cafe on my days off?"

She turned and her bright-blue eyes blazed momentarily, but there was no real anger on her face as she playfully thumped him. They hugged affectionately. "I do find the house empty though, don't you?"

"I enjoy the peace. We have to accept this is a different stage in our lives, love. We've done what we can to give our kids a good start and you must admit they've doing us proud. There'll be grandchildren one day, and they'll fill our hearts if not our house. Lucky we are and don't forget it."

"I know how lucky I am," she said, as they kissed affectionately.

Gwyn looked in the door at that moment and gave a theatrical sigh. "Not you two as well! Everybody's kissing. Mam and Dad and now you two!"

He was smiling as he collected the coat he had forgotten.

"I hope you don't think we're too old, young man," Lewis said warningly.

"Nearly, but not quite," was Gwyn's parting shot.

When Jack called on his grandmother one evening after school Gladys reminded him that she was still looking for someone to help with the cleaning. "D'you think I might ask Victoria's mother, Jack?"

"No, Grandmother. I would not be happy about you employing my wife's mother. There must be someone willing to give you a couple of mornings."

"Mair was all right, but she's working full time now. I've interviewed several young girls, dear, but none of them are suitable. So clumsy and uncaring. I'd lose all my lovely ornaments in a month."

"I'll ask in school. Someone will be found."

"The wedding isn't far off and I want the house looking its best for that, even if Megan is determined to have a small affair." She looked up at him, and pleaded gently, "You don't think Mrs Collins, just this once, might . . . ?"

"I'll do my best to find someone, Grannie dear."

"Grandmother, Jack, you know I consider 'Grannie' to be common!"

Jack was smiling affectionately as he left. Whatever problems the Westons had suffered, or would in the future, Grandmother Gladys would never change.

Victoria's mother enjoyed working at the house on Chestnut Road but she preferred it on the days when Martha Adams was out. Then, Sam Lilly relaxed and they worked together, enjoying the tasks Martha had set, stopping for a cup of tea at ten thirty which, weather permitting, they drank in the garden.

Sam's sight was not very good, but he managed to help with most of the work, cleaning windows when they needed an extra rub, moving furniture and polishing the floors with the mop Martha provided. She had got rid of most of the carpets, considering then unhealthy.

"I'd love to have a garden for the children to enjoy," Mrs Collins said one morning, as they sat in the early spring sunshine. "I've never had a garden."

"You live in a house, so isn't there a backyard? Somewhere to sit and feel the sun on your face?"

"There's a yard, but no flowers and looking at a grey, old blank wall isn't the same as sitting in a garden with flowers and greenery."

"Do you know anyone who would do a bit of gardening, Mrs Collins?" he asked later. "A handyman rather than a professional."

"Well there's Frank Griffiths, he's often looking for a few hours work." She explained where Frank could be found.

"Thank you, I'll go and see him. Mrs Collins, look, can I use your Christian name? Mrs Collins and Mr Lilly seems very formal between friends. I'd be pleased if you'd call me Sam." She didn't reply for a long moment and he thought he had embarrassssed her. "I'm sorry, I didn't mean any offence."

"You didn't offend me," she said softly. "I've never been called anything but Mrs Collins – or Mam." She added, with a smile, "Even my husband called me Collins. I have such a silly name you see, for someone in my position."

"And you can't tell me?"

"I can't tell you," she repeated sadly. "I'm sorry. Perhaps one day."

"When you accept that you and I are friends." He took her cup and they walked back into the house both very thoughtful, the word 'friends' hanging enticingly in the air between them.

Sally's ploy to keep her boarders at a distance failed. She came back from the shops one day to find Maxie cutting the grass. She saw that he had already weeded one of the flowerbeds, and had made himself a cup of tea. This was too much.

"I made him the tea, mummy," Megan told he when she began to complain. "He was working so hard, doing those jobs we can't find the time to do ourselves, that I thought he deserved it. Did I do wrong?"

"No, dear, of course not, it's just that Mr Powell is getting too friendly. I prefer the guests who wear an air of mild offence and complain with tedious regularity."

"I'll make sure I do nothing to encourage him again," Megan promised. "As for now, isn't it a relief not to have to face grass cutting this weekend?"

Outside the back gate, peering through a weak section of the privet hedge, Ryan watched and glared.

"There's a man watching the house," Maxie reported when he carried the bags of grass cutting to the compost heap. "Anyone you know, is it?"

"He's my husband," Sally explained.

"I thought you were a widow, Mrs Fowler-Weston." Maxie

feigned surprise, even though Carl had forewarned him. He glanced at Ryan and for a moment, seeing the angry-looking man watching him and feeling his anger from the length of the garden, he felt a strong desire to run. But Sally's nervousness stilled him and he went to her and reassured her, even though he knew nothing of the situation. She was afraid and that was enough for him. He led her away from where Ryan could see them, his arm protectively around her shoulders.

Seeing Ryan standing there, silent, and so obviously disapproving, she began to talk. Forgotten was her intention of treating the boarders indifferently. Shaken by seeing Ryan staring at the house she needed a comforting shoulder. She explained to a sympathetic Maxie about Ryan's breakdown, his occasional and frightening violence, and of their separation. Afterwards she was angry with herself for being so weak. "So much for my decision to be aloof," she said to Megan.

Frank was in such a euphoric state having been invited to supper with Mair that his grin was beginning to alarm his friends. "He's got more teeth than Charlie Perkins's horse," Hywel muttered as he glanced at his happy son. "An' all because he's been to supper with Mair, a policeman's daughter. What's the matter with the boy, Janet? Where did we go wrong?"

The smile on Frank's face remained undimmed, his happiness bursting out of every pore, so that when Sam Lilly called at the cottage to ask him about some work, he thought the man was mad.

"Of course I'll do a small gardening job." Frank beamed when Mr Lilly had explained. "When d'you want me to start? Certainly, certainly. As quickly as I can. I'll work all night if it's urgent, I'm so pleased you asked me." Mr Lilly glanced nervously at Janet and Hywel who had offered tea, and were sitting one each side of the fire on which a stewpot simmered.

"A woman," Hywel hissed in explanation, and Janet nodded soberly.

When Mr Lilly left, having been shown round the property and been introduced to dogs, cats, pigs, chickens, ducks and goats and a couple of ferrets, he wondered whether he had been wise.

His next step was to visit Mrs Collins's daughter, Victoria, and he went, after enquiries, to the neat little house in Philips Street and knocked at the door.

"My name is Sam Lilly. You don't know me," he began when he had ascertained that the person he was speaking to was Jack Weston, Victoria's husband, "but your mother-in-law, Mrs Collins, helps my sister in the house and, if you have a moment, I'd like to talk to you."

"There's nothing wrong with Mam, is there?" Victoria asked, appearing beside Jack.

"Your mother is well and so far as I can tell, happy," he assured them both.

Going inside the small room, he was surprised at how attractive it was. When he commented on the pleasant decor Jack told him that most of the work had been done by Frank and Ernie Griffiths.

"What a coincidence! Frank is one of the reasons I'm here." Having been reassured that Frank was a trustworthy person, which Jack did with tongue in cheek and with nudges from his wife, Sam explained his plan.

"Your mother tells me she has never had a garden and, with Frank's assistance, I thought I might provide her with one. Planters, shelves on a whitewashed wall, you know the kind of thing."

His idea was welcomed and their promise of help willingly given.

Frank and Jack met that evening in the Railwayman's and discussed what was needed. They arranged to meet and look at the yard behind 17 Goldings Street when Mrs Collins was at work a few days later.

Jack and Victoria spent some time looking around a local nursery and making lists of suggested plantings for Frank and Sam Lilly to consider. It became a secret enjoyed by many. Frank and Sam used Hywel's battered old van to transport containers and plants to one of the many sheds around the Griffiths's cottage, where the planning and planting was done. The shed became a meeting place for Jack, Sam and Viv, as well as for Frank and the rest of his family.

On the day they intended to make the transformation, Jack and Victoria arranged to take Mrs Collins to west Wales for a drive. The youngest two children went with them and the others were being looked after by Rhiannon helped by Dora.

The day was warm and Jack and Victoria had packed a picnic. Doubtful that the beginning of April was a suitable time for eating out of doors, Mrs Collins was assured that they could eat in the car if the sun didn't oblige.

Lewis, Charlie and Gwyn went along to Goldings Street and were quickly found jobs to do, the first of which was white-washing the walls.

"Half the town's involved, and how Mrs Collins hasn't heard the whispers I'll never know." Sam laughed, as he and Frank began loading the van to take the shelves and containers to Goldings Street on that Sunday morning.

With everything prepared in advance, Frank and Ernie quickly fixed shelves to the newly painted walls. Hywel brought in the simple table and benches he and Basil had made from discarded floorboards taken at night from a due-to-be-demolished house. Sam Lilly moved the items around the small area until he was satisfied. With much huffing and puffing and moaning about people who couldn't make up their minds, from Charlie Frank and Viv, the job was finally done. Climbing into the van with the tools and oddments of wood, they drove off to return the tools they'd borrowed, satisfied with their day's work.

Unsure how long the job would take, Jack didn't bring his family back until early evening. Dusk was closing in and, the street lights were becoming stronger and as he stopped the car, he said, "Come on, Mother-in-law, on with the kettle, we could all do with a cup of tea."

When she was encouraged to go outside, she gave a gasp of delight. "How –? When –?" she gasped. Then she smiled wider and said, "Mr Lilly?"

"And the Lewises and Jack and Frank and Ernie and Hywel." Her daughter laughed. "Half the town was involved."

"I must go and thank them all," she said as she walked around the garden, which was lit with a bulb fixed near the back door and the light shining out from the living-room. "I never imagined the old yard could become a garden." She touched the pots and rubbed a hand across the smooth wood of the table. "He's so kind, I must go and thank him, at once, and all the others too."

"Cup of tea first," Jack insisted. He filled the kettle and set it to boil. Then smiling widely, enjoying her pleasure, he said, "All right then, if you insist on thanking everyone . . ." He went to the front door and whistled and the work force trooped back in followed by her children with Dora and Lewis, Janet and Hywel Griffiths and more hesitantly, Sam Lilly.

Mrs Collins gave Sam a hug, as he modestly accepted her thanks, which resulted in a spate of wolf whistles and silly remarks which both participants clearly enjoyed.

Gladys heard a knock at the door one afternoon in early April. She looked around checking that the room was tidy enough for visitors, pushing a cushion more neatly across the arm of the heavy couch and pulling the table runner into a slightly more central position. She took a deep breath. She hated answering the door herself. It had been one of the many things she had enjoyed about having a servant. She could decide who to invited in when she wanted. Besides, she discouraged people from calling without an appointment being made.

A tall, rather thin woman stood on the step, dressed in black. Her pale face reminding Gladys of a mourner at a funeral. It was raining heavily, the day was dark, and the large black umbrella which the women held above her head, added to the funereal effect.

"Yes?" Gladys enquired haughtily. "What do you want?"

"It's more what you want, I believe," the woman replied in a surprisingly well modulated voice.

At once Glady's voice softened and she asked, "How can I help you, Mrs – er?"

"I believe you need a cleaner. I'm very experienced in looking after a home and, if the conditions are satisfactory, I'd like to apply for the job."

"Come in, Mrs – er— ?"

"My name in Dreese. I am a widow and my husband was German." This was spoken as though in preparation for an unpleasant response, but Gladys was desperate to have some help and the thought of a servant who was well spoken had already made her anxious for the woman to accept the job. "A German? How interesting," was all she said.

An hour later, after sharing a pot of tea and some excellent home-made apple strudel which Mrs Dreese had brought with her, the arrangement was made. Accepting an hourly rate that was going to shock Arfon out of his chair, Mrs Dreese was to begin her 'training' as Gladys put it, on the following morning. The references submitted by Mrs Dreese seemed short lived. She didn't appear to have worked for very long.

"My husband had a successful business you see, and we lived comfortably and well." She described her previous home in one of the better areas of a nearby town and Gladys was visibly impressed. "Then we had a disaster, another firm came in offering lower prices until we were driven out, and then the prices went back up and we had nothing left."

"She's a widow, dear," Gladys explained to Arfon when he admitted he was suspicious. "I don't think she needed to work while her husband was alive. She's a person fallen on hard times." She lowered her voice sympathetically.

"Then make sure you don't put temptation in her way," Arfon warned. "Hard times can make thieves of the best of us!"

"Arfon, dear. Don't say such things." She knew he was referring to his own lapse that had almost ended with him facing a prison sentence. "The Westons don't consider such things. I'll treat her as I would anyone else, unless I have reason to change my opinion."

"German you say?"

"Yes, but the war is over."

"I wasn't going to criticise—"

"People do, dear. I could see it in her eyes. Even the best of us have some prejudices and you'll have to be careful what you say."

"I wasn't going to say anything!"

"Of course you were dear, but you'll soon accept her for what she is, a decent woman."

"Gladys! I wasn't going to—" He gave up.

Mrs Dreese went back to the two rooms and a kitchen she called home. She wondered what her son, would say. He hated her using her real name and telling people about his father.

The two rooms for which she paid a weekly rent of ten shillings were small and very dark due in part to the overgrown hedge outside the back window of her living room. She had offered to have them cut them down, but the landlord had refused permission.

The door from the living room led into a narrow kitchen. Along one wall was a bath, covered with a board, which she removed when she took the weekly bath she was allowed. She also removed it to do her washing, in the two hours allotted to her on Monday afternoons. At the moment the wooden board was propped against the wall, the clothes and bedding having just been washed, but left in the bath waiting for the weather to be suitable for drying it in the overgrown garden.

There was a small food cupboard, and she took out a packet of ham and a loaf of bread. Filling two plates with small, neatly cut sandwiches, she covered them with a clean cloth and went to find her son.

She called to him as she knocked on his door, "There's a sandwich if you'd like it."

"What's this about you applying for a job as a cleaner?" he demanded as he pulled the door open. "And with someone like Gladys Weston too."

"It's what I do best, looking after a home. I kept our home beautifully, didn't I? Now I no longer have one, apart from those shabby rooms, I think I'll enjoy working for the Westons and pretending their house is mine."

"Oh, Mother, why did it all have to go so wrong? How could my father end up bankrupt?"

"I don't know, Carl, but I do know we have to try and put it right."

Carl Dreese, who called himself Rees, took the sandwiches and for a moment resented his promise to his mother that they would work and save until his father's debts had been cleared. He had given up so much: a career, the girl he loved, and his home. Sometimes there seemed little chance of living long enough to do more than pay off the debts. He knew his mother had given up her chance of a happy life, too, but there were times when he still resented his sacrifices, believing that his were greater – promising he would avoid girls and meeting Mair in secret so his mother wouldn't be upset. It was hard.

His mother saw the doubt on his face and said encouragingly, "It won't be much longer, Carl. Another year or two and we'll almost be there. Selling the house gave us a good start. Thank goodness the house was mine, or that would have been lost to us too."

Five

E dward Jenkins was absent from the sports shop more and more frequently as Easter approached and arrangements for his special day were filling his time. Gladys was heavily involved. Megan discouraged her grandmother as much as possible but, as she explained to Edward, she didn't want to upset her.

"Dear Grannie had such plans for my sister and cousin Jack and me," she told him as they went through the guest list in Edward's flat one evening. "I think she had been saving for our weddings for years and if the family business hadn't failed we would each have had a splendid affair and invited half the town."

"I don't think so. Jack and Victoria ran away from her dream of a large white wedding, remember? Going off to Gretna Green like a couple of kids. And when your sister Joan married Viv Lewis they cut her ideas severely, didn't they?"

"And now we've done the same. Poor Grandmother. She did want to pretend the Westons were royalty for the day."

"What about the reception? We still haven't decided."

"You're sure you don't want to have the reception in Montague Court? It was your home."

"My sister is still there and I don't trust her not to try and spoil it. No, we've ordered the cake, and for the rest we'll ask Dora Lewis – if she can find someone to help her on the day. Mair perhaps? We can't expect your Aunt Sian to organise the catering for our wedding, even if she is Dora's partner. We'd never get that one past your grandmother!"

"So, it's Gomer Hall and Dora and partner, then? You are sure, Edward?"

"We'll go and see Dora this evening, shall we?"

Dora invited Sian to discuss the young couple's arrangements and they planned the buffet lunch for Tuesday, April the third. With Sian helping Dora with the advance preparations and Mair agreeing to help on the day, everything was quickly arranged.

The day broke calm and dry. Dora was in the hall before seven, checking that the tables were set up and the ordered food had arrived safely. Mair met her there and they decorated the tables and the walls so that the rather drab room was as festive as they could make it.

In the big house overlooking the docks Gladys was almost in tears. "Arfon, what is the matter with our girls? Imagine another Weston wedding in that awful, common, place."

"Imagine a white wedding with the bride carrying her daughter into the church!" Arfon replied in his pompous manner. "D'you want the girl to be a laughing stock as well as the source of gossip, woman? Megan has a child and the man she is marrying isn't the father. Stop wishing for the impossible and settle down to enjoy the day. It is a celebration after all." He rested a hand on the back of a chair and leant at an angle as he prepared to make a speech. "Two people setting out on life's path and—"

"Do shut up, Arfon dear and let me wallow in misery for a hour or two. Then I'll put on a brave face like I always do."

Arfon chuckled then. "They've caused a bit of grief here and there, our girls, haven't they?"

"Always talked about, always setting the trend for others to follow, but this, our dear little Megan having a child out of wedlock and now marrying the owner of a shop! It's too much sometimes, Arfon dear, it really is."

"The Jenkinses were landed gentry," he mocked, "once!"

"All right, you can mock me dear, but I did hope that one of our three grandchildren would make us proud."

"Rubbish, woman, I'm proud of them all and so are you."

Megan was leaving her daughter with Rhiannon during the service and then, much to her grandmother's dismay, she was going to walk out of the church with the baby in her arms. Never one to worry about the town's gossips, she determined to show them that their words would have no effect on her or on Edward. Megan and Joan's maxim was, if you do something unconventional or even outrageous then do it boldly, not secretively as though ashamed, there's less to talk about if you show you don't care what the gossips say. Today was going to be a test of that attitude, without doubt.

Megan's mother, Sally, was so besotted with the baby she had long forgotten any thoughts of shame. She helped Megan dress her granddaughter in the new outfit they had chosen with such care, and then braced herself for meeting her husband. Today, Sally and Ryan were going to the register office together as though none of their difficulties had happened. He was meeting her at their house in Glebe Lane. She was anxious, not for fear of him hitting her but afraid he would do something to spoil their daughter's day. She stood, dressed in her pink and grey outfit, waiting for him to arrive, half hoping that he wouldn't, wondering if he would be able to cope with the ceremony and with giving his daughter away as he had grudgingly promised to do.

Edward was wondering if his sister Margaret would appear. Rather reluctantly he had issued her an invitation, but not to Megan's Uncle Islwyn. That would be taking tolerance too far.

The room in the register office was small with no space for more than the immediate family, but once outside, the happy couple were swamped with well-wishers as they made their way to the hall. Rhiannon was there with her husband and stepson, all dressed in their best: Rhiannon wearing a long coat to hide the swelling of new life within her. Lewis was with them as Dora was in the hall putting the final touches to the wedding breakfast. Janet and Hywel Griffiths were there with their family, including Basil and Eleri and their two small sons. Ernie's wife Helen was conspicuously pregnant with a baby due the following month and she was in no way shy about showing it. Her mother kept pulling her daughter's jacket across her front, even pinning it in place at one point, but Helen only laughed and let it hang freely again. "At least try and hide it until people have forgotten the date of your wedding," Gloria Gunner pleaded, to no avail.

Frank wasn't with the rest of the family. Learning that Mair was helping Dora with the catering he had gone ahead to see whether he could help.

"I'll go down and walk with Mair to the bank every evening you're away," he promised Edward.

"You can keep an eye on the shop by painting the understairs cupboard while we're gone, if you like," Edward suggested, and was amused at the look of delight on the usually solemn face of the tall, skinny young man. In the past, Frank had earned a few shillings walking with funeral processions, setting the solemnity of the occasion with his long, droll features, and to see it smiling was an unusual sight.

Sally was standing alone, remembering the moment she had seen Ryan coming and the way her heart had begun to race. He had looked calm, but he had also looked unwell. He was pale and his eyes were heavy as though from lack of sleep. She tried not to fuss over him, but it was difficult to forget the habits of years. She had been glad her sister Sian had been with her when he had thrown down the buttonhole she had offered him. Grateful too that Sian had held her arm as Ryan disparagingly said that the wedding was a farce and he would not take part in it.

"Get someone else to give the girl away. I won't be there to see it."

As he had turned and walked away, Sally had started to run after him but Sian had stopped her.

"Let him go, Sally. We'll ask Jack. He and Edward are friends and he is Megan's cousin."

Sadly Sally had agreed.

William Jones, the retired draper who had once owned the shop that was now the sports shop, was there with his landlady and they both carried small, gaily wrapped wedding presents as well as some confetti to throw over the happy couple. Gwennie Woodlas who ran the ladies gown shop which offered, 'Clothes for the Discerning Woman', was there. Viv and Joan looked round the gathering throng and thought that if anyone did start any criticism, there were enough of the couple's friends here to stop it before it did any harm.

Sally was startled to see Maxie Powell there, also carrying a very large and beautifully wrapped gift. He hadn't been invited but was obviously not going to allow that small detail to stop him enjoying the occasion.

"I'm here to represent all the people you look after so well in Glebe Lane, Mrs Fowler-Weston," he said, smiling and handing the box to Mair, to add to a growing pile.

"I can't get rid of the man," Sally whispered to her sister.

"Don't worry, there are always a few gate-crashers and he looks harmless enough," Sian reassured her. Megan had a quick word with Jack who led the man away. Maxie wasn't upset or embarrasssed.

"I only wanted to deliver the present," he said cheerfully. "I didn't intend to stay."

Sally saw what was happening and she felt mean. "Please stay and share the food, Mr Powell," she called. Sian and Jack shrugged acceptance of her decision and a delighted Maxie was allowed to return to the crowd in the hall.

"First dance please, Mrs Fowler-Weston," he said, as he waved his thanks to Sally and Sian.

At first Mair was too busy to note who was there and who was not. The food was simple, most of the work being done before the guests arrived. The cake, made by Sian and Dora a few weeks previously, stood in isolated splendour on a separate table where it could be admired. Barry Williams had already taken a photograph of the couple pretending to cut the cake so he and Caroline and young Joseph-Hywel could sit together and enjoy the occasion.

The babble of voices crowded out Mair's thoughts. She gathered plates, cut food and served it, stacked used dishes and brought out clean ones, concentrating on the job and trying not to think of the hours she had spent dreaming about such an occasion with herself and Carl as the leading players. The sound of voices swelled around her as the meal progressed. Conversations building as friends exchanged gossip and others introduced themselves and searched among their known acquaintances to find someone they both knew, so they could deepen their friendship, for the afternoon and evening at least. Laughter and chatter filled the room, yet Mair felt more alone than she had ever been. If only things had worked out between her and Carl, she would have been laughing and enjoying herself too.

Then she saw him. He had entered the hall, uninvited, and walked towards the top table. The buzz of dozens of conversations died down as he handed Megan and Edward a long box.

"He's my cleaner's son you know," Gladys's loud voice announced, as Arfon asked the man what he wanted.

"I was asked to deliver this," Carl said, with a bow.

"By whom?" Edward asked, standing to accept the gift-wrapped parcel. He looked at their names scrawled on the label and put it aside and sat down. He whispered to Megan. "It looks like it's my sister's handwriting. I think we'll open it later."

Basil and Eleri Griffiths's four-year-old Ronnie had a different idea. While the toasts were being drunk and his parents' eyes were not on him, he tore open the box and revealed a doll. A cheap doll, with a gaudily painted face, which he held up in great excitement before running to give it to his baby brother.

Edward tried to hide it from Megan, but she saw it and laughed. "How nice, a gift from my Uncle Islwyn and his mistress, Margaret," she muttered.

"I'm sorry, Megan. I hope your Aunt Sian doesn't see it."

"I have," Sian said briskly. "It makes me more sure than ever that your Uncle Islwyn leaving me for Margaret Jenkins was the best thing that's happened to me in a long time."

The uneasy moment was passed off as a joke, and Sian went into the kitchen to make sure Dora and Mair were coping. She found Mair in tears and Dora comforting her.

"What's the matter with everyone?" Sian demanded. "You're staff and aren't supposed to cry!"

As a contribution to the day, Gladys had paid for her cleaning lady to help clear up after the wedding breakfast and Mrs Dreese arrived soon after her son had delivered the parcel. As she was outside the kitchen she heard Mair telling Dora and Sian why she was so upset.

"It's Carl. He said he loved me and, and," she sobbed, "and now he's told me goodbye."

"Without telling you why? But why would he leave you if he loved you?" Sian demanded. She wondered, because of the depth of distress in the usually sensible Mair, whether he had left the girl expecting a child. "You haven't done anything – er – silly, have you?" she whispered. Mrs Dreese watched the scene and was angry. How dare they talk about her son like this?

"Don't say I could be having Carl's baby," Mair wailed. "I'd die of shame!"

"I doubt it," Sian said dryly. "You'd cope with it like the rest of us."

"Sorry, I was forgetting about your niece. I didn't mean to be rude. What a thing to say, on a day like today, too. I – oh, er –" she clasped her stomach and wailed, "I think I'm going to be sick." Dora helped her out of her chair and directed her towards the toilets, before sharing a knowledgeable glance with Sian.

Carl was standing just inside the hall, a drink in his hands, talking to one or two of the guests. Edward had wanted him to leave, to take the insulting gift back to his sister and Sian's husband, but decided it was better not to make a scene. Instead, he continued with the pretence that sending the doll as a wedding gift was simply a joke.

Mrs Dreese didn't go into the kitchen, she opened the door to the hall and called her son. "I thought you'd promised me to stay away from women? These people are talking about you and a woman called Mair. Asking if she's expecting, and considering you the father."

"Mam? What are you saying? Keep you voice down!"

Mair, coming out of the toilets, said, in surprise, "This is your mother? Carl, why didn't you tell me? Why so many secrets?" Turning, Carl collided with Mair, nearly knocking her over. She staggered backwards against the wall before sliding down onto a pile of empty boxes. Without waiting to see if she

99

was hurt he burst through the double doors and out into the street.

Frank had been looking for Mair, still hoping she would find time to talk to him and he could offer to walk her home, even though she had told him to get lost, twice already. When he saw the way Carl pushed her aside he went to help her.

"Go after him!" she said. "Why are you letting him get away with pushing me like that?" She was red faced with crying and her hair was stuck to her cheeks with spent tears. Her eyes blazed angrily at him as though he were the one at fault.

"I can find Carl any time," Frank said. "I stopped to make sure you were all right."

"Oh, you're useless." She sobbed. "Get lost!"

Frank loped home dismayed, wondering why he was always in the wrong. He sat in the back porch waiting for the rest of the family to return and thought that his life was utter misery and showed no sign it would ever improve.

The wedding party finished at eleven thirty and Mair walked home alone. Several people had offered to see her safely back and to each she had explained that she had someone waiting for her. The night was cold, an easterly wind biting her flushed cheeks with an iciness that she welcomed. Although there was no moon it wasn't completely dark for someone like Mair, who was used to walking home alongside the dark trees and far from street lamps.

The woods were comfortingly quiet, she had no fear of an attack, although once she reached the darker stretches of the lane, she did wish she had agreed to her father coming to fetch her as he had pleaded to do. Why had she sent Frank away? He'd have at least made sure she was safely home. Instead, she had stupidly hoped that Carl would miraculously appear and walk with her. When would she learn?

She was hardly out of sight of the last of the houses, having just passed the telephone box where she and Carl had sometimes met, when she heard someone coming up behind her. Some instinct told her it wasn't Carl. Increasing her speed she went on into the dark, narrow, tree-lined lane, looking ahead for her first sight of the lights in the cottage.

The hand on her arm was sudden and heavy. It was Carl after all, was her first thought. The blow to the side of her head was unexpected and she was disorientated as more blows rained down on her. She tried to run but tripped over the grass at the edge of the lane and fell to the ground. Her head, her legs and her arms were beaten and kicked until she was crying, pleading with her assailant to leave her alone. Then she stopped speaking, lost in a whirlwind of pain and fright, just concentrating on trying to avoid the punches and kicks, listening to the grunts as her attacker aimed each one. The beating slowed down and instead of grunts, she heard panting as the person grew tired.

The attack stopped as suddenly as it had begun and she lay for a while, aching and sore and very frightened, half expecting the person to return. The phone box wasn't far and, slowly and painfully, she made her way there. She had lost her purse but got through to the operator who, eventually, rang her father's number. She sobbed as she tried to explain what had happened, then slumped to the floor and waited for him to come.

"Who was he?" he asked, once he had got her home and they waited for the doctor. "Did you recognise him?" "No, I don't know who it was. But Dad," she said in a whisper, "I think it was a woman."

In the days following the unexplained assault, Frank was a regular visitor to the Gregorys' cottage. Mair refused to see him for the first few days, but he brought gifts, leaving them with her father, or outside the back door. He delivered fresh eggs, a chicken, a rabbit – stolen – and, with acute embarrassment, a bunch of flowers which he hid under his coat until he had entered the kitchen. When she finally saw him, Frank asked her if the man who had made such a cowardly attack had been Carl.

"No, it wasn't a man's voice," she told him emphatically. "The sounds I heard were very brief, but I'm sure it was a woman." Frank was convinced she had been mistaken.

Rhiannon opened the shop early one Monday morning and was surprised to have several customers before the usual time of nine o'clock. When she saw Barry Williams later that morning she suggested to him that she could try opening at eight thirty each morning. "Just for a trial," she said. "See if it's worth it. Most people start work at nine so there must be plenty of passing trade between half eight and nine. Pity to miss it."

"Won't it be a long day for you?" Barry asked doubtfully.

"I don't mind. Charlie and Gwyn go off to Windsor's garage before eight and I'm up to cook their breakfast, so it isn't as though I'd need to rise earlier."

"Well, if you're sure." He drove off in his van to a town in west Wales, where he had arranged to take photographs of a wedding party that afternoon and a golden wedding celebration that evening. With the promise of plenty of orders he was going to have a good day.

Carl Rees was one of Rhiannon's customers who called before nine o'clock. He came in and looked surprised. "Didn't expect to catch you this early." He smiled. He chose a box of Milk Tray and a bag of toffees.

"Who are the chocolates for – Mair?" Rhiannon asked, as she packed his purchases. She received only a grunt in reply. "Sorry, I wasn't being nosy," she said untruthfully. Mair hadn't explained, but Rhiannon knew she had been upset at Megan and Edward's wedding.

"Jumping to conclusions is worse," Carl said, slapping the money on the counter.

At lunchtime, Rhiannon usually went across the road to start preparations for the evening meal but today she went up to the High Street. Walking into the sports shop she called to Mair.

"I think I offended your boyfriend," she whispered. "I only asked whether the chocolates were for you again, and he seemed a bit angry. Sorry."

"So am I," Mair replied. "He's never given me any chocoates and anyway, we're finished. So whoever he's buying them for, it isn't me!"

"Oh dear. I've really done it, haven't I? That's the last time I try to be friendly."

Rhiannon left Mair, feeling very embarrassed at her innocent remarks and quickly did her shopping. Mair stood thinking about the strange courtship that had ended so mysteriously. She thought about the attack. If it had been a woman, could it still be connected with Carl? A wife? A jealous girlfriend? She had never been given an explanation for his secretiveness. He owed her that, at least. She decided she had to have a serious talk with Carl.

Her opportunity came when he passed the shop an hour later. She called to him and he stopped and came in. Edward was away buying stock and she offered Carl a cup of tea. As he sat and drank it, she asked, "Who's my rival then? Who's the mysterious woman you're buying chocolates for?"

"None of your business," he said, the sting taken out of the words by a wide smile. "I'll tell you one day, but not now. Right?"

"I'm not a very patient girl, Carl," she said.

"Then waiting to learn my secret will be good for you," he retorted.

"But if it's over, and we won't be seeing each other again, the least you can do is explain. Please, Carl?"

Thanking her for the tea, kissing her lightly on the cheek he left, whispering, "All right, meet me tonight and ask me again."

"You mean it's on again?"

"No, I can't go on seeing you, but we can meet one more time."

"And we'll talk?" She smiled as he nodded, although she half dreaded hearing what he had to tell her, convinced he had a wife; a jealous wife who had taken revenge on her in that dark lane. Her father would be out at some meeting or other and wouldn't be back until ten. Plenty of time to persuade Carl to reveal his secret. For the rest of the day she puzzled over it and at five thirty, when she left for home, she was still wondering.

She was edgy walking home even though it was not yet dark. She jumped at every sound and was relieved to see Frank and for once didn't tell him to get lost. She thanked him for his gifts during the days she had been off work recovering from her injuries.

"I know you don't know who was responsible," he said, "but I'm glad you and that Carl Rees are finished."

She didn't reply.

On her way back from the cinema that afternoon, Jennie Francis walked past the premises she had once leased. The window was still empty. That, and the absence of a sign made it clear that no one had so far rented it. It was already beginning to look neglected and shabby. If only Peter had supported her and she had been able to stay a bit longer, she might have turned the business around. Saddened by the finality of the brief visit, she went for a walk.

She knew she would have to get a job, but until she had persuaded Peter to sell the house, she had no intention of helping him with the finances. She was in debt, with the end of her business, but not by much. Once she was earning she would easily settle the few outstanding bills. The sale of the house would give her a little capital, enough to start her savings plan towards a fresh business of her own. Really her own. This time she wouldn't begin it in debt to Peter's parents.

She wandered aimlessly along the streets, her feet slowly and almost unknowingly, taking her to the popular Pleasure Beach where several stalls and shops were preparing for the forth-coming holiday season. It was almost dark by the time she reached there but there was still plenty of activity. Ladders had sprouted like exotic plants, propped against shop fronts supporting men wielding paint brushes with more enthusiasm than skill. Windows were being cleaned of the grime of the winter months and buckets of water were thrown across paving.

Whitsun was the big opening and the proprietors of the cafes and shops were going to be ready. One cafe seemed to be open for business and she went in. It was filled with the local traders. All of the customers were dressed for work. Mostly paint-stained trousers and shirts, or dungarees with paint brushes and small tools jutting out of every pocket. Men were arguing about the best way of repairing gutters and complained about the mess they had to clear out. The women wore coarse aprons with pockets bulging with dusters and tins of polish.

"We're closed, Missus," the man behind the counter said. "Only for the traders this is, see."

"I'll buy her a cup of tea, Wyn," a familiar voice called, and Jennie turned to see Carl sitting at one of the tables.

"I'm repairing some of the shop signs," he explained as he stood and offered her a seat. "This is Jennie, my ex-boss," he said, by way of explanation.

When she was sitting with a cup of tea in front of her, Carl asked, "Have you decided what you're going to do, yet? Will you reopen when you've sorted out your finances?"

"I'll do something, run a shop of some kind but so far I haven't decided what business it will be. I should have stuck with my original plan and made it a gift shop," she said bitterly. "A place selling really special gifts, something for everyone. Once I'd become well known, I'd have persuaded people to come long distances to buy from me because of my unusual stock and wide choice. I'm sure it would have been successful."

"Get in touch if I can help," he said.

"Thanks. Now, what about you, Carl? How is that girlfriend of yours?"

"What girlfriend? I don't stay with a girl long enough for her to call herself my girlfriend." He took a sip of tea and added, "Too wily for that, I am."

"What about the one called Mair? Mair Gregory, wasn't it?"

"Only occasional friends. Nothing serious," he assured her as he stood to get back to his work.

An hour or so later, Mair was getting ready for Carl's visit. Despite his saying they could not go on meeting, she had convinced herself that this would be the day he would tell her everything and propose. They hadn't known each other long but the passionate nature of their brief relationship was proof that love wasn't slow to grow. Thank goodness Dad would be out.

Carl must have been watching for her father to leave because he knocked on the back door only a few minutes after the constable had ridden off on his bicycle. He stepped inside and at once took her in his arms. There was a scraping sound from outside, which they both recognised as her father's bicycle being propped against the wall, and instead of standing there as her father re-entered, Carl darted out of sight and crept up the stairs.

"Forgot the minutes of the last meeting," her father explained as he retrieved his papers from the living-room table and left once more.

"Where are you?" Mair whispered, a giggle of amusement in her voice.

"I'm up here, stuck under your bed," Carl hissed back and the unnecessary struggle to pull him out ended in the way his secret visits had always ended, in her bed, both swearing undying love.

It was past nine o'clock before they came down and Carl was anxious to leave.

"Don't dash off, my father isn't an ogre," Mair pleaded. "Why don't you stay for supper, there's plenty for three unless – unless you're full up after eating those chocolates Rhiannon thinks you buy for me?"

"Look, Mair, I think it's best we don't see each other again. For a while at least."

"What? But I thought we were together again?"

"No. Believe me it's best this way."

"How can you say that after all we said and did upstairs?"

"I meant all that, every word. But I have a problem and until it's solved I'm not free."

"You're married!"

"No, I'm not married. But this problem, well, I can't talk about it. You'll have to trust me. I know it's asking a lot, we haven't known each other very long, but I have to deal with it on my own."

"How long?" she asked. "You promised to tell me, get everything out in the open. You told me you loved me, Carl!" Questions crowded her brain and were about to tumble out, eventually, in anger.

Carl put a finger over her lips. "Please, Mair, please trust me."

"How long?" she repeated.

"Months. Maybe years," he said, lowering his head in apparent dismay.

The sound of the bicycle scraping against the wall again alerted him and he kissed her hurriedly and left by the front door. She hid her dismay from her father, talking lightly about her day in the sports shop as she prepared supper, but all the time she was hurting inside. Ending it without any explanation and after telling her he loved her, what had gone wrong?

When she slipped into her bed, remembering with such pain how Carl had shared it with her so recently, she realised that she still didn't know who was the recipient of those chocolates, or why he had run so desperately fast from Gomer Hall. She had to face facts. All his previous behaviour pointed to there being a wife. The attack made by a woman added credence to that theory. What should she do?

When Jennie heard from a neighbour that her mother-in-law was recovering from her spell in hospital, she rather reluctantly went to call on her. It was seven o'clock on a mild May evening and she wore a summer dress for the first time. That alone will be enough to start her off, she thought irritably. Never cast a clout, and all that. Well, she wanted to get out of the heavy winter clothes. And her mother-in-law's house was so gloomy she needed to cheer herself up before going inside.

Peter was there as she had hoped. He looked nervously at her as though she would undoubtedly bring bad news.

"Mam isn't well enough for visitors," he said at once.

"Oh, in that case, will you give her these?" She handed him a bunch of mixed spring flowers, but he shook his head.

"Flowers always make Mam sneeze, you should have remembered that."

"In that case, as I'm not allowed to behave like a daughter-in-law should, can I have a word with you?" She gritted her teeth as he looked around him, trying to think of an excuse. "It's all right," she hissed, "I haven't brought reinforcements."

"You'd better come in I suppose."

"No! Just meet me at the estate agents tomorrow at five o'clock. The house is going to be sold." She left him standing there and hurried off, wondering how she could have possibly loved him, wondering why she had ever thought he would be a supportive partner.

For a while it had been wonderful, she being the strong one. Peter had needed her and together they had defied his mother and bought a house, refusing to live in two of her spare rooms. They had decided to start a business which she would run until it was established, they would then run it together: fine glassware and china; novelties and seasonal offerings, perhaps paintings as well, later on. A happy business expanding as their fame spread, their reputation for having something for every purse and every occasion. It would have been so wonderful. Tempted though she so frequently was, she had never once said to Peter, 'told you so', when the decorating business his parents had insisted on, had failed. He was there, outside the estate agents when she arrived at five the following day, but he did not look as though they would agree about the house. She took a deep breath and prepared to argue. "Look, Peter. You let me down about the shop and I'm not willing to let you win this one. I want the house sold. It's pointless me staying there on my own." She waited for him to speak and when he did, the next stage of her argument was forgotten.

"I want to come back," he said.

She looked at him for a long time in silence.

"How is your Mam?" she asked in a polite voice.

"Oh, she's a bit better, but she isn't strong."

"You're still having to shift for yourselves? Find your own food?"

"Yes, I – no, Jennie! That isn't the reason I want to come back." She weakened momentarily but knew their marriage was over. It had been over the day he had insisted she close down the business and return the loan his parents had given them. Without loyalty there was nothing. Hardening her heart and, avoiding looking at him, she said coldly, "You left me, Peter. I was working all the hours I could to get our business underway, and all you could do was criticise me for not being the perfect wife. I was working for us. You and me. I could never trust you again. You supported your parents instead of me once too

108

often." She pushed her way into the estate agents' office and announced loudly. "Mr and Mrs Peter Francis. We have an appointment. We're putting our house on the market. Aren't we, Peter?"

Peter could only nod.

When she went home she sat in a chair for a long time, getting colder, her thin dress no protection against the chill of the evening, too upset to light a fire. The room grew dark and she couldn't raise the enthusiasm to turn on the light. She felt the grumblings of hunger but when she did move, she went straight to bed. Today she had ended her marriage. She was a bully and she felt ashamed.

Mrs Collins had never been called by her first name: her husband had called her Collins; the children called her Mam; everyone else called her Mrs Collins. The invitation to call Sam Lilly by his first name had alarmed her. If she did so, she would have to admit to the foolish name her parents had chosen for her. How could she do that?

Sam had been so kind to her. Generous, too, helping with the work his sister Martha paid her to do and preparing the wonderful surprise garden.

Before leaving for work that morning, she went out into the yard and admired the sturdy geraniums with their burgeoning buds of pink, red and white, and the more delicate lobelia which were already sending out branches of blue flowers amid the stocky sweet alyssum and forming a frame around the larger flowers to come. Small shrubs in a corner promised green throughout the year and nearby, marigolds and nasturtiums were arranged to fill an old coal bucket and drift over a pile of stones. There were even a few hollyhocks Frank had found a place for against the wall where the concrete had weakened and allowed him to prepare a bed.

What would happen if Mrs Martha Adams discovered how her brother had been spending his spare time? Sam hadn't said, but she had guessed that he had not told her about his help with the housework. She pushed aside the small hope that if she were told to leave he would still be a friend. She was a widow with seven children and a stupid name. What was she thinking of, imagining someone like Sam was more than a generous and kindly man willing to help anyone? Why think for a moment that he thought of her other than as a deserving case? 'A deserving case', had been most people's opinion of her, both before her husband had died and since. Nothing was ever likely to change that. Certainly not the kindness of Sam Lilly.

She dressed the two younger children and delivered them to her daughter. Victoria had agreed to look after them for the morning. Then she caught a bus on the High Street. She was due at Martha Adams and Sam Lilly's house in half an hour and she wished she was not. Because of her fanciful thoughts of a friendship that would grow and perhaps become something stronger, she was embarrassed when she walked into the house in Chestnut Road to begin her work.

Martha was dressed to go out and, giving Mrs Collins her instructions for the three hours for which she paid her, she left to meet her friends at the Rose Tree cafe. Hoping that Sam was also out, Mrs Collins gathered her dusters and polishes, mops and brushes and started on the bedrooms. Singing coming from the bathroom unnerved her and she coughed and called to let him know she was there.

"It's me, Mr Lilly, I'm starting on the bedrooms."

"Good morning, and call me Sam," he said as he came out onto the landing. "Now, what d'you want me to do first?"

"Really, you shouldn't. You've done so much for me already. Mrs Adams pays me to do it."

"I'll take the rugs into the garden and beat them. Best make the most of the dry day, eh?" Ignoring her protests he tackled the rugs and then came back in time to help her put fresh covers on the bed. With few words necessary, they dealt with everything on the list and went out into the rather chilly garden to drink a cup of tea.

"I hope we don't have a frost tonight," he said, looking up at the clear blue sky. "Pity to see those geraniums of yours damaged."

"What can I do? Frank told me to cover them with newspaper."

"Worth a try. But don't worry, they're tough enough." They walked around the garden when they had drunk their tea and Sam explained to his interested companion the names and habits of the plants in the flowerbeds.

"The lady who lived here before you, Mrs Nia Williams, loved her garden," Mrs Collins told him. "So sad that it killed her, wasn't it?" She told him about the accident in the garden when Nia been trying to cut down a branch that she considered dangerous. Lewis Lewis, who had shared the house with her at the time, had been promising to deal with it for weeks and one day, perhaps to surprise him, she had tried sawing through the branch herself. It had fallen on her and killed her.

"I think it must have been worse for the man. He must feel guilty every day of his life," Sam said softly. "I know I would."

"He went back home to his wife eventually and I think she has helped him deal with it."

"Nice to have someone who cares, isn't it?" he said.

"There are times when it can save you from despair," she replied, as if from personal knowledge, although there had never been anyone in her life to whom she had been able to turn. As if sensing this, Sam took her arm and walked side by side with her back to the house.

There was a sensation of contentment between them, as though a corner had been turned as they washed their cups and Sam walked her to the bus stop.

"If you won't tell me your name," he teased, as the bus came into view, "tell me again the names of your children."

"My husband was a great royalist so the first three were called Victoria, George and Albert – our Bertie. Then we have Elizabeth and Margaret. Then war began so we added, Winston and Montgomery." She laughed. "We're a family for grand names and no mistake."

"No Eisenhower?"

"The cat was called Ike."

"And yours?"

The bus stopped and the conducter called, "Hurry along please."

"Seven is enough to be getting on with," she replied. She was smiling as the bus stopped then started on its slow journey back to her children and the need to cook supper.

Frank was still happy. His observations told him Carl no longer visited Mair. Hope was such a powerful tranquilliser that he did the chores requested by Hywel without argument and even dug a patch of ground ready for planting out lettuce without being asked. Mair would soon forget Carl. She'd soon realise what a waster he really was. He went several times to the sports shop hoping to see her but Edward would explain that she was out, or busy, or in the stock room. It took a long time for him to realise she was avoiding him. She made it clear when they did eventually meet. Hanging around in the lane waiting for her to get home from work, he stepped out and offered to carry her shopping bag.

"Mair, it's smashing to see you."

"Is it?"

"Yeh."

Reaching the gate she went through and closed it after her leaving him firmly on the outside.

"Nice meeting your dad the other night. He and I could be friends now I've given up poaching and all that, couldn't we?"

She looked at him with utter disbelief.

"Mair, I was wondering—"

"Get lost!"

"All right." He sighed. Hands in pockets, long legs bending and straightening like an automatic doll, he headed for home, accepting the inevitable disappointment like a small boy.

Mair almost called him back. She was going to be alone that evening. Her father had some meeting to attend, then he would be working through the night. She wasn't in the mood for a solitary meal, the wireless and bed. She didn't think she'd eat and she was doubtful of sleeping. She had a lot to think about and none of it was pleasant.

Six

Ryan Fowler walked to Glebe Lane and stood watching the house he had once called home. He hadn't stayed. To have had a job, a home and a family – including the fussy Gladys as a mother-in-law, then almost overnight to lose it all, had been a distressing experience, but now he didn't think he wanted any of it back. He wasn't lonely. He hardly missed them. Contented – that would describe his present existence. Living in a flat, being paid moderately well for doing a non-stressful job that he could forget the moment the clock reached five p.m. each day, and pleasing himself how he spent his spare time, it was no hardship.

He stood for a long time looking over the back gate, half hidden by the overgrown lonicera. Cutting that straggling mess, a most tedius job, was no longer his responsibility, he thought with a smile. He watched as Sally went in and out of the kitchen serving her paying guests with their evening meal. It was only the thought of Sally finding comfort in the arms of someone else that occasionally kept him awake at night. He didn't want to go back to her, but he admitted to a little jealousy when he thought of someone else sharing her bed and being fussed over by her in a way he could no longer tolerate.

He walked back to the basement flat. Gradually his mood of relaxed acceptance changed, he wanted everything to go back to how it had been a couple of years ago: Sally as a loving wife; himself as master in his home. It had been strange, even frightening, to look in at the house where he had lived for almost thirty years, seeing it carrying on with its life without him. It was as though he were dead; a restless spirit come back to haunt the place where he had been happy. He wanted to go back, walk in

113

and make himself a cup of tea, read a newspaper in his favourite chair. But he couldn't. To do that too soon could delay the moment for months. His shoulders drooped as he accepted the reality that to go back was his dream.

Anger swelled. For a while he allowed it to grow, enjoying it, feeling ill treated and sour. He turned on the television and stared with half his mind involved and the other half seething at the unfairness of life. He blamed his parents-in-law, Gladys and Arfon, and his daughters and his wife. They were all to blame. Unable to cope with his turbulent thoughts, he went out again into the dark night.

His feet took him once again towards Glebe Lane. He was still apportioning blame on everyone around him. His daughter Joan had married Viv Lewis, who had pushed him out of a well-paid job. Megan had shamed him by becoming a mother before she was a wife. Then there was his wife. Sally had embarrassed him, robbed him of his authority by turning their house into a guesthouse. She had made it blatantly clear to the whole town that he was incapable of being boss in his own home. Hardly surprising that he'd lost his temper.

Looking into the kitchen, he saw that Sally was washing dishes and being assisted, not by Megan but by a stranger. One of her guests probably, he decided. As he watched, the man touched her shoulder and Sally moved away. Ryan smiled. It wouldn't be long before she was fussing over someone new. Then he'd really have a reason to be angry.

He roamed the streets through the early hours and could hardly remember where he had walked. In a back lane behind Hartley Street one or two dustbins had been placed outside the gates ready for collection later in the week. One had been tipped on its side and the contents spread across the ground. Stale food was exposed and a pair of boots lay abandoned, decorated with potato peelings and stalks of cabbage. Distastefully, he picked one up and walking briskly, purposefully, went back to Glebe Lane and threw it through Sally's window.

He felt exultant, a conquering hero, as he hurried home, as though he had won a great victory. But as soon as he reached the back lane behind the High Street and went into his flat, he began to sob.

Mair walked home from the shop slowly, her feet dragging. She was in no hurry to shut herself inside the lonely house. Her father would be out again and apart from preparing a meal there was nothing urgent to do to fill the long lonely hours. She was tempted to call on the Griffithses. Frank would probably be there, working in the garden or talking to the goats, she thought disparagingly. But even Frank was better than no one today.

There was a knock at the door and as her thoughts had been on Frank it was he whom she expected to see. It was Carl. Relief spread across her face and she stood back for him to step inside. He looked around as though the trees were hiding spies.

"It's all right, Carl. No one can see you!" she snapped.

"I'm sorry, Mair. It's difficult."

"So I gather. Your mother, is it? Not wanting to lose her darling son?"

"It *is* partly my mother, but you'll have to trust me on this. If we're careful, make sure no one sees us, we can go on meeting."

"You haven't told her about us, have you," she stated.

"She's afraid I'll marry and leave her. You know what mothers are like."

"No, I don't. My own mother died years ago. I do know that my father wouldn't try to spoil my chance of happiness and a life of my own."

"Sorry, I'd forgotten." He put an arm around her and kissed her forehead gently. "It must have been hard for you without her."

"Can't you imagine how worthless and foolish you make me feel, pretending you don't know me? Why can't you show everyone that we're friends? More than friends – lovers. Are you ashamed of me? Is that it?"

He held her tightly against him, cheek to cheek, feeling the hot tears that ran down her face on to his lips. "I'm sorry, my darling girl. But I have something to sort out, something that stops me from telling the world how I feel about you. I can't tell you, but if you could be patient for a little while, then one day it will be different. I promise you." He let his lips caress her cheek, her neck. "Please Mair, let me stay."

She looked up at him, his eyes so pleading and his lips so tempting, but she turned away, opened the door and waited in silence as he stepped out. She locked the door and waited, leaning against it, a barrier of just a few inches. She expected him to knock, to plead for her to open it again, but all she heard were his footsteps as he walked away.

An hour after Carl had gone, there was another knock and with her heart filled with hope, Mair ran to answer it to see Frank standing there.

"Don't say 'get lost,' " he pleaded, as she began to close the door. "Our Mam's invited a few friends round and I thought you might like to come. Rhiannon and Charlie will be there and our Basil, Eleri and their boys. There's Jack and Victoria and our Ernie and Helen and—"

"Yes, I'll come. Thanks."

"Oh, you will? Good. Smashing!" He had been taken by surprise by her acceptance and he grinned widely and said hopefully, "Call for you shall I?"

"About eight?"

"Smashing!"

"The grin's back," Hywel whispered to his wife as they watched their lanky son dash in and drag the bath out of the shed. "Mair!" they said in unison.

"You invited that policeman's daughter then, our Frank?" Hywel teased as Frank began filling the boiler to heat water for his bath. "Dangerous that is, mind, remembering where most of the meat for tonight's food came from. Pheasant, partridge and rabbit pie made by your mam, and eggs from Booker's hens. Mad you are, boy, encouraging PC Gregory's daughter."

"I like her," Frank replied. He went to talk to the goats. He didn't mind a bit of teasing, but Mair wasn't a subject for jokes. When he went back to check on the boiler, Hywel was still in the same mood.

"All the girls in Pendragon Island and you have to go and

choose that one." Hywel sighed dramatically. Frank pushed him out of the kitchen and locked the door to have his bath in peace.

By half-past eight the small cottage was crammed full and still more people came. Janet made sure there was a comfortable seat for Rhiannon, who had made her announcement about the baby she carried, and one for her daughter-in-law, Helen who was eight months gone.

"Make sure you stay in one piece, mind," Hywel whispered to Helen as she sat awkwardly on Janet's wooden rocking chair. "I'm no good with people, only goats."

"Don't worry, there's a month to go yet." Helen laughed. But as she spoke she felt a sharp twinge and grasped Ernie's hand for comfort.

"Hell's bells, Helen, I'm not ready for this yet," Ernie spluttered as he saw her face tighten with the discomfort.

Frank was looking less than cheerful. Mair had been ready when he called for her but since arriving at the cottage, she had ignored him. She was sitting beside Rhiannon and whenever he got close enough to listen, they were talking about babies. He went out and leant over the goats' pen. A bachelor, that's what he'd be, for the rest of his life. Minding Mam and Dad when they were past minding themselves; a boring old uncle, and growing old himself, all alone in this place.

He was whispering to the goats, telling them his tale of woe, when Mair came to find him.

"Sorry I've been talking to Rhiannon for so long," she said, and at once his spirits lifted. "It's about babies, see. She likes to talk babies now she's going to have one."

"Her and our Helen. Nothing but baby talk," he said. "We're better off out here talking to the goats."

When they went back inside she stayed with him for the rest of the evening, looking at him to share a joke and singing along when the regular choruses ended the evening.

Frank saw quite a lot of Mair over the following days. Edward and Megan took the baby out and about as the days lengthened and the sun became warmer, and Mair was left in charge of the sports shop. Willie Jones who used to own the premises, which he had run as a draper's shop, called several times a day, and would sometimes stay to allow Mair to dash to the cake shop to buy something for her lunch. Frank made the excuse of sizing up a few jobs still needing to be done, and assured Mair that he was there if she needed any help.

Mair didn't admit it but she was often glad he was there, especially when she had to walk to the bank to put the bag in the overnight safe. After that unprovoked and unexplained attack on her, she had become less confident. He would walk beside her jauntily, as though riding shotgun on some stagecoach of old, Mair thought with a smile, as he glanced around him, both looking out for trouble and in the hope that some of his friends would see them together.

There had been no sign of Carl for several days and one evening, when the bag had been safely posted through to the night safe, he felt emboldened to ask, "D'you fancy going out later? Pictures? A walk?"

"All right. But I'll have to get our Dad's tea first. He's on nights again this week."

"On nights a lot isn't he, your old man?"

"I think he changes with one or two of the others. He doesn't mind it."

After walking her home they arranged to meet at seven and Frank strolled back to the cottage, whistling cheerfully. It seemed that the gossips had been right, and Mair and Carl Rees no longer met. This evening, with her father on nightshift, there might be a chance for them to talk, really talk, and perhaps put their meetings on a regular footing.

They came out of the cinema at ten thirty and almost immediately bumped into Carl. Leaving Frank with a few hurried words, Mair ran after him and began talking to him with some urgency. Frank stood in a shop doorway wondering what to do. It was clear from the way Carl had responded that he didn't want to talk to Mair. As she clutched his arm, he edged away, trying to pull free. She held her ground and he stopped, but his reluctance was plain from the stance of his body. He wanted to get away.

Frank decided to wait. She might not want him to see her if she were upset, but there was no way he was going to let her walk home alone and Carl couldn't be relied on to care for her properly. Leaning his long frame against the door of the shop, he settled in his patient way to watch and wait.

"Carl, I have to talk to you," Mair said, as Carl insisted he was in a hurry. "I have something to tell you."

"Sorry, Mair, but I don't think it can be any concern of mine. It's over. I'm sorry, but you were right it has to end. There are things I have to be free of before I can get involved with anyone."

"But—"

She tried to interrupt but he hushed her, talking patiently to her as though to a child. "I can't discuss it, but one day you'll understand. I have responsibilities. Not a wife, I swear to you that I'm not married—"

"Good," she said. "Glad of that I am, you not having a wife. Because I think we're going to have a baby!"

Frank was watching and although he couldn't hear what was said, he knew it was something serious. Carl looked as though someone had shot him. He held both hands to his chest and stared down at Mair.

"Rubbish," he said, finally. "Don't think you can trap me with that old trick. If you're expecting, it isn't mine!"

Mair stepped back and Frank guessed that this time she was the one receiving the shock. His heart was racing, he wanted to go and thump Carl, whatever was happening. His muscles were aching, longing for the sensation of landing his fist on Carl's chin. Then he saw Carl swivel on his heels and hurry off.

He waited a moment or two, until he saw Mair start to walk in the direction of her lane. He followed but didn't try to catch her up. Best let her recover from whatever argument they'd had. She passed the phone box and hesitated and he thought she might be thinking of ringing her father to ask him to leave work and see her home, afraid of facing the dark lane. He stepped forward and said, "I'll see you safe home, Mair."

He walked silently beside her until she went through her door. She seemed hardly aware of him. He stood for a long time in the darkness beneath the trees, waiting, hoping to see Carl, longing for an opportunity to pick a fight with him. He didn't need a reason; he badly needed a fight. At two a.m. he went home disappointed.

Victoria and Jack walked home from the pictures that evening and they were silent too.

"Don't be unhappy, love," Jack said comfortingly when they got back to their little house in Philips Street. "Having a baby is such a wonderful thing, it's well worth waiting a few more months for."

"Rhiannon is expecting. Helen Griffiths has a baby due any day. I'm so disappointed, Jack."

Jack held her and whispered, "Another month longer to have you all to myself."

He had spoken to a doctor and been told that tension, longing for a child so much, could in itself be the problem. "Tell your wife to relax, forget about conceiving and just be a loving wife," had been his advice. How could Jack tell her that?

He knew that relaxing while they made love was almost impossible for Victoria, brought up in a house with a drunken father and a mother who spent most of her married life either feeding a child or preparing for another. The sounds of lovemaking had been frightening to her as a child and the memories were slow to leave. Decorating the bedroom in cheerful, light colours had been his idea. Making it as different as possible from the rooms she had known as a child. It seemed to have made a difference at first, but soon her beautiful, gentle face had slipped into the same expression of dread as soon as they walked into the room and approached the big, comfortable bed. He didn't know what to do.

Victoria changed the subject. She was aware of a big difference in her mother. "It's since she's been working for Martha Adams and Sam Lilly, isn't it?" she said to Jack. "D'you think there can be a romance developing?"

"It would be wonderful if there were. Your mother is still young. She's kind and loving and gentle – just like you, my darling girl – and quite a catch for someone. Even with six children to care for," he added with a smile.

"Sam Lilly seems very fond of her. He helps her when she works for his sister, makes sure Mam doesn't have any heavy lifting. And now he's invited her to take two of the children to Tenby for the day."

"And he planned that surprise garden for her. That's the act of a besotted man if anything is."

Two of Victoria's brothers were working. They had both found jobs in a store selling animal feed and some of the other needs of farmers and small holders. One of Victoria's sisters delivered morning papers and, with the few piano lessons her mother gave and the money she earned from cleaning, the family managed quite comfortably. Jack and Victoria helped a little, buying clothes as birthday presents to eke out the family finances. Even Gladys Weston offered cast-off clothes on occasions, although her choice of garments, beside being too large for the dainty Mrs Collins, were hardly suitable. Mrs Collins was a skilled needlewoman, however, and she used the material to make smaller garments, sometimes to sell.

"Poor Mam. She's so busy, she never has an idle moment. That's why I was pleased by Sam Lilly's invitation."

"They're going for the whole day?" Jack asked.

"Mam and the two youngest. I said we'd look after the others, get them their meals. Is that all right?" she asked. "You needn't come if you don't want to. I'm sure Viv would be interested in a fishing trip if not."

"Now that *is* a good idea." Jack smiled.

Mair and Rhiannon had not been close friends, but gradually, over the past weeks they had begun to see more of each other. Leaving a few minutes early for her lunch break one day, Mair ran down to Temptations hoping to catch Rhiannon before she closed. Rhiannon was just locking the shop door but she hesitated when she saw Mair coming down Brown Street.

"It's all right, I'll open up for you," she said, as Mair puffed and panted towards her. "Sweets, is it? Or a birthday card you've just remembered?"

"I wanted a chat if you've got time. I've brought a couple of pasties and some cakes. If you'll provide the tea we can eat and talk."

Delighted with the unexpected visitor, Rhiannon led the way across the road to her house.

"Right opposite your Mam and Dad, lucky thing," Mair commented, glancing across the road. "All right for a babysitter, eh?"

"I'm not thinking that far ahead," Rhiannon said, and Mair saw from her friend's face that she was a little troubled.

"Didn't you want a baby?" she asked, as Rhiannon set out cups and saucers and filled the kettle.

"Of course I want the baby. But I'm afraid to bank on everything being all right, after last time," she added.

"Oh, Rhiannon, how thoughtless of me. You lost a baby last year, didn't you."

"Mam said women often do lose the first. I don't know if that's the truth, mind. Trying to comfort me she was."

"I wish it was true," Mair said, eyeing Rhiannon to see her reaction.

Rhiannon looked at her, a quizzical frown on her face. "You don't mean – Never!"

"I haven't been to the doctor yet. But yes, I think I'm going to have a baby, sometime in December according to my reckoning. What can I do?"

"See a doctor. That's the first thing. I'll come with you, if you want me to."

"Thanks."

"The father, he does know?" Rhiannon asked, hesitantly. "Don't say if you'd rather not, but you have to decide whether or not you want to marry him, or go it alone, like Megan Weston did. Brave that is, mind."

"He knows, but he won't marry me. He's going to deny ever seeing me except on a bus or in the pictures."

"Carl Rees!"

"His real name is Dreese, and his mother works for Gladys Weston. Would you believe that? He doesn't use his father's name and won't say why. A great one for secrets, is Carl Rees. I wonder what else he hasn't told me."

"Something shameful his father did, perhaps?"

Mair only shrugged.

The kettle was boiling, the kitchen was filling with steam, but neither girl seemed aware of it. Mair was silently wondering if she would be lucky and lose this poor unwanted baby as Rhiannon had done and have the problem solved for her.

"Do you know who attacked you that night?" Rhiannon asked as she turned away at last to deal with the kettle. "Was it Carl?"

"No, and that's for definite! It was a woman."

"You're not covering up for him?"

"No! I wondered if it might have been his wife although he swears he isn't married. A wife or perhaps a jealous girlfriend?"

"I'll ask Jennie Francis when she comes into the shop. She might know something about him." Rhiannon changed the subject slightly then, to talk about the preparations for her anticipated new arrival. She was positive about the situation and tried to present images of them both walking their babies in summer sunshine, and growing up and becoming friends as they headed for school.

"I'm afraid of the pain as well as the gossip," Mair admitted. "Do you feel any different yet?"

"I feel really well. Although, I do have a bit of backache. I daren't mention it though, or Charlie will ask me to give up work. Which reminds me," she added, looking at the mantlepiece clock, "I'd better get back to Temptations or the job will leave me!"

"You should tell Charlie," Mair said. "How can he look after you if you don't tell him everything?"

Thinking about her friend's words later, Rhiannon told Charlie after they had eaten, that she was a bit uncomfortable and, at once, he took her over the road to number seven.

"Mam?" he said as Dora opened the door to them. "Rhiannon is having a bit of backache and we've come for reassurance, right?" He knew how afraid Rhiannon was that her second pregnancy would end the same way as the first, and he tried to take away any slight alarm as soon as possible.

"Are you sure you're all right to drive that far, Sam?" Martha asked her brother when he told her of his plans to take Mrs Collins and the children to Tenby. "You know you need your glasses changing and the sun can be very harsh this early in the year."

Sam didn't tell her that his sight had deteriorated and he was avoiding having a test, in case he was warned of the possibility of giving up driving altogether. Just one summer, then he would face the unpalatable fact. Just one summer to give Mrs Collins and her children a few treats.

He called for the three Collinses at ten o'clock and they set off with the car packed with blankets, hampers and flasks, intent on finding a place to have a picnic lunch. He had also brought a beachball, plus a few buckets and spades in case the children wanted to build sandcastles. "I hope they aren't too sophisticated," he confided in their mother, "I'm rather looking forward to castle-building myself."

"Winston will build them but I'm afraid Montgomery will prefer to jump on them." Mrs Collins laughed.

They were leaving Tenby after a few pleasant hours and were on the way home when Sam stopped the car to allow the children one last run around on an area of open grassland. He sat beside Mrs Collins and said, "Friends are we?"

"Of course we are. You're a wonderful friend to us all, Sam." She used his first name deliberately, knowing what he was about to ask her. "And," she went on, "if you promise never to tell anyone –" she waited for his nod then went on – "then my names, my stupid names, are Gloriana Fleur. Now can you understand why I never admit to them?"

"Glory. I will call you Glory," he said softly.

The mood had changed when they set off again. Their friendship had broken through a barrier leaving them more relaxed, less formal, their affection for each other easily seen. Sam kept glancing at her as if to reassure himself she was comfortable and happy. He was smiling and Mrs Glory Collins thought he was the kindest man she had ever met, that the day the most perfect she had known, and that she was the most fortunate of women. The euphoria lasted about ten minutes, until Montgomery began to feel sick, his wail of misery and disbelief bringing them down to earth with a bump.

Sam slowed down, looking for a convenient and safe place to park where he could allow Montgomery to get out and breathe some fresh air. Approaching a left-hand bend, he glanced back to see if the boy was able to wait a while longer, and he drifted out too wide. The car was hit by a car of equal size coming the other way.

Neither car had been travelling fast but the bump, plus the drivers' reaction, turned both vehicles and Sam's car ended up facing a hedge, while the other careered across the road, the driver pulling frantically at the wheel and over-compensating madly. After circling around, his eyes wide with panic, he finally stopped his car immediately behind Sam's.

The shock of the sudden collision, plus the terrifying sound of scraping metal, had frightened the children and they were screaming. It was minutes before Glory and Sam were satisfied they weren't hurt. The drivers got out and each admitted to a lapse of concentration. The other car had two dogs in the back and these, the man explained, had begun to fight.

"One of my passengers was feeling sick," Sam said, and Glory added that the sudden bump hadn't avoided that problem!

Mopping up and making sure neither car had suffered serious damage took some time, but within half an hour they both drove off having exchanged names and addresses, but each certain they they would do nothing further. Both drivers were convinced that the fault lay with him.

When Sam told his sister what had happened, she at first only wanted to reassure herself that no one had been harmed. It was later that she began to wonder whether Sam's invitation to Mrs Collins was simply altruistic or whether he was about to break his promise and find a woman to share his life, leaving her alone.

Martha was a war widow and Sam an apparently confirmed

bachelor, so they had pooled their money and bought the house on Chestnut Road from Barry Williams. If Sam broke his word and left her, she wouldn't have the money from the half share of the house to buy anything to compare. She also wondered if Sam had told Mrs Collins about his failing eyesight and whether she would be willing to look after him if he became blind. That had been her promise to her brother, that she would stay with him and care for him.

Several people had been to look at Jennie and Peter's house. Jennie met them and showed them around the home she and Peter had once built up with such pride, now nothing more than a property someone would take off her hands. Everything in it had been purchased to make it more their own, a place with a character they had helped form, a unique atmosphere they had fashioned for themselves and which was like no other. Now it was something to destroy, break up and disperse like a stage set when the run had ended.

At the end of April they had received an offer for the full amount and Jennie went to see Peter, to arrange a time to go to the estate agents together and set the sale in motion. He refused.

"But Peter, we agreed!" She was exasperated. "This is what we decided. You and I no longer live as a married couple, so we cut everything we have built in half, and go our separate ways. It's what happens when two people no longer love each other."

"I think we should give it a bit longer, give ourselves a chance to work things out."

"Why? We might wait months for another chance to sell. I want to start living my life again, not spend week after week sitting here waiting for you and your precious mother to make up your mind!"

She argued with him for almost two hours, while he sat in a chair in what had been their living room, straight-backed, feet neatly together and remained obdurate.

The following day she went to talk to his mother.

"The value of the property will go down, not up, with the paint work already showing the effects of several winters. There are rooms that need decorating and the place will soon have that abandoned atmosphere that puts prospective buyers off quicker than noisy neighbours," she explained calmly.

Later that evening, Peter put a note through the door telling her he would be at the estate agents the following lunchtime. Instead of being pleased, Jennie was sad. Sad to be reminded once again that it was his mother he listened to, and that a discussion with her, his wife, had made no difference at all.

Peter was aching with misery. He wanted to go back to his marriage, but how could he? If he made all the promises Jennie wanted him to make and even if they moved away from his parents, as she also wanted, nothing would really change. She would still be overbearingly stubborn and insist on having a say in everything they did. She accused him of being weak where his mother was concerned but couldn't see that she was any different.

After meeting her at the estate agent and dealing with the initial steps towards selling their house, he didn't go back to the office. He couldn't face the routine as though nothing had happened. Not caring where he went, he wandered through the town, and out towards the lake. A cafe tempted him to rest and he went inside where, the first person he saw was Viv Lewis, the manager of Westons, the man who had bought the stock from his wife when she closed down her business. He recognised Viv although they hadn't met. For no particular reason he went over and introduced himself.

"Peter Francis?" Viv frowned. "Oh, are you related to Jennie Francis?"

"She's my wife."

"How is she? Has she decided on a new venture?"

"We're separated, that's how she is," Peter's voice was bitter.

"I'm sorry to hear that. But it can't have been because of the business failure surely? She'll try again and I'm sure that next time, with a better position or a different stock, she'll be successful."

"Why does she want to run a business, be independent? I can

afford to keep her and she could be a proper wife. Oh no, that isn't for Jennie. She has to show everyone how clever she is."

Seeing that the man was distressed, Viv motioned to his mother and Dora came over with a pot of tea and some cakes, left them, and quietly walked away. Viv poured the man a cup of tea and pushed it towards him.

"My wife loves being in business. We work alongside each other without a moment's disagreement. That's my mother who served the tea. She and my father are both happy working and enjoying their spare time together." He crossed his fingers superstitiously when he said that. "We're all different and we have to do what's best for us. Your Jennie will run a successful business one day. You ought to be proud of her."

"She makes me feel less of a man. Emasculated, that's what I am, not having any say in the way we live. She refuses to accept the traditional role of caring wife and mother, and without it, everything falls apart. My mother has never worked. She spends all her time looking after my father and me. Cared for us wonderfully she has. What's wrong with that?"

"Nothing, for your mother. But that wouldn't be enough for my Joan or my mam. I suspect that Jennie is more like Joan than like your mother."

"We're selling the house."

"Divorcing?" Viv asked.

"No!" Peter looked shocked. "No talk of divorce."

"Sorry, I thought . . ."

"We're living apart for a while, that's all."

"Where are you living?"

"Back with Mam."

"Big mistake that is, man. Going back to Mam? Never should have done that."

"She looks after me well."

"Then you should move out straight away and show that wife of yours you can look after yourself!"

"What would you do if Joan left you?"

"Anything necessary to get her back. Anything. I'm so proud of her, she makes me feel twice my size every time I look at her and realised she's chosen me. Less of a man? What a lot of ol' rubbish."

Peter was very thoughtful when he left Rose Tree cafe and walked home.

In the Griffithses cottage, Caroline was dealing with her week's washing and great clouds of steam were issuing from the boiler. The back kitchen floor was covered with bowls filled either with newly washed garments or piles of soiled linen waiting their turn. A huge galvanised bath was resting on a wooden stool and, beside it, Caroline was rubbing a pair of Joseph-Hywel's trousers up and down on the rubbing board. Putting the soap in its rest at the top of the board she paused a moment and leant across the side of the bath. Perspiration seeped in bubbles from her skin and her face was red with the energy she was expending on the tiring task.

It was Wednesday afternoon and she knew that Barry would be waiting for her in his flat above Temptations. They had been meeting there regularly for some time: a pretence that their farce of a marriage still had a core of life worth reviving. Today she had decided not to go ever again. It was over and she knew she would be happy to live the rest of her life without him. She and her son were content here in her parents' home, with her brothers and their wives always calling in. She had missed the noise and laughter of the place when she had gone to live with Barry. The long hours spent alone while he was out working had been too much for her to bear.

Her mother said nothing as the time passed, two o'clock, three o'clock, until she knew her daughter would not be going to meet Barry. Now, at four o'clock, Caroline was unnecessarily washing clothes that Janet and she would normally deal with at the weekend.

The dog barked and she looked out of the window to see Ernie walking towards the door. What was he doing here when he should be at work?

"Ernie love, is everything all right?" she asked as her son fought his way through the kitchen, coughing exaggeratedly in the steamy air. "The baby isn't on the way is he?"

"Helen is fine apart from the occasional twinge. And I'm all right, I suppose, Mam," he said as he flopped into a chair. "I didn't feel like another couple of hours at work so I said I was feeling sick and they sent me home."

"But you aren't sick?" Janet questioned.

"Sick of work, sick of everything."

"Oh no. Not another Griffiths failing to settle down. Why can't you be like our Basil? Took to married life like a duck to water he did. What terrible thing is your Helen supposed to have done?"

"Helen isn't the problem. Happy we are, looking forward to the baby coming. No, everything's fine between Helen and me. But living with her mother is driving us spare."

Janet sighed with relief. This was something soon sorted. "Get yourself a place of your own, even if it's only a couple of rooms, Ernie. Every married couple needs space. Ask around and see if you can't find something not too expensive and near enough for your mother-in-law to be able to call. Near us too if you can. We want to enjoy this new baby when he comes."

"I don't think Helen will want to move for a while, not with the baby and all."

"And can't you cope a bit longer, for her sake?"

"I'm not allowed to sit in the armchair and eat my sandwich at supper time. I'm not allowed into the living room – that's the lounge – until I've changed out of my working clothes. Mam, I wear my second-best suit and she still won't let me in there! Oh, and we only watch interesting programmes on the television, no comedy, and no music. The woman's barmy, our Mam." Ernie looked up to see both his mother and his sister stifling giggles. "All right, joke over. What am I going to do?"

"There's always the shed," Caroline laughed. "Threaten that and perhaps she'll behave."

When Ernie went on his way, slightly more cheerful than when he had arrived, Janet put her hands on her hips and said, "That's our Ernie sorted. Now, Caroline, what are we going to do about you?"

*   *   *

130

Mair tried not to think about the baby she carried. It could only be a couple of months, there was plenty of time. If her father had been suspicious, he might have noticed that she walked away from any talk about babies, even shutting off the television when anything remotely connected with children was shown. She still hadn't spoken to a doctor, although she had almost decided that if nothing had happened by the middle of May, she would accept Rhiannon's offer to go with her, and make an appointment. She continually put it off, knowing that once it was official, she could no longer pretend it wasn't true.

Once she began avoiding anything to do with babies, she seemed to come across the subject everywhere. Shops advertised maternity outfits, toys were recommended for every stage of childhood. Even on buses there were women knitting small white garments and every magazine she bought had something to add to the knowledge she did not want to gain. She was beginning to feel trapped.

The worst occasion was when she accepted an invitation to go to the pictures with Frank. The film was boring, so instead, they went to find some supper at the cottage Frank shared with his parents. Helen and Ernie were there, all lovey-dovey, talking about the flat they were going to find once the baby was born. Seeing Helen's swollen figure and the way she was boasting about her appetite, eating for two, Mair wanted to run straight out. She went into the kitchen where lines of washing had been hung to dry, and made tea, helped by the very attentive Frank. When the sounds of groaning and panting and cries of alarm filled the small house, she looked at Frank and said, urgently, "I think I should go home."

Shouts and wails and calming whispers played counter-point as Hywel begged Helen to get to the hospital and told Ernie off for not keeping her at home, and Janet soothed everyone and calmly asked Frank to run and phone for a taxi.

"There's the van," Frank suggested, but Ernie shook his head. "Quicker it'll be mind, and I'll let you drive it," Frank offered, aware of Mair's embarrassment. "You could go now, this minute and be there in no time."

"Go, Frank, and phone the hospital," Janet urged.

Reaching for Mair's hand, Frank pulled her out of the house and headed for the phone box at the end of the lane.

It was then that Mair had her idea. Frank wasn't very bright. She might be able to persuade him that the child she carried was his, if she could change her attitude towards him and get him into her bed within the next few days. She wouldn't let him down. She'd be a good wife and he'd have no cause for complaint. Frank's biggest asset as a prospective husband was his slowness. He had that highly desirable facet of his character that every woman dreamed of: Frank Griffiths was malleable.

Carl had done her a favour denying they had been lovers. Apart from Rhiannon, no one would think it strange that she had been seeing Frank and not talking about it. He wasn't considered a great catch. The Griffithses and her father were hardly likely to welcome the idea of a romance between them so it would hardly seem surprising that they had kept their meetings a secret.

When the telephone calls had been made, she led Frank back to her cottage, explaining that with her father once again on nights, she didn't fancy being alone tonight. "It was knowing that Helen's baby's birth is imminent," she said. "I don't know why, but it made me want company tonight."

Frank saw no point in asking for further explanation.

"Charlie Perkins's horse impressions again," Hywel whispered to Janet when Frank arrived home in time for an early breakfast.

Seven

F rank ate an enormous breakfast after his return from Mair's cottage. He was finishing off with some thick toast made on the bright fire in the living room when his brother Basil came in.

"Any news about Helen's baby?" Basil asked, and with his mouth full, Frank shook his head and nodded to the pile of freshly toasted bread. When Basil had found himself a plate and was spreading the toast generously with butter, Frank managed to say, "I think Mam's at the hospital now."

"You look pleased with yourself," Basil said, as Frank happily munched his way through his food. "Your face isn't a natural smiler. So, what's happened?"

"I saw Mair last night and she's given that Carl Rees the push."

"Sure of that, are you?"

"Well, I hope so, but I'll keep an eye on the pair of them just in case she changes her mind."

"Don't build your hopes up, brother Frank. Mair's had a few boyfriends in her time, and besides, you'll give our Dad a heart attack if you start talking of wedding bells and a policeman's daughter in the same breath, mind!"

Frank looked uncomfortable. "Who'd have a bloke like me?" he said, but he was soon thinking of the way he and Mair had spent the previous night while her father was out, and the smile came back.

Basil waited awhile but as there was no sign of Janet coming home he left and returned to Trellis Street. He had wanted to talk to his parents, as his landlord had increased the rent and he had

133

heard rumours that he was intending to get him and his little family out of their flat altogether. He had a regular job, but nothing saved, and he didn't know how to deal with the threat.

As he left the shabby cottage, where he had had such a happy childhood, he stopped and looked thoughtfully at the outhouse which had been a bedroom until he and then Ernie had married and left home. Was it a possibility? He shook his head abandoning the idea as soon as it had been born. He couldn't bring Eleri and the boys to live in what was little more than animal shelter. Things had changed and it was no longer possible to think of bringing up a family in such an inconvenient place. Eleri had lived with her first husband, Lewis-boy, at Dora and Lewis's house. He had only provided a small, overcrowded flat and he couldn't expect her to accept anything more lowly than that. What could he do?

He climbed the gate into the lane, his long legs making this easier than unlocking the gate and relocking it after him. He stood again, looking back at the shed-cum-extension and he was standing so still, so quiet, that he heard the sibilant hiss of tyres on the surface of the lane while the cause of it was still some distance away. Automatically, from ingrained practice, he stepped silently back into the shelter of a tree and watched.

Constable Gregory sailed serenely past on his bicycle, and when Basil called, "Good morning," he had the pleasure of seeing the man wobble and almost lose his balance. The policeman stopped and glared at him. "What you doing skulking about in the hedges, Basil?" he asked.

"Wondering what you're up to when you should be asleep." Basil replied, remembering Frank telling him the man had been working the previous night.

"Sleeping? That's a laugh. Off to work I am, watching out for the likes of you and your family! So behave!"

"Going in the wrong direction aren't you?" Basil nodded in the direction of town and tilted his head enquiringly.

"None of your business where I've been or where I'm going, Basil Griffiths. Remember I'm after villains so watch it. Right?" Wearing a haughty, righteous expression he sailed on. Basil

wondered which of his brothers had been wandering around
Farmer Booker's woods, or if his father had been the one most
recently aggravating the man. The idea had its appeal and he
went back to the cottage and collected a few things. Tonight he'd
set a few traps. A rabbit made a good nourishing stew.

That night, Frank walked to Mair's cottage and stood watching,
half expecting and half dreading the sight of Carl Rees arriving.
Mair's father was at home, but that was no reason why Mair
couldn't go and meet Carl at a given time.

At nine o'clock the back door opened and Frank's spirits
dropped but it was her father who stepped out. He was not in
uniform but he moved with care and went silently through the
woods, unaware of being followed by Frank.

The night was dark and still, with not even a light breeze to
move the branches. All his senses alert, Frank trailed Gregory's
progress through the trees. Then he heard the unmistakable
sounds of someone else stepping cautiously through the trees.
Such faint sounds that the constable seemed unaware of them.
The thought that it might be one of his brothers or his father,
made Frank take action to warn him. He shook a branch and
ran through an area he knew was best avoided if he wanted to
walk in silence; it was covered with dry, brittle twigs, the
remnants of an aborted attempt to clear some of the intrusive
brambles. His feet made a lot of noise and the constable turned
and headed straight for him. Frank saw him with his night-
trained eyes and easily avoided him, turning back to stand and
watch once more across the lane from Mair's home. He didn't
know who had been wandering the woods, but he thought, by
the professional way the person had walked with hardly a
sound, that it might have been his father, or Basil or perhaps
Ernie, even though he should have been home waiting for news
of his child.

A short distance away, his brother Basil picked up his abandoned equipment and continued setting his traps. His smile was
reminiscent of Frank's.

*   *   *

The following morning, Frank poured himself a beer from the flagon in the corner and told his mother that he was going to start on the bedroom for Jack and Victoria at last.

"You'd never believe the colour, our Mam. White woodwork and the door panelled in hardboard and painted yellow to match the walls. Could you sleep in such a room? Damn it all, it would be like sleeping in the daylight."

"And when has that bothered you, Frank?" Janet teased.

"Well, I suppose it's modern. But yellow? Now a soft blue or pink, that's all right, mind. I like a bit of colour, but it has to be soft and soothing, not 'wake up it's morning.' "

Janet was laughing while she helped Frank to gather together his painting and wallpapering tools, when a red-faced Ernie came bursting in to tell them them he had a son. "Another grandson for you Mam. Where's our Dad? Chuffed he'll be for sure." Frank was pleased with the news, thumping Ernie on the back and telling him well done. Janet began to cry but insisted the tears were happy ones. Hywel muttered something about being front line now there was a younger generation to push them up a notch and Ernie drank Frank's beer. Frank remembered just in time not to start a fight.

As an excuse to call, Frank went to the sports shop to tell Mair of the arrival of a new Griffiths, and invited her to go for a walk with him that evening. Then he ran down to Temptations to tell Rhiannon, and the news began to travel.

That evening, Rhiannon and Charlie went to tell Dora and Lewis and, as they approached the house, they heard quarrelling. Dismayed, they called from the doorway before walking in. Rhiannon looked suspiciously from one to the other. "Not arguing, are you?" she asked.

Dora snapped, "Of course we are! Your father wants to fill the garden with vegetables we no longer need and I want a lawn and flowers!"

Rhiannon was so relieved she giggled and Dora joined in.

"I know what you were thinking," she whispered when she and her daughter were making tea, "afraid I was about to throw your father out and you'd have him back as a lodger!"

*   *   *

136

"You should have seen their faces," Dora told Sian the next morning when they were opening the Rose Tree cafe. "Terrified they were. Poor Charlie was forcing such a smile, he looked as though he was being strangled!"

"Are their fears ungrounded?" Sian asked as she grated cheese into a bowl. "You don't regret having Lewis back?"

"I wish I'd come to my senses sooner," Dora replied. "I'm really happy now Lewis and I are back together again. Although, there's still a sense of waiting, as if something has yet to fall into place. I'm happy, don't doubt it, but – I don't know – we aren't complete somehow."

"You still remember the early days, when the house was full to bursting, and there weren't enough hours in the day to do all you wanted to achieve," Sian suggested. "Life changes and we sometimes find it hard to accept it."

Dora nodded. "You're right about that. The house seems too big. All those empty rooms. I open the doors sometimes and look in and it's as though I'm a stranger there, as though they belong to another life, ghosts have taken possession. In my melancholic moments I can almost hear the children shouting and laughing and then I return to the present and become engulfed by sadness. We rattle about like peas in a colander, me and Lewis, and I think we both feel it."

Aware of having said too much, she turned to Sian and asked brightly, "And what about you? D'you hear anything about your delinquent, Islwyn? Or Issy, as that Margaret Jenkins insists on calling him?"

"So far as I know he and Margaret Jenkins seem to be content, although I do wonder sometimes. She must hate working as a housekeeper in the house her family once owned. And, Islwyn, well, he was never one for hard work. I doubt he's changed even for his new love! I don't think she can be exactly happy, do you? And she must hate seeing her brother Edward so successful and happily married. I don't think Margaret is the sort to take pleasure from the happiness of others."

"Poor Islwyn."

"Not really. When you think of what he did – taking money

from my parents' business and doing nothing for it, cheating on the accounts to take even more, well, I think he's lucky to have what he has got."

"And you wouldn't take him back?"

"No! There are better men than him in the world and if I wanted a new husband, I'd find one."

"And, would you? Look for another husband?" Dora dared to ask.

"I might, once Islwyn has agreed to the divorce."

Dora was surprised. If anyone had asked her, she would have been certain that Sian had no interest whatever in finding another man to share her life.

"It just shows," she said to Lewis later, "You never really know another person, no matter that you believe them to be a close friend."

Dora's daughter looked up smiling as the confectionery rep got out of his car and hurried towards the shop. Before she had married Charlie, she and Jimmy Herbert had been close friends and it was as a friend she greeted him. It was raining and she opened the door for him to run straight in. Jimmy held a briefcase rather ineffectually over his head as he ran from the car.

"Tea?" she offered as soon as he had closed the shop door.

She usually persuaded him to stay a while when he called for an order. They reminisced about the dance class in Gomer Hall that they had enjoyed for a while, and discussed mutual friends, before he settled down to take her order. Jimmy worked for the same company as Rhiannon's father, which gave them another link.

He was still there when Jennie Francis came in for some toffees. Seeing Rhiannon greet her as a friend rather than an unknown customer, Jimmy took out a sample of toffees and gave them to her. Rhiannon introduced them and went into the kitchen to find another cup. Before Jimmy left, he had learnt something about Jennie's situation and had told her of a job going in a shop at the Pleasure Beach, selling nothing but seaside rock – in every imaginable shape and size.

"It isn't what I want," Jennie confided in her friend when

138

Jimmy had gone. "But with the house being sold and me having to find somewhere to live, I have to earn some money. It would only be a stop-gap, while I sorted out my finances and got myself started in a business of my own."

"No chance of a reconciliation, then? You and Peter?"

"I have hoped for things to come right," Jennie admitted. "But whenever decisions have to be made, Peter always choses his mother to discuss them with rather than me and I can't see that ever changing. She'll get older and more demanding and he'll become more and more guilty if he doesn't do what she wants. I don't want to be second best for the rest of my life. Would you?"

"No one deserves that," Rhiannon said. "For a while I thought Barry Williams was the one for me, but he wasn't as loving and caring as Charlie is. Better to wait for the right one, don't take a chance telling yourself it will get better, because it almost certainly won't."

"The house will be sold in a couple more weeks. It doesn't take long for your life to be pulled apart," Jennie said sadly. "A few months ago I had a struggling business, a husband and a home. Now they've all gone. It's hard to believe sometimes."

"Come back and have some lunch with me," Rhiannon said. "I boiled a joint of ham yesterday, we could have a sandwich. Then," she added, "you could take a bus over to the Pleasure Beach and see about the exciting job selling sticky rock!" She was pleased to see Jennie smiling as she pulled down the blind and locked the shop door.

With some misgivings, Jennie took the job in the small shop overlooking the beach. She knew she had to earn some money, enough to find a room and feed herself. Imagine ending up in a bed-sit in some crummy old ruin, after owning a house. It was crazy. The debts accrued from the business should have been shared. Peter should have been with her, helping to sort out the end of her enterprise. Instead, she had a mental picture of him of standing beside his mother looking at her with disapproval as she struggled. Selling rock and listening to inane jokes as people bought sweet dummies and talked about the recipient's reaction as though they were the first person to think of such a thing. She shuddered. At least it would bring in some money while she looked for something better. There was a part of her too that hoped the news would shame Peter into some offer of assistance once the house was gone and she was installed in her drab room. She was determined it would be a drab room. That way there was the greatest incentive for her to get out and move on.

Peter heard of her new job from Carl, whom he met in the High Street.

"What is she thinking of?" Peter was shocked. People he knew were likely to see her there and that would be embarrassing for him. And what would Mam say? He had to stop her before someone told Mam.

The house was empty when he got home. His parents were out on a rare visit to the pictures and his meal was on a saucepan of simmering water keeping warm. He hated that, eating alone with the gravy forming a dark rim around the plate. He thought of Jennie and wished things could have been different. If only she and Mam had got on.

His thoughts drifted back over other girlfriends he had brought home. Mam never approved of any of them. In a rare flash of honesty he knew that she had firmly discouraged them. It was Jennie who had fought against his mother's determination to keep her away from him, and he had been flattered at the way she had fought for him. Even when they were married, Mam was always reminding him that nothing was for ever, that divorce was always an option and no longer considered as shaming as it had once been. She had warned him not to have children, too. Perhaps she had thought the arrival of a child would make the marriage more permanent, less easy to dissolve? Had Jennie been right? Had his mother been constantly undermining their marriage? Nonsense. She just wanted him to be happy.

Jennie hadn't wanted children, this was the one subject about which Jennie and his mother didn't argue. Mam always insisted that for them to have a child would have been a mistake. For the first time, he wondered why.

*   *   *

140

Edward and Megan Jenkins loved their daughter Rosemary but since their wedding, Edward was a little worried. The baby's father was his cousin, Terrence and although Terrence had shown no interest in the child, Edward was well aware that should he want to, Terrence could make life difficult for them.

"Megan, how do you feel about my adopting our daughter?" he asked one evening as they were settling the nine-month-old into her cot. "That sounds ridiculous, but she is ours and I love her dearly. I just think that if I formally adopted her, there wouldn't be any problems to rise up and bother us in the future. What do you think?"

"I want her to be ours, legally ours, Edward. I'll start making enquiries tomorrow."

"Should we write to Terrence and tell him what we plan to do?"

"Better to leave him out of it until we know the facts and are ready to start proceedings," she replied. "I doubt he'll be bothered, but he might try and make some money out of it, don't you think?"

"Make us pay to stop him formally protesting you mean?"

"He's always broke and he's quite capable of it, isn't he?"

"Yes, you're right. We'll make enquiries and say nothing."

In the large kitchen of Montague Court, Edward's sister Margaret was browsing through an old newspaper, before wrapping up vegetable peelings in it and putting them in the waste bin. Her eye caught a picture of her brother. It was an account of the wedding of Edward to Megan and, as she read it, she felt unreasonably angry. Because Edward had refused to stay at Montague Court and help her build it up into a prestigious hotel and restaurant, she had lost it. Now he was successful in his small-minded way and she was working in a menial job in the place around which she had spun her dreams.

For a while she had accepted her situation but, seeing Edward's smiling face looking out of the local newspaper, reminded her of all she had lost. She sat there for a long time, thinking of her brother and his wife, Megan, one of the once high and mighty Weston family, and their daughter, Rosemary.

Rosemary was not Edward's child she thought with some relish. Perhaps a word to her cousin Terrence might be interesting. Complacency was always Edward's failing. He let things happen and didn't worry too much about what the future might hold, only about the immediate situation. She very much doubted whether Edward had contacted Terrence to ask if he wanted any part in baby Rosemary's upbringing. With time on her hands, bitterness in her heart, Margaret started to write a letter. Money. That was always the best way of persuading cousin Terrence to do something. Money was something of which Terrence could never have too much.

"Darling," she said, when Islwyn came in with some freshly laundered bedding. "I've decided to write to my cousin Terrence."

"Why bother?" Islwyn replied. "He'll be here looking for money before the ink's dry!"

"I might have a way for him to earn some," she said, gathering him into her arms.

Basil and Eleri were worried about their housing situation. Every day, Eleri went to various estate agents and looked at every flat they had on their books. She also toured the shops, looking for notices of places to rent and looked at any she saw advertised. The result so far and been disappointing. They simply couldn't afford anything decent.

Basil asked everyone he knew and investigated every avenue without success.

As she often did, Eleri went to talk to Dora, of whom she was very fond.

"We could put a notice in the cafe for you." Dora suggested. "But wouldn't it be better and simpler just to pay the extra rent and stay put? It's so costly to move, even from rooms. Nothing fits and you get rid of things you'd rather keep and buy stuff you like less. And there are the boys. They might not be as happy as they are now, close to the shops and the park you are, and not far from the school."

"I'd have to work."

"Yes, and pay for someone to mind the boys. I'd look after them for you, you know that, but with the cafe, there's only the evenings."

"I've thought of everything and there doesn't seem to be a solution," Eleri sighed.

Dora's blue eyes were bright and thoughtful for a long time after Eleri had gone.

Lewis came into the cafe soon after Eleri had left with her two boys. Sorry to have missed them, he abandoned thought of a cup of tea and went straight out again, hoping to offer the little family a lift home. Instead he saw Mrs Glory Collins getting off a bus, struggling with a large parcel. He stopped and invited her to get into the car.

"It's some sewing I've done for Mrs Adams," she explained as Lewis took the heavy parcel from her. "Curtains that needed lining. Sam – Mr Lilly – offered to come down and fetch them but I thought I could manage. Glad to meet you I was, believe me."

"Why do women have to try and be independent?" Lewis smiled. "You can talk of equality all you like but we're built differently for different tasks. Right?"

"Leave the heavy stuff for the men, is that it?"

"Why not?"

He waited while she went into the house on Chestnut Road, the house where he had lived so happily with Nia Williams before her death. He had accepted the loss of his love and knew he was happier than he deserved to be with his wife. Dora loved him and had been able, eventually, to forgive him for his long-standing relationship with Nia. But there were moments when he longed to see Nia's gentle, smiling face, hear her softly spoken voice telling of her love for him.

He was quiet on the way back to Goldings Street and Mrs Collins looked at him aware of his good looks: black hair, slim moustache, slightly tanned smooth skin and those devastatingly appealing eyes. He was always neatly dressed; shoes shining, dazzlingly white shirt, well-pressed suit with just a line of a handkerchief showing in a top pocket. She wondered whether he was true to Dora now, or whether those attractive features had led him into further liaisons. Knowing Dora, she hoped not.

There was another woman filling Lewis's thoughts, but Nia was dead and he couldn't imagine loving anyone else as he had loved her. Pulling his mind back from melancholy, he stopped at a florist and bought flowers for Dora, and a smaller bunch for a delighted Mrs Collins.

Mrs Dreese, quite enjoyed working for Gladys and Arfon Weston. Gladys's imagined importance amused her and she flattered the old woman and pretended to admire her in a way that delighted Gladys. There was no malice in Mrs Dreese's actions, she just liked pleasing her employer. It amused her to see Gladys's behaviour, the way she scored points over her friends, her pretence that she was from a grander background than she could truthfully lay claim to.

Before her husband's troubles had taken everything from them, Mrs Dreese had owned a larger house than Gladys's and had employed several people to help, including a full-time housekeeper and a gardener. About this she had said nothing. After all, it was the present that counted and, apart from the few pieces of furniture she managed to cram into her and Carl's rooms, she owned next to nothing.

She was aware that one of the things that gave Gladys pleasure was the fact that she was well spoken and well mannered. She knew that when she went through the wide, hall with its oak panelled walls to answer a knock at the door, Gladys would sometimes stand listening while she asked the visitor's name and business before showing them into the hall and asking them to wait while she enquired.

One morning, Gladys's curiosity got the better of her and she asked her tall, elegant 'servant', to join her for her morning coffee.

Sophie Street

"How long have you been a widow, Mrs Dreese?"

"Not long. My husband died of a heart attack when my son, Carl, was twenty-two. He was a clever boy, but all hope of college was abandoned when we realised how little money we had."

"How sad," Gladys commiserated. "He does some carpet-fitting for my husband's business, doesn't he? Doesn't mix socially much, I gather, apart from some fishing with my grandson, Jack. Jack was brilliant you know, but he was determined to be a teacher. He had a call, you see. He could have done anything he wanted, but it was as a teacher that he was called."

"How wonderful," Mrs Dreese said. "To give up on a great career because he was called to help in the local school."

"Of course your son is rather fond of Constable Gregory's daughter, Mair, isn't he?" Gladys whispered conspiratorially. "Poor Mair. She worked for me for a while you know, but she wasn't trained."

"I wouldn't know about his social life. I don't interfere," Mrs Dreese replied evasively.

"Your husband was in business, was he?"

The firm and very emphatic "Yes," with no further supplements, made Gladys realise she had asked too many questions, too soon. Perhaps she would go and see Joan and Viv to find out more. Carl did carpet-fitting for them from time to time and they might have learnt something about the man. "Time we were getting on, I think," she said, dismissively, as though it had been she who had ended the conversation. Mrs Dreese smiled, gathered the cups and returned to the kitchen.

When she went home, Mrs Dreese knocked on the door of her son's room before entering her own. Carl answered and rather ungraciously invited her inside.

"There's still gossip about you and this Mair Gregory," she said at once. "You have to be more careful. You don't want to face defending yourself in a paternity order. Or worse still, get married."

"There's no chance of either of those things happening. I have been careful. No one has seen me with Mair except in very public

145

places. Anyway, it's not your concern. I'm twenty-eight years old, for heaven's sake!"

"Of course it's my concern! You have a debt of honour to repay. You promised. You can't forget it and play around dangerously like this. You've taken her out, you can't deny that. Spent money on her, money we can't afford to spend." She sat down on the edge of the couch that was also his bed, drooped a little and went on, "Don't give up, Carl, please don't give up on your promises."

"Don't give up? Giving up is all I ever do! And all in the name of my dear departed father! He let *me* down! I had to give up on college, give up on girlfriends, give up all thought of doing something for myself! Why should I carry on? He's dead! Nothing I give up will change that!"

"He was a good man," she said softly.

"A foolish one! And I'm wasting my life because of his foolishness! He ran his business into the ground, giving to people he thought were in need. Gullible to every pleading face, that's the truth of it, isn't it, Mam?"

"No. He was trusting. Too trusting. I'll admit he was too trusting. But foolish? No. How can you say such a thing?"

Instead of answering, Carl grabbed his coat from the back of a chair and left her. Standing in his room, staring at the swinging door which led into the narrow, stale-smelling hall, she looked less confident, even a little afraid.

Her own rooms were larger than those of her son. From her sitting-room, french windows opened onto a rather bedraggled garden which gave her a sense of greater space and freedom. She went in, pulled back the heavy maroon velvet curtains, and opened them, then held the kitchen door ajar with a pair of boots Carl had given her for the purpose. The breeze was refreshing. Staring out into the bright garden, her dejected mood making her aware of the untidiness, rather than of the beauty of the fresh green of the trees and the cheerfulness of the flowering shrubs. She wondered how much longer she could persuade her son to carry on.

Carl came back after an hour and knocked on the door of her

room. She raised her arms and they hugged in silence.

"Let me have a look through father's papers, "he said as he sat on the board which covered the bath in the kitchen. "If I had some idea of how much we still need, I might be encouraged." Mrs Dreese shook her head. "No, Carl, my dear. I don't want to take them out of the box. I want to leave them just as your father placed them there when he entrusted me with all this. You know the full amount, fifteen thousand pounds, and I won't open the papers until we're almost there." She opened her purse and showed him a couple of five pound notes. "This is what I'm contributing this month. Not bad, eh?" She put it inside a teapot on a high shelf.

He hugged her again and handed her a ten shilling note. "Mam, I'm sorry. Take this and treat yourself to an evening at the pictures. I was going to join Viv Lewis and Jack Weston for a pint. Better you have a night out instead. You're working so hard. You make me ashamed for losing heart sometimes like I do."

Sally went back to Glebe Lane one afternoon, rushing because she was late, thinking ahead of the meal she had to prepare. She had been up to Rose Tree cafe to see her sister and had stayed too long. Now she was carrying the new potatoes she had extravagantly bought, which she was intending to serve with poached salmon and salad. It had been the ease of the simple meal that had encouraged her to take an hour off. An hour that had extended into two, and now she was late. New potatoes took forever to scrape.

She unlocked the front door and stepped inside. There was an hour before any of her guests were due. She didn't encourage them to return before six o'clock. That gave her plenty of time to prepare the meal and gave them time to change.

Some of them bought wine, a growing habit, she understood, and one which restaurants were beginning to take seriously. She kept each bottle in her larder clearly labelled with the owner's name and brought it to their table each evening. Her shopping bag contained a bottle of wine she had bought as a spare. It might be worth offering a glass and making an extra profit, so long as no one reported her for selling without a licence, she thought with a surge of guilt.

The girl she had recently engaged to help with the cleaning had gone and she was pleased with the clean, lavender smell of furniture polish that met her as she went inside. She was humming as she dropped her shopping bag in the hall and began taking off her coat. Then a sound in the kitchen startled her, her first thought was that Ryan had come back.

"Hello, Mrs Fowler-Weston, I thought I'd make a start on the dinner as you were a bit late back."

"Mr Powell! What are you doing here? I have repeatedly explained that my kitchen is out of bounds." Startled, she sounded more upset than she would normally have been. The guests did sometimes return early, but they always went straight to their rooms.

"Maxie, call me Maxie," he said as if there had been no reaction to his interference. "I've cooked potatoes and opened a tin of meat so we can have a cottage pie," he said smiling as he helped to hang up her coat. "Vegetables will have to be carrots and swede, they won't mind missing greens for once. Feed us well you do, Mrs Fowler-Weston."

Sally stared at him. "Mr Powell, I do *not* need your help in dealing with the running of this place. I have dinner arranged. Will you please leave my kitchen!"

As she spoke she was planning how she would tell him to leave and not come back. She would do it this very evening, once she had sorted out the meal for the others. She couldn't have this. She had to be strong. Oh, how she wished Ryan were here, or even Megan. Someone to stand with her when she told this amiable but unwanted man to go. Maxie Powell didn't make her nervous, like others had done, but she couldn't cope with someone interfering and using her kitchen as though it were his own. It just wouldn't do.

When she went into the kitchen she saw that the pie had been made, neatly marked with a fork and decorated in attractive swirls on the creamy potatoes, and was ready to go into the oven. Carrots had been carefully sliced into even sticks and swede was already on the cooker top waiting to be boiled.

A tray had been set with a cup and saucer and a plate of biscuits. He turned away from her and poured boiling water into the teapot and said, "There, you sit down and drink this, I'll go and pick a stalk or two of parsley to decorate the pie, shall I?" She might not have spoken for all the notice he had taken.

Unable to decide on the best action, she allowed the meal to pass without saying anything to Maxie or even glancing in his direction. When the others guests praised her for the delicious food, only then she did look at him. But like the others, he was looking at her and joining in the comments on her excellent cooking. It was bizarre to say the least.

"Freshly poached salmon and new potatoes, tomorrow," she said weakly.

She was washing up when he came into the kitchen and this time she was going to make sure he understood.

"Mr Powell. I appreciate your concern when you thought I was too late back to prepare dinner, but I do *not* want you to come into the kitchen again. Ever. Do you understand? If you do, I will ask you to leave and not come back."

If she expected him to be subdued by her words she was wrong. He smiled widely and opened his arms.

"Don't fight it, dear lady," he said, and she stepped back as though stung. "I know that what has happened between us is sudden and hard to believe. But I knew the moment I saw you that we were meant to be together. You need a man here and, with your husband gone—"

She slapped his face so hard her hand hurt. "Please leave. Now, this minute!"

"I've spoken too soon, have I?" he said, rubbing his face ruefully. "Proud woman that you are."

At the back gate, Ryan watched the scene in the kitchen and at once ran up the path and burst into the house.

"What's going on?" he demanded.

"Nothing I can't handle," Sally said. "Will you both leave at once."

Ryan looked at Maxie, who was still rubbing his cheek.

"I thought she and I were friends, that's all," Maxie said. "I've

149

helped cook the dinner and done everything I can, and now she's telling me to go," Maxie spoke as though in shock.

To Sally's increasing alarm, Ryan took Maxie's part.

"You should be ashamed. Taking advantage of the man who pays to be here. If you can't manage this stupid idea of yours of running a lodging house, then admit it and give it up."

"Guesthouse," Sally protested in a whisper. "And I *can* manage." Leaving the two men commiserating with each other on the unfairness of it all, Sally ran to her room and locked herself in.

Maxie left after breakfast but on the following Friday when he was next due to stay with her, he came back as though nothing had happened.

Frank was surprised at the change in Mair's attitude to him. Instead of telling him to get lost whenever he invited her out, she actually instigated some of their meetings. Besides visits to the pictures, which he didn't really enjoy, the seats being very uncomfortable for his long frame, there were walks during which they stood and kissed and suppers at her home where her father was sometimes present and sometimes not.

Mair became a regular visitor at the Griffiths's untidy cottage, calling in after the sports shop closed, certain of a meal and a pleasant evening. Gradually, the idea of being married to Frank and being a part of this unconventional family was no longer a thought to be dreaded. She sometimes wondered, when she saw Janet looking at her when Janet thought she was unaware, if Frank's mother had guessed the situation and knew the reason for her sudden interest in her son. Perhaps, one day, she'd admit it, but not yet. She had to show Janet and Hywel that, if she married their son, she would be a good wife and a loyal one. Only then could she contemplate admitting how she had used him.

Rhiannon also wondered about Mair's change of heart and as she thought of the interest Mair had shown in her plans for the new baby, she was suspicious of the girl's motives.

Frank talked to his brother about it one morning. He met Basil as he walked towards the factory where he and their brother Ernie now worked.

"D'you think there's a chance she'll marry me? I don't have anything saved, or a job, but if I thought there was a chance I'd look for work and even promise her dad I'd give up fighting and poaching."

"Duw, there's love for you!" Basil teased. "You'd get a job?"

Ignoring the jibe, unable to see the funny side of his situation, Frank went on, "Has she just turned to me because she misses Carl? Viv said something about marrying on the rebound. Is that all it is?"

"If it is, then I'd work fast, Frank. Ask her before she either goes back to Carl or finds someone else to grieve with."

"I'll go and see her when she closes the shop for lunch talk to her and ask her how she feels about me."

"You're sure, are you? There's more to marriage than savings and a job, mind. Take this problem we have with the flat. I think we'll be evicted before the summer's over. I have to deal with it, find a place that's comfortable and that we can afford. Would you be able to sort out problems like that? You can't take on a wife and not be prepared to look after her proper."

"I don't expect where to live would be a problem, she'd want to stay and look after her father, wouldn't she? That cottage belongs to him. We'd be all right there."

"You sleeping in the same house as a policeman? You'd never feel safe enough to close your eyes!"

"Oh, I would," Frank said with a sideways grin. "Already tried it, haven't I?" He left Basil at the plastics factory gates, staring at him in surprise, and walked back the way they had come. He wouldn't wait for the shop to close for lunch, he'd go and see Mair now, this minute.

Sam Lilly was another man with marriage on his mind. They hadn't known each other long, but he wanted to take care of Glory, give her some of the ordinary treats that her life had sadly lacked. Since the accident on the way back from Tenby he had been afraid to invite her to go for a drive, although, when she

151

referred to the incident she never suggested that any of the fault was his. If she knew about his poor eyesight, that was never mentioned either.

When she turned up for work one morning and told him that Jack had offered to teach her to drive, he was delighted. If he ever felt he was no longer able to drive his car, then Glory would be able to take on that task for him. He offered her the use of his car, but declined to give her lessons himself.

"I don't think I'd be such a good teacher as Jack," he admitted. "I once tried to teach my sister and we didn't speak to each other for a month!"

It was only much later that he felt the beginnings of doubt. What was he doing? Training Glory to be his slave? He hadn't thought about how she would feel, acting as his eyes, and perhaps giving up all thought of her own needs and desires to look after him. He felt ashamed. How could he be so selfish?

For the next few weeks he was out when she arrived for work, although she noticed he had attended to many of the tasks he habitually dealt with. There was no word and he never called to see her and check on the lovely garden he had given her and in which he took such a pride and pleasure.

They met once in the High Street, when she was looking for some material to make dresses for her daughters, Elisabeth and Margaret. Caroline Williams, Barry's wife was serving her with buttons and cotton when Sam walked in with his sister. He greeted her with obvious pleasure and, at his invitation, the three of them went to the Blue Bird cafe for a cup of tea and some cakes.

The talk was trivial: Glory and Martha discussed the material she had bought and the style of dresses she would make and Sam sat for the most part in silence, watching her and obviously pleased to be there.

"How are you getting on with your driving?" he asked as they prepared to part outside the cafe.

"Very well," she replied. "I enjoy it more than I'd imagined."

"Use the car whenever you need to practice," he said again. "If anyone would like to give you an hour or so."

She was aware of him standing watching as she walked away and turned for a final wave. She wondered why he had suddenly begun to avoid her when he still enjoyed her company and cared about what she did. Was he afraid she had begun to think about marriage? 'Be wery careful o' vidders all your life', Dickens's Sam Weller had warned, she remembered with a frown. Perhaps she had better look for another house to clean and leave Sam Lilly well alone. The thought was inordinately sad.

That she had made the right decision seemed to be confirmed when she told Mrs Adams the following week that she no longer wanted to work for her.

"I thought you'd be off as soon as you knew," Martha said and Glory was startled by her bitterness.

"Know what?" she asked. "I've simply decided to look for something closer to home, somewhere I can walk to where I don't have to catch a bus."

"You don't convince me. You can't face it, can you?"

Puzzled, Glory went to see her son-in-law and asked him what Mrs Adams had meant.

The following day Jack called at Goldings Street and told her that Sam's sight was failing and that within a couple of years there was a chance he'd be registered as blind.

"Why didn't he tell me? Why didn't he trust me?" she said, hurt more than dismayed by the revelation.

"Give him a chance to tell you. He might just need more time."

"I've told Martha I won't be going there any more."

"Go back and talk to her, tell her how you feel, tell her you've changed your mind. Women do, all the time." He smiled, and led her out to his car and gave her a lift back up to Chestnut Road.

It was Sam who answered and invited them in. Jack left the room and closed the door as she said, "Sam? Are you avoiding me?" There was a pause, then she went on, "You are, and I find it very hurtful. Is it because you can't talk about your sight problem? A problem that hasn't even begun?" Another pause, then, "That accident was not your fault, Sam. You can see perfectly well or you wouldn't consider getting into a car and driving. You're thinking too far ahead. Any changes in the future can be dealt with as they arise.''

Jack was shamelessly listening at the door and he smiled as he heard his mother-in-law's gentle laughter after listening to Sam's response.

Eight

When Rhiannon knocked on the door of 7 Sophie Street one morning in June, she was frowning. Without waiting for her to say anything, Dora asked, "What's wrong?"

"I want to come back home to live," Rhiannon replied.

"What's he done? I'll kill 'im!" Dora's blue eyes blazed, yet her heart was calm, belying the angry words and outraged expression. She knew that Rhiannon and Charlie were happy, waiting for the birth of their child with great joy and excitement, she knew that Rhiannon was teasing.

Unaware that her mother hadn't been taken in by her attempt at portraying misery, Rhiannon's face creased into laughter as she said, "They're coming to do repairs to the house and we need somewhere to stay for a couple of weeks!"

Rhiannon's house had originally been a terraced property but bombing of Pendragon Island during the war had damaged it and caused the one adjoining to be taken down. The pine end had been shored up with huge bulwarks of timber ever since. Their name had at last reached the top of the list on the council's order of repairs and a letter had arrived that morning telling them work would begin the following week and expected it to take about a month.

"It will be good to have you, you know that," Dora said, after pretending to be shocked by the teasing. "I'll get the rooms sorted so you can come over as soon as possible. Your dad's got some holiday to come so he can help Charlie empty the rooms on that side of your house."

They parted then, Rhiannon to open Temptations and Dora to catch the bus up to the lake and start work at the Rose Tree cafe.

*   *   *

The postman brought a surprise letter for Megan and Edward Jenkins too, with a London postmark and handwriting Megan vaguely recognised. She frowned as she slit the envelope and took out a single page. She scanned it quickly and handed it to Edward.

"From your dear cousin, Terrence," she said, as he began to read.

Dear Megan,

It is such a long time since I had word of you and our daughter, so I have decided to call and see for myself how you both are. I can't tell you how much I am longing to hold the darling child in my arms.

My fondest love to you both,

Terrence

"What a lot of bunkum!" Megan said, as Edward looked up, his expression one of dismay.

"But he says he wants to see Rosemary. He'll want to take her from me. I couldn't bear that, darling. Can he have heard of my plan to adopt her d'you think?"

"I can't think how. I do think he has an extra sense about things that might mean money. I imagine that's what this is about, don't you, Edward? Money?"

"I hope so. I'll pay anything so long as he leaves us alone." He sat down crushing the flimsy sheet of paper in his hands. "How could he know? I didn't think anyone kept in touch with him, now grandfather has gone."

"Your sister Margaret?" Megan suggested.

"Of course! I'll go and see her and ask what this is all about. Even in my most pessimistic moments, I can't imaging cousin Terrence wanting to be involved with bringing up a child."

"I agree. So, it's money and – I don't know about you, darling, but I don't want him to gain anything from a threat to harm our happiness. Whatever he wants, the answer is no. Do we agree?"

"I don't know," Edward looked very doubtful and Megan hugged him.

"Darling, it's a form of blackmail. He'll be back again and again if he thinks we can be squeezed for extra money. Oh, it will be pleasantly done. He'll be at his most charming. But it will still be blackmail. So we don't give him a penny. We are agreed, aren't we?" There was a firmness in her voice as she repeated her decision, demanding that he shared it.

He smiled at her but there was a slight quiver in the corner of his mouth. "I think we should wait and see what he says. We can't decide on any action until we know what he wants."

"But we don't hand over any money. We have to be certain how we feel about that before we see him."

"All right," Edward said, but Megan had a feeling that he was not as strongly convinced as she.

Terrence stepped out of his car at the entrance to Montague Court and looked around for someone to help with his luggage. The place hadn't changed much apart from some fresh paint and slightly more orderly grounds. Shrubs that had been overgrown and spread across the grass had been cut back and the edges neatened. He smiled at the realisation that he would never have noticed such things before meeting Coral Prichard, widow and his most recent conquest.

He opened the boot and strolled towards the entrance. No one about. He was sure that the new owners would have someone available to handle his cases. He went into the reception area and called. A man in a smart suit and a cap came forward and as Terrence recognised him, he burst out laughing. "Islwyn? What on earth— ?" Still laughing, he pointed to his car and said, "My man, gather my luggage and take it to my room, would you?"

Islwyn glared at him and walked away.

A lady appeared then, opening the door glass door of the office, stepping out and smilingly asking how she could help.

"I have a booking for three nights, Mrs er—?"

"Grant," Annie supplied. "And you are Mr Jenkins?"

"My family owned this place until recently," he said.

"Then we'll have to make sure we look after you well, won't we?" Annie smiled.

"With my cousin Margaret and Islwyn Weston attending my every whim, it's a facinating thought." Terrence smiled. "Imagine you succeeding in making him work. So many have tried and failed. What a delightful prospect."

Annie Grant made no comment. She had thought when he telephoned that he had come to gloat. She had noticed that the car he drove was an expensive new one, and guessed he was going to make sure his cousin Margaret noticed it too.

Terrence had to carry his own bags to the room he had been allotted on the first floor. It had once been his Aunt Dorothy and Uncle Leonard's room, he remembered, full of ancient, heavy furniture, with thick curtains draped across the windows, and cobwebs regularly appearing in the corners. The room had been so dark it had frightened him as a child. He remembered running along the corridor when he had to pass its door, feeling the threat of attack between his shoulder-blades.

Now it was cheerful, the once sombre walls painted a delicate lemon, with a blue carpet and pale oak furniture, and the ghosts had gone. Outside, the month of June was behaving itself and the sky was clear, the view across the gardens calm and soothing. He was surprised at how much the Grants had changed the place. His aunt and uncle would have hated it though. Change had been an anathema to them. They had been obsessed with tradition to the detriment of progress, comfort and profit. He guessed that cousin Margaret hated it too. The thought made him smile. Served her right, the bad-tempered old witch.

After unpacking and sending for a drink, which he hoped Islwyn would bring, but which was delivered by Annie Grant's husband, Leigh, he went out to find Megan and Edward intending to play the doting father for a while.

In the Rose Tree cafe that afternoon, Dora was thinking about what she had to do at home to prepare for sharing the house with Rhiannon and her family. At five o'clock when the customers had dwindled to just one or two sitting drinking tea, she asked Sian, "D'you want the last of these pasties?"

"No, you take them. Jack and Victoria have invited me to dinner this evening. They've promised me a rich rabbit stew."

"Bought? Or courtesy of the Griffithses?" Dora asked.

"Jack said it had a notice tied round its neck stating it was the property of Farmer Booker." She laughed. "But it won't taste any the worst for that!"

"Frank Griffiths, I'll bet. He loves outwitting Booker and Constable Gregory. Courting Gregory's daughter would just be adding to the fun."

"There's some soup left if you want it?" Sian offered as they gathered up their things preparing to leave.

"The pasties will do for Lewis and me. I need a quick and easy meal tonight," Dora explained. "I want to start emptying drawers and cupboards, and getting rid of surplus furniture, ready for Rhiannon and Charlie and Gwyn."

"I thought you might," Sian smiled. "Want any help?"

"No thanks. We'll put the spare stuff up in the loft for now."

"For now? That's fatal, that is. In the loft they'll stay and you'll forget what's up there. You'd never believe what I found in ours when we moved to Trellis Road. Toys Jack had grown out of, and books galore."

"That's a point. It might be worth having a scout around up there. I think we put some old toys away too. Years ago. Rhiannon might like some of them."

"And she might not! I don't think today's mothers fancy old things, they want everything new, and who's to blame them? We had enough of second-hand stuff to last two lifetimes, didn't we? Leave them there, the Lewis family might have some family heirlooms to discover one distant day."

Lewis was late home that evening and Dora put the pasties in the oven to heat slowly and looked up at the landing, where a trap-door opened into the roof space. It was no use trying to stand on the banister and stretch up, like Lewis did. She wouldn't be able to reach even to open it, let alone climb into it with some of the items she wanted to move. But she was too impatient to wait for Lewis. Manhandling the ladder with difficulty, she succeeded in propping it up against the wall and, climbing up, she threw back the trap-door. Another struggle and she had the ladder touching the entrance and up she went. They was a light, and gingerly touching the edge of the wooden surround, she flicked the switch and flooded the area with a sickly yellow glow. Why did men economise with a low-wattage bulb where it was needed most and used so rarely it hardly mattered? she grumbled.

It was her intention simply to move a few boxes, to make room for the things Rhiannon would need to bring. But she was quickly distracted, lifting lids that hadn't been moved for years, poking about in cartons to find school reports and once favourite annuals, *Rupert*, *Radio Fun*, *Beano* and *Dandy* and many more. Why had they kept them? Viv and Rhiannon's school reports amused her. 'Could do better', was the usual remark. What would those teachers think of them now? Both managing a business, both happily married. She avoided searching deeper into the box, she knew that the reports of her other son, Lewis-boy, would be there and she didn't think she could cope with seeing them even now, almost five years after his death in a stupid road accident.

Then she opened another box and found aeroplane models that Lewis-boy had made. Handling them brought tears then a smile or two. None of them had been finished. Always too impatient to move on to the next thing, that was our Lewis-boy, she thought. Braver now she had coped with finding Lewis-boy's treasures, she lifted the lid of a thick cardboard box she had unearthed in a corner under some remnants of carpet intended to lag the water tank.

The box contained old newspapers, yellow and brittle with age. She had no recollection of saving them. What could they be? Curious, she carried them to the edge of the trap-door and went down the ladder, pulling the box after her. Carefully taking out one of the crisp newspapers she saw that it had been folded to reveal a court case about a local prostitute called Miss Bondo. She knew the name vaguely and was curious, but seeing the time, she put the box into a cupboard and washed her hands, and started to set the table. The date on the paper had been before she and Lewis had bought the house, over thirty years ago. One day, when she had more time, she'd investigate. Now, she had to prepare for Rhiannon and Charlie and Gwyn. They were far more important than some old newspaper reports.

"Who's Miss Bondo?" she asked when Lewis came home.

"Molly Bondo, d'you mean?" he asked. "What makes you ask about her? She's the local tart. A friend of Barbara Wheel, who married Percy Flemming. Why?"

She didn't have time to explain, so she said, "Oh, the name came up somewhere, that's all. Now, hurry and eat up. We've got work to do."

"Are you going to tell me what? And why?" he asked. "Don't tell me we've offered a home to Basil and Eleri and the boys!"

She laughed. "Of course, you don't know. Our Rhiannon and Charlie and Gwyn will be staying with us for a while. Their house is being repaired." He still looked puzzled. "Come on, the ladder's up ready, you'll have to shift a few things to make room for them."

"What things?"

"Oh small tables and a couple of chairs. Nothing much," she said. She was thoughtful as she took in his words. Eleri and Basil and the babies living here? Now that would liven the place up, no mistake.

A few days later Dora suggested to Lewis that they spent a bit of money strengthening the fences around the garden.

"What on earth for?" He laughed. "Rhiannon's baby isn't due for months. And I don't think we need worry about Gwyn escaping, do we?"

"No," she conceded, "but it does look untidy. A bit of paint and a few repairs will save more work later on."

Lewis looked at her quizzically. "Dora? What are you thinking of?"

"Well, when Eleri and Basil visit, and for Rhiannon's baby later on, we'll need to be sure the garden is safe."

Lewis was suspicious but said nothing more.

On Saturday morning, Terrence walked into the sports shop in the High Street and was surprised at what he saw. Remembering the state of the shop when Edward had first considered buying it, he had expected a temporary, hastily decorated place with some cheaply made fittings. Instead, there were smart displays of a wide range of sports equipment and sports wear. Full sized models showed the latest in golfing clothes and tennis outfits. Shelf upon shelf showed how well stocked they were and Edward, Megan and Mair were all busily attending to customers. An old man appeared from the back room carrying what looked like a cigar box and which on closer inspection, turned out to be fishing flies.

Disappointment flooded through his mind. He hadn't expected dull, boring Edward Jenkins to have achieved all this. He looked around while the four assistants continued to serve, the constantly ringing till painful to his ear. Where was the baby? Were they able to employ a nanny as well? At least it looked likely that they could afford to pay him something to compensate for losing his child, he thought sarcastically. He'd put on a good act and then reluctantly agree to allow Edward to be known as the father.

He had a moment of panic at the thought that Edward might not want that, that he would welcome the appearance of the real father, grateful to hand over some of the responsibility and expense. As Megan looked up and saw him, he was tempted to run from the shop.

"Terrence?" Megan said questioningly.

"Megan, my dear. How are you? And, how is my little girl?"

"We are all well. So, if there's nothing else, we are rather busy."

Her abrupt manner was no surprise to him, Megan always spoke as though she were a dowager reprimanding a servant. It was one of the things he had liked about her, the way she was never embarrassed, never acted as though she were in the wrong. He remembered once when they had broken down and were lost, she had gone into the hallway of someone's house and, receiving no reply to her call for assistance, had used the phone to get help. The owner came back and had demanded to know what she was doing and, with a few words, Megan had the poor woman apologising for her harsh words. He came out of the brief reverie to see Edward standing beside Megan.

"I want to see my daughter."

"Dorothy, you mean?" Megan asked, her head tilted pertly in query.

"Of course, Dorothy. How is my little Dorro?"

"I have no idea. My daughter is called Rosemary," she snapped. She turned away then and began showing a small boy a collection of kites.

Terrence laughed. "I knew you were teasing," he lied. "Now, I want to see my daughter. Can we go somewhere and talk?"

The rush of customers had slowed down and leaving Mair and Willie Jones to see to the remaining few, Megan led the way upstairs to the flat.

Rosemary was in her cot, her arms above her head, her cheeks flushed with sleep. Terrence looked down at her and tried to look interested. He turned to face them and said, "She's beautiful. I suppose you want to adopt her, Edward?"

Edward didn't reply, he was hushed by a glare from his wife.

"I could be persuaded to sign her away," Terrence said, "although it would be a wrench."

After trying in vain to convince them that he would prefer not to lose contact with his child, Terrence managed to bring the stilted conversation around to money. "For a thousand pounds I'll sign anything you wish," he said.

"Come on Edward. It's time we went back down to relieve Mair. Rosemary will be awake soon and she'll need changing. Although," she added, "you can deal with her, can't you, Terrence? While we give Mair and Willie a break?"

"I have to go. I'm meeting someone," he mumbled. "But I'll be back. If you want me to sign adoption papers you'll have to be generous."

"Generous, Terrence? I'm surprised to hear that word falling from your mouth."

Megan and Edward watched him leave, running down the stairs and out of the shop, getting into his smart car and driving off with a snort of the powerful engine.

"He means to make trouble," Edward said.

"I don't think so. Not when we've told him that he's welcome to have the child for a day every week and every other weekend. Fatherhood is the last thing Terrence needs."

Terrence was not too disappointed about the money. Coral Prichard, his latest 'love', had enough of that. But he had hoped to persuade Edward out of a reasonable sum to add a touch of class to his courtship. With a thousand pounds he could have taken her away to spend a weekend in Paris that she would remember all her life. It would have set their relationship on a firm base. After that she would believe him when he told her he didn't need her money.

A foolish investment soon after they married would be believable. He would have her sympathy and he already knew how generous she could be. Being married to Coral Prichard and living in her large house in Richmond with two servants to deal with his every need was what he had been born for. He'd always known that. Yes, with a thousand from Edward he would be settled for life. And, Coral was fifty-five and not in the best of health. He would like a thousand pounds to flatter her with a good courtship. He had to persuade them to give him the money, and Edward was his best chance.

It had to be Edward. He doubted if his sister Margaret had anything left after her disastrous attempt at running a smart restaurant with the lazy Islwyn Weston. And Megan's family were no longer wealthy. No, he had seen the fear on Edward's face and knew that he was the most likely one to part with money. Edward loved and wanted the child and that was what he would count on.

Megan's mother was considering money that day, too, wondering if she would be wise to sell the guesthouse and find a small house in which she could live on the proceeds. But when she counted the cost of moving and the fact that her husband was entitled to half of the money, she knew she would be unable to manage. No, she would have to continue running the house for paying guests and now Megan was gone, she would have to manage alone.

The girl she had employed for three mornings each week, was very willing, but it wasn't enough. It had been all right when Megan had been there to help out at busy times and for a few weeks following her daughter's wedding it had been manageable, but slowly the work had become more and more tiring. This was her excuse for allowing Maxie to stay and to help.

Having ignored her request to leave, he continued to come on the same two days each week as though nothing had been said. He gave her no cause for complaint and she gradually accepted he was there to stay. He sat with the other guests and ate the evening meal, and only after the others had gone back to their rooms or into the television lounge did he overstep the mark and walk into her kitchen carrying trays of dishes and begin to help her deal with them. It was so casually done she found herself handing him things to deal with, and without being told he seemed to know where everything was kept and rarely made an error. When the kitchen was tidy, he would start setting the tables for breakfast, covering the table with a cloth, exactly as she always did. He would then make a pot of tea and set a tray for her and carry it through to her private room and leave it on the oval table outside her door. Then he would leave her with the admonition to sit and relax for a hour, before going back to his own room.

How could she complain? How could she tell him to go? She admitted to herself that on the nights he stayed she was glad of his help. But it couldn't continue. She knew that. She had to discuss it was someone and her sister was the only one who would help.

The Rose Tree cafe usually had a slight lull in their busy day just before lunch, so she went about that time and asked Sian to spare her a few minutes. When she explained the problem of the guest who refused to leave, Sain asked her why she wanted him to.

"From what you say, he isn't a problem, more an asset to a

busy woman like you." Sian frowned. "Unless he is threatening in some way. Does he make you nervous, Sally?"

"He doesn't do anything I can complain of, really he doesn't. He just likes to help. But why does he spend time working in my kitchen when he pays for me to look after him?"

"Have you asked him?" asked the pragmatic Dora, and Sally shook her head.

"It seems such a silly thing to ask, 'why are you doing my work for me?' Well, could you say it?"

"I see what you mean. But perhaps *you* could, Sian," Dora suggested.

"No, I'm being silly. I'll ask him myself and suggest that he doesn't need to, and see what he says." Sally looked very doubtful.

She went home still unsure of what she would do, but when Maxie came into the kitchen that evening, she took a deep breath and said, "This is very kind of you, Mr Powell, but I really don't need your help. You pay to stay here and you shouldn't feel obliged to do my work for me."

His reply suggested that he hadn't heard a word.

"D'you know, Mrs Fowler-Weston, I worry about you."

"Worry? About me?"

"I come and stay twice every week and I do what I can to ease your burden, but what about the other five nights, you have all this to do on your own."

"I don't mind," she protested. "It's my job."

"That girl, the one who comes in to clean. Why don't you ask her to help you on three or four evenings, see to these dishes for you? You do the cooking, mind. Good at that you are and we'd all hate for someone to take that over from you. But clearing up after, well, she could do that and then I wouldn't be so worried. Do simple meals on the other days and you could sit and relax in the evenings instead of standing here slaving away for us ungrateful lot."

"I don't know . . ." She was confused. Wasn't she the instigator of this conversation? Wasn't she going to be strong? Then why was it ending with him giving her advice? "I'll think about it, Mr Powell," she said meekly.

"Call me Maxie. Everyone does," he smiled cheerfully, as he placed the last drinking glass on its allotted shelf.

Money was on Basil Griffiths's mind that Saturday too. With the increase in their rent, Eleri was having to consider working full time. She had once worked as an usherette at the cinema and, with the children so young, that seemed the only work she could do. Basil would be home each evening and she would be leaving as soon as he got in. Not much of a life.

Several people were looking for suitable accommodation for them, something decent that was cheaper, but every place he had investigated was either too small or too shabby. He thought again of the room where his brothers had slept, and went back to look at it. It had once been a separate building, stone built and with a thatched roof, now replaced with corrugated iron. Perhaps someone had lived there in some far off day, there was even a fireplace of sorts, although within the Griffithses memory it had been nothing more than a place to store animal feed and to provide shelter sometimes for the few sheep Hywel had once kept in an ajoining field.

To accommodate his growing family, Hywel had joined it to the house with an extension linking it to the back porch. Basil went inside. It had an air of despair about it. The window let in little light. Spiders were already colonising the corners between walls and roof and creating net curtains across the glass. Some of Frank's clothes still hung like a dusty scarecrow, on a hook behind the door. It was nothing more than a glorified shed. He couldn't ask Eleri to accept this. He ambled into the kitchen and made himself a pot of tea from the constantly humming kettle at the side of the fire.

Janet came in while he was drinking his second cup and he told her of his worries.

"I wish we could help," she sighed. "But even with our Ernie gone, there's still your sister. Why she can't live with Barry and act like a married woman should, I don't know. But there isn't room for the four of you, even if she and little Joseph-Hywel moved out."

She promised to ask all her friends and tried to reassure him. "There's a place waiting for you, and you'll find it when the time is right. I'm sure of it, son."

"I wish I could believe you," he said as he raised his long skinny form from the chair and set off back home.

Janet wished she believed it too.

The following day, Mair had arranged to meet Frank to go for a walk. She had suggested taking a picnic and had bought bread and an assortment of sandwich fillings plus fruit and a chocolate cake. Frank brought the makings for tea, piling kettle and pot and china into the old hamper the Griffithses had used for years. Janet had added a few pasties and Mair remarked that they had enough to survive for several days.

"You don't know Frank like I do!" Janet replied.

Mair was pleased: a sunny day and plenty of good food. She wanted it to be special. Today, she had decided, she would have to tell Frank about the baby. Any longer and it would be too late, the gossips would tell him first and she didn't want that. She was already changing shape and having to loosen her belt, although only three of the nine months had gone. Several friends had looked at her with suspicion and some glee, the promise of some gossip clearly anticipated with the usual pleasure.

Frank had borrowed the van and they drove to a small bay and carried their food to sit among the rocks, just out of reach of the incoming tide, the line of flotsam and jetsam a guide. She set out the food, while Frank built a fire and set the kettle he had brought to boil.

"Frank, I have something to tell you," she began as the kettle began to hum cheerfully. Frank's face drooped. She was going to tell him goodbye, tell him there was someone else. He turned his soulful eyes on her and waited to hear the dreaded words. "I'm going to have a baby. Our baby, Frank. I went to the doctor on Friday and he confirmed it."

The expression on his face underwent a transformation, the lugubrious heavy-eyed look opened out and he stared at her like a child opening a present on Christmas morning. "And we'll get married?" he said.

"You don't have to," she said, lowering her gaze dejectedly. "Not if you don't want to."

"Want to? Of course I want to! When shall we tell Mam and Dad? And your father of course. Oh heck, he won't be well pleased, will he, you marrying a Griffiths?"

"I don't care what he thinks, as long as you're happy," she said.

Awkwardly he hugged her and slowly they kissed.

"He'll be beautiful," he said a look of such rapture on his face that Mair wanted to cry. "He won't be long and skinny like me, will he? I want him to be like you."

"Short and fat, you mean?" she laughed, breathless with the excitement emanating from him. For a moment, his joy had made her forget the true situation.

"No, no. Cuddly, dark-haired and – oh, Mair, he'll be perfect!" Then his eyes opened wider still. "Mair, what if it's a girl? Mam's got grandsons and a girl would be just perfect." He went to hug her again but held back. "Daft isn't it, being shy, after all that we've been up to, but that's how I feel. Shy and a little in awe of you," Frank said. "We'll be Mam and Dad. Oh, Mair, I can't believe my luck."

"Nor me, Frank. Nor me."

After the picnic, of which Mair ate little and Frank demolished much with great enthusiasm, they drove home. "Come over tonight, and we'll celebrate proper. Dad's working from ten o'clock," she said as they parted.

"It won't harm – I mean—" he said shyly.

"Everything will be fine, Frank."

He wondered in his slow way, why PC Gregory was so frequently on the night shift. He decided it was a good time to find out. Tonight he'd follow him and see whether he went to report for work or had found somewhere else to spend his nights. If there was something suspicious going on, it might be useful to know. It might stop Gregory from playing the irate father when Mair told him her news, and stop him killing me, Frank thought grimly.

169

When he told Mair that he wouldn't see her that night, she was upset. She didn't show it, she just smiled and said, "Tomorrow then?" and went in with the remnants of the picnic, turning at the door to give him a rather sad wave.

He was going to change his mind! He would talk to his parents and they would persuade him against marrying her. Desperation overcame her as she prepared supper for her father and packed his snack box. As soon as she had seen him off on his bicycle, in his uniform, presumably not coming back until the following morning, she grabbed a jacket, locked the door and set off in the same direction. She would have to try again to talk to Carl.

Only minutes before she left the house, Frank had moved out of the trees and followed her father. Constable Gregory didn't ride fast on his ancient sit-up-and-beg style vehicle. He just sailed along, with his headlight piercing the darkness like a nervously held sword, making it easy for Frank to keep up with him. As the lane twisted and turned, Frank slipped through the fields and trees and waited for him at the next bend. It was soon quite clear that the man was not going to the police station. So where was he going? Frank's heart swelled with hope as the bicycle turned away from the town and into the small road where several houses had been turned into bedsits and flats. He was going to discover something useful that might save his life.

Constable Gregory propped his bike against a hedge and Frank watched as he slipped through the hedge and tapped gently on a french window. Heavy curtains moved aside. It opened, and Gregory went inside. It was obviously a regular arrangement.

Counting the gates, he went to the front of the houses and counted along again until he was certain which one Mair's father had entered. He made a mental note of the number and decided he could make some enquiries the following day. The postman and the newsagent were usually happy to talk. Once he knew who lived there, he could start working out why Constable Gregory called there so regularly, although it was almost certainly a woman. "Dirty old devil!" he said aloud. "Just let him say a word to me and I'll have 'im."

He heard footsteps then and he pushed himself deep into the hedge and lowered his head so his pale face wouldn't be seen. Someone was going to call at the same house but this time at the front door. How many more called here at night? It had to be a woman, but what was going on?

Hardly daring to breath, he stood perfectly still as the footsteps approached. Not a man this time, but a woman, he realised as they drew closer. Then the gate opened and a figure stepped so close to him he could have touched her. She knocked at the front door and waited.

After a second knock the door opened, a light switch clicked and a weak bulb bleached the night air. In the dim light he saw to his dismay, that the man answering the knock was Carl Rees and the woman who pleaded to be allowed in, was Mair.

Nine

F rank saw Carl Rees open the door wider and invite Mair in. Watching her take the single step that took her inside and out of his reach was as painful as anything he had ever experienced. In just a few seconds he had lost everything. Before she had turned up and knocked on Carl's door, he had been full of excitement at the thought of marriage to Mair, a child, a home where he could look after them both. Now it was all gone. He had never felt more like crying. His shoulders drooped and his face took on the lugubrious expression so useful in the days when he had walked beside funeral processions and led the mourners.

What could he do? Facing Mair again was going to be difficult. Would she carry on as though this secretive visit to Carl hadn't happened? And if she did, should he do the same? That would be the easiest thing to do: carry on, make arrangements for them to marry. But if he did that, all the time he would be watching her, waiting for her to leave him and go to Carl. It was Carl she loved and if Carl proposed, she would accept and tell him – poor, dull Frank Griffiths – 'sorry, and goodbye'.

He didn't leave the shelter of the hedge. He wasn't sure why, but at the back of his mind was the certainty that whatever was happening inside the house, Carl couldn't be relied on to make sure Mair got safely home. There had been no explanation yet, of why some weeks ago she had been attacked and, besides, Carl wasn't the caring kind.

It seemed hours but in fact it was only ten minues before the door reopened and Mair's huddled figure came out. The door closed behind her before she had left the step. Frank didn't reveal his presence but waited until she had passed him before starting to follow her. It was late, after eleven, and quite dark. She had a hood over her head as she bent forward and began to run. By simply lengthening his stride, Frank had no difficulty in keeping up with her.

At the telephone box she hesitated as though considering making a call and he waited. She went inside, dialled and then replaced the receiver. Running now, along the dark lane, a barely concealed shadow, he heard a low wailing and realised with deep sadness that she was crying.

When she was safely inside the lonely cottage at the edge of the wood, he stood for a long time watching, guessing her movements and remembering with heart-wrenching unhappiness, the room where she slept, which he had sometimes shared over the past weeks. If Carl had agreed to marry her, would she have passed the baby off as his? That thought increased his wretchedness.

Seeing the light go on in her bedroom he turned away and went home to seek comfort from the warmth and friendliness of the goats. There was no point in trying to sleep. As dawn broke he was back in the woods, armed with a shotgun and an empty sack. Patiently waiting at the edge of a field where rabbits regularly fed, he watched until a group of three grazed close together. His shot killed two and dazed the third, which he quickly dispatched. He put them in his sack and slowly walked home. He was preoccupied with his cruel disappointment, and made no attempt at evasion as he passed close to Farmer Booker's farmhouse. He wasn't surprised or particularly disappointed when Farmer Booker appeared and demanded he open his sack.

"The police have been informed," Booker told him, and Frank didn't argue. "See you in court, then?" was all he said.

An appearance in court, well, it wasn't exactly excitement, but it would remind him that life goes on, even with a broken heart. He was in this maudlin state of mind, a lovelorn, simple man undeserving of the cruelty of the fates, when he suddenly remembered Mair's father. It was the constable whom he had set out to follow, and he had gone into the same house as Mair. What was going on?

*   *   *

174

Mair lay on her bed all that night, switching the light on, then off, trying to read then throwing the book from her, unable to sleep, wondering if she had lost Frank. It was so unexpected for him to say he couldn't see her and not explain why. Perhaps he had talked things over with his parents and they had guessed that the child wasn't his. Yet how could he? there hadn't been time. No, any change of heart had been Frank's. Memories of her late-night pleading with Carl returned: the humiliation of being turned away; the long, lonely walk back through the lane, her distress numbing her fear; her aborted telephone call to her father, knowing she didn't want to talk about it to anyone, certainly not to him. As on other occasions, she wished her mother had lived, or that she had a sister with whom to share such moments.

She rose at six and made a cup of tea. Dad would be in soon, perhaps she'd have the fire lit for him. Even in June the house needed the comfort of a fire for at least part of the day, shaded from the sun as it was, by the thickness and height of the surrounding trees.

Frank saw her stepping outside in her dressing gown, to collect coals and some sticks. He wanted to go and take the heavy bucket from her, offer to get the fire going while she made them a cup of tea, but he didn't. She didn't want him, he reminded himself. It was Carl she loved and for a while she had thought he, dopey Frank Griffiths, would be an acceptable second best.

Unaware of his nearness, Mair wiped away persistent tears and wondered if she dare go and visit the Griffithses and try and talk to Frank. All she would lose was pride, and Carl had taken most of that from her anyway. If only she could stop crying.

At seven o'clock, Dora was up, dressed and out in the warm, misty garden.

Lewis called from the bedroom window, "Dora? What's the matter, I haven't overslept, have I?"

"No, I was just measuring up the garden. Which way should we extend the lawn d'you think? Somewhere that gets the best of the sun. The swing can go further down, near the lane. What d'you think?"

"I think you've gone mad! Wait, I'm coming down." He reappeared a few moments later, with a dressing gown flapping around his pyjamas, his hair still a little tousled, his fine dark eyes wearing a slight frown. Very handsome. Dora sighed as she watched him approach.

His film-star looks had made him attractive to women of all ages – his looks and his charm. Lewis had frequently found their adoration impossible to resist and his affairs had caused Dora many distressing moments. She promised herself that now they were together again she would live with it, and not accuse him of infidelity if something happened to make her suspicious. Nia Williams had been her greatest threat and now she was dead, she believed the worst of the danger had passed.

"I love you in the mornings, Lewis," she said softly, and the slight irritation faded from his face and he hugged her.

"I'm glad, Dora Lewis. Very glad. But," he added, "I still want to know what you think we're doing, setting up the garden for children. Rhiannon and Charlie and Gwyn will provide all their baby's needs, it isn't for us to do."

"I know love, but 'Heshe' will spend a lot of time here. We've got a better, bigger garden for one thing, they only have an ol' yard."

"All right. What d'you want to do?"

"Make a bigger lawn."

"It's the wrong time for seed."

"Turf," she said. "I've already made enquiries and it isn't very expensive. And a swing."

"A swing. For a baby who isn't born yet."

"Ready for when its needed." She didn't tell him of her other plan. Lewis had to be coaxed. If she came straight out with it now, he'd say no. There was time to persuade him, plant the idea at the same time as they planted the new lawn. That way he'd be half convinced that the idea was his, a sure way to make certain that when the question was raised, he'd say yes. She made tea and toast and they sat outside, discussing the position of lawn and swing and even a sandpit, before they went in to dress.

*   *   *

Rhiannon was already in Temptations talking to Barry, when Dora dashed past hurrying to catch her bus. She waved to her mother and said to Barry, "Always in a hurry, our Mam. She does so much before she goes to work you'd never believe." She was smiling as she turned back to Barry and the discussion about when Rhiannon would leave work and prepare for her baby.

"How do you feel?" Barry asked. "Will you be able to work a few more weeks?"

"I've got more than two months to wait, if I stopped now I'd be bored silly in a week!"

"Caroline said you were complaining of backache, is it better now?"

"I feel fine. If I could stay on until August, then the last few weeks would fly."

"So we need to start looking for your replacement in about a month."

"If I hear of anyone, I'll let you or Caroline know." She coloured up and then said, "Barry, I'm sorry. I'm looking at this from my point of view. You and Caroline might prefer me to go now, and not work here until I'm waddling around like a duck."

"Stay as long as you can, that's what Caroline and I want." He smiled. "You'll be hard to replace."

A routine visit to the doctor a few days later changed Rhiannon's mind. The doctor recommended that she spend an hour or two each day resting with her feet up. The work at Temptations meant standing for long hours and she had to admit that there were days when she felt very tired. She said nothing to Barry, giving herself another couple of weeks before making up her mind to leave. Her successful, problem-free pregnancy had restored her confidence and she no longer worried so much about losing the child. She told Charlie, but played the doctor's advice down a little, only saying she should consider stopping work sooner that she had intended.

"How soon is 'soon'?" he asked anxiously.

"How long is a piece of string? I'll give it two more weeks then tell Barry to look for someone else. Right?"

*   *   *

177

Jennie met Carl one day, quite near the shop she had once rented. He walked her past it swiftly. She thought he was being kind and not allowing her to mope over the loss of her business. As they crossed the road, he asked her about the sale of the house.

"It's going through and I have to get out in a couple of weeks," she replied.

"You have somewhere to live? Or are you going to live with Peter's parents?" he asked.

"Not a chance! No, I haven't found anywhere yet. I haven't treated the problem as urgently as I should, it hasn't seemed real somehow. I suppose I didn't really think our marriage would end so – so – casually. I'll have to do something soon, though, or I'll be sleeping on the beach beside the dreaded seaside rock shop!" she laughed.

"You know Sally Fowler-Weston, don't you?" Carl said. "She has paying guests. It might be an idea for you to take a room there, at least until you decide what you're going to do. Better than rushing into something you might not like."

"I hadn't thought of that. Meals provided too, it does sound tempting."

"You can keep an eye on one of the lodgers," he said confidentially. "Mrs Weston is nothing to me mind, but I do wonder about a man called Maxie Powell. He's a labourer on one of the sites where I sometimes do a few days work. He was boasting one day that he intended to flatter her into accepting him as a permanent part of her life. He needs watching and I think she'd be better off having another woman in the place."

"I'll go and see her. If she has a room vacant, I'll take it, for a while anyway. I'll quite enjoy being spoilt."

"And you'll watch Maxie Powell?"

"I'll watch Maxie Powell," she agreed.

Jennie found the days at the beach selling seaside rock very boring. She knew she should put aside all thoughts of what might have been and forget the business she had begun and lost, but she was still very bitter. One morning, leaving the house early, she was more dejected than usual. She had signed the contracts for the sale of the house where she and Peter had begun their marriage with such hope and optimism. They hadn't met for over a week; even the contracts had been signed separately, each going into the office when an appointment had been made and dealing with the simple action that was going to change everything so dramatically.

One morning a few days after she had spoken to Carl, she was too early to catch the bus. The seaside shops and stalls and shows didn't open until ten o'clock, there being few visitors to the beach before then. She turned down the road by the church and, after trying not to look, stopped and went across to her old shop. Something was happening. The window was covered with stuck-down newspapers, making it impossible for anyone to look inside. The glass door, too, was covered with hardboard and, even pressing her nose to the edge of the window, she couldn't see anything of what was going on inside. She walked on and stopped at Temptations to talk to Rhiannon.

"What's happening to my old shop, do you know?" she asked as she went inside.

Rhiannon put down the duster she was using and shook her head. "I haven't heard any rumours. Is it re-let, then?"

"Apparently. The windows are covered and something is going on. I wonder what kind of a shop it will be?"

"If I hear anything, I'll let you know," Rhiannon promised. "How is the job at the rock shop making out? Interesting, is it?"

"It was – for the first ten minutes!" Jennie sighed. "Can you imagine, everyone comes in and, as though they're the first to think of such an audacious idea, decide to give some rock in the shape of a dummy, to their big brother, or their boss, or their grown-up son. Or rock in the shape of a fried breakfast to give their husbands after promising breakfast in bed. For a while I forced a laugh and declared that it would be such fun and how did they think of such a hilarious idea. Now I want to scream!"

"Thank goodness we have more variety here in Temptations. I think I'd be screaming after a week of that."

"I'm looking for something else, but not over the beach. I think I'd rather sell second-hand socks to tramps."

"What about this place?" Rhiannon asked quietly.

179

"Me manage Temptations? Of course, you will be leaving soon. But won't Barry have someone in mind?"

"I'll have a word if you like, find out if he has offered the job to someone, but I don't think he has."

"Thank you. I'd like to work here."

"You'd have to see Barry of course. But the wages aren't bad – enough for you to pay for a room and feed yourself."

"It's Wednesday and, although the beach shops stay open, it's my half day, so I'll call and see him on my way home, shall I?"

"Er, no, not on a Wednesday," she said, unaware of any change. "Barry and Caroline consider that their special time and they don't make any other arrangements. Come tomorrow morning on the way to work and I'll try to make sure Barry's here."

"Their special time? Barry Williams and Caroline? I thought they were separated?"

"They are, but they're working on it."

"Good luck to them," Jennie said sadly. "All right, I'll see you tomorrow morning."

She hurried out wishing she and Peter were working on their disaster of a marriage. Mother-in-law trouble was often used as a basis for jokes but it wasn't really funny. Not funny at all.

Instead of going to the bus stop, Jennie went to Glebe Lane to see Sally. There was a room vacant, but Jennie didn't take it. There were a few days to go before she had to leave the house and it would have been a waste to pay rent unnecessarily.

"I'll come back next week and see whether the room is still available," she promised Sally.

Waiting at the bus stop, guilty that she would be late opening the shop, the van she had sold to Carl approached and he stopped to give her a lift.

"Thanks, Carl. I'm late. I've been to see about a room in Mrs Fowler-Weston's house."

"Good."

"I haven't taken it, but I think I will, next week when I have to leave the house."

They drove out of town and along the road towards the Pleasure Beach. A few coaches were pulling into the car parks and excited holiday-makers were spilling out, carrying picnic baskets, sunshades and towels wrapped like sausage rolls around swim suits. Before she got out of the van, Jennie asked, "Have you heard who's taken the shop?"

"Rumours flying," he said, "everything from fish and chips to books to sweets to clothes. Look, I have to go, I'm blocking the road." Waving cheerfully, he drove off and Jennie walked towards the shop planning her apologies.

Terrence had failed in his attempt to get Megan to part with some money. He knew Edward was the weak one but he didn't seem able to get him on his own, and work on his anxiety. He would have to change his tack. Failing Edward and Megan, perhaps Megan's grandmother might be persuaded if he threatened to publicise the fact that he was being denied access to his child? The local newspaper wouldn't be interested in their petty squabbles, but Gladys might not know that. He set off optimistically to visit Arfon and Gladys's large house, hoping to find Gladys on her own.

As he touched the front gate he heard voices. Instead of knocking at the door he went round the side of the house and looked into the garden. Megan and her grandmother were laughing at the little girl as she kicked and struggled to roll over, on a fluffy white blanket spread on the lawn. In the shade of a tree, Edward and Arfon were smiling as they watched the scene. Terrence went back out to the pavement and waited.

When Edward and Megan left he met them by accident, or so it seemed, and at once said apologetically, "Megan, I'm ashamed of myself. I don't know what got into me. It was wicked, asking you for money. I would never do anything to hurt you. I won't raise any objection if you and Edward want to adopt our daughter legally." Megan thanked him rather grudgingly. "There is one thing," he said, leaning over the pram where Rosemary was now sleeping. "I really do need a loan. I would appreciate you lending me a thousand pounds. I don't want you to think my signing away my daughter is anything to do with this, but I am rather embarrassed financially at the moment and I'd be very glad of your help. It's only temporary. You have my word on that."

Edward hesitated, frowning as he tried to think of the right words to use. Megan tightened her jaw, her eyes sparkled with irritability as she said, "No, Terrence! We don't have any money for one thing, the business needs building up. For another, I wouldn't give or lend you money if I were the owner of thousands."

"But—" Edward began.

"Don't think for a moment that Edward and I will feel sorry for you, and we won't submit to blackmail." She glared at him angrily. "So, there's nothing more to discuss, is there? If you'll give us your address, we'll send the papers on when they arrive."

Terrence smiled. "Still the same old hard-faced bitch you always were, Megan. Really, cousin Edward, you have my sympathy. Well, perhaps I'll be hard-faced too and forget my promise to sign away Rosalie, or move and forget to give you my address? You'll have to wait a long time then, won't you? Always worrying whether I'll turn up and demand to see my child?"

He hurried off and Megan and Edward walked home in silence.

When Rosemary was in bed, Edward said, "Don't you think that was unwise?"

"No! and I don't want to discuss it, Edward." Her next outburst revealed to Edward how upset she really was. She pointed out that he didn't even remember the baby's name. "Rosalie. He called her Rosalie! Can you believe the man! The other day he didn't correct me when I called her Dorothy. What does he care, apart from using her as an excuse to get money from us? He won't succeed, I won't let him use Rosemary this way and you shouldn't consider it either."

Edward lay awake long into the night, wondering how real Terrence's threat was and whether he should defy his wife and pay the man.

* * *

In the Griffiths's cottage, Caroline lay awake too, wondering where her life was taking her – if anywhere. She and Barry had stopped meeting regularly every Wednesday afternoon in the flat above Temptations, when, for a few hours they pretended to be a courting couple sneaking a few hours away from everything else to talk, and make love and dream of that wonderful future where everything was perfect. After so many false starts they were both hesitant about trying once more to make their difficult marriage work and Barry's suggestion when he had met her to drive her home from work that afternoon, had thrown Caroline into confusion. He had begun by telling her about the possible applicant for the job of managing Temptations when Rhiannon left to have her baby.

"Who is she?" Caroline asked. "Do I know her?"

"She's called Jennie Francis and she used to run the small paint, wallpaper and carpet shop near the church. Fancied herself as a rival to the Westons she did, for a while. Then something happened and she suddenly closed down. From what I've learned from Rhiannon, she and her husband have separated and their house is being sold. So," he went on hesitantly, "this Jennie Francis needs accommodation as well as a job."

"There's nothing we can do about that," Caroline said, "but I'll ask around, see if there's a suitable place near enough for her to get to the shop. That is, if she's suitable."

"If she is, how d'you feel about her having the flat?"

"You moving out, you mean?" Her heart began to race, but not with excitement at what he was certainly going to suggest, but dismay. "Where would you go?" she said, pretending to be stupid. "We've sold Chestnut Road and there's hardly room for you over your showroom-cum-studio."

"We aren't short of money. Isn't it time we bought a house and began to make a home, for the three of us? Joseph-Hywel should have a brother or a sister before much longer, or he'll be more like an uncle to the new arrival. Caroline, we've lived apart for so long, and we're drifting further apart. Isn't it time to try again, and this time with a determination to make it work?"

She lay in her lonely bed, with the sound of trees murmuring outside the windows, her small son sleeping peacefully beside her. Joseph-Hywel would be four next month. Barry was right, if they were to give him brothers and sisters they shouldn't wait much longer. But the thought of being a wife, twenty-four hours of every day, was not a prospect that excited her as it should. She tried to work out why this was so. She had been so comfortable living with her parents that, unlike many young women, she had never dreamed of marriage as a way of escaping. She had loved Joseph, Barry's brother, completely and she would have travelled to any part of the world if he had wanted her to. Losing him while expecting his son, and before they were married, had numbed her senses. Marrying his brother had been a necessity and nothing to do with love at all. She had tried for a while to love Barry, but now, once more facing the prospect of living with him, sharing everything, being a loving wife and all that entailed, she knew it would be wrong. She felt tears trickle onto her pillow as she confessed silently that she didn't even want to share her son. He was hers; hers and Joseph's and, pretend as she might, that could never change. She would never love Barry in the way he deserved.

She slept finally, having made the decision to tell Barry as soon as possible that it was over, she was staying with her parents, probably for the rest of her life.

Jennie arrived at Temptations the following morning with a couple of references, and she and Rhiannon waited in the shop for Barry to appear. They didn't see Caroline walk up the back steps and go into the flat. But Rhiannon heard voices behind the door from the shop, and quickly realised that Caroline had called. As the voices became louder, she knew Barry and his wife were quarrelling. This was disturbing. Caroline was a quiet, gentle person and Rhiannon had never heard her raise her voice before. She wondered what had happened, and hoped that her curiosity would be satisfied. She had known Caroline and Barry a long time, knew of the problems they had encountered and wished them well, but she was human enough to want to know what had caused Caroline, the most peaceable of the Griffithses, to become angry enough to shout.

When all had gone quiet, she waited, wondering whether to knock on the door to the flat to remind Barry of Jennie's appointment, or to wait, in the hope he would remember and come down. She went into the small kitchen beyond the shop and made tea, giving a cup of tea and some biscuits to Jennie while she waited.

"Is there a cup for me, Rhiannon?" a voice called, and Barry came through the shop door, from the street, not from the flat as she had expected. His rather pugnacious face was flushed, but his voice seemed calm as he asked, "Are you Miss Francis?"

"Mrs Francis, yes," she said, taking his proffered hand.

Barry asked few questions, his mind seemed elsewhere, but he quickly learnt of her circumstances either from Jennie herself or from what he remembered Rhiannon explaining previously. After ten minutes, he had offered Jennie the job and had also told her that if she could wait a month, the flat might also be available.

Pleased for Jennie, but saddened at the knowledge that the shop she had been so happy to manage was hers no longer, Rhiannon told Barry that she would like to work two more weeks, one on her own, as usual, and the second beside Jennie, so she could explain how everything was run. Still distracted Barry appeared only to half listen to her suggestion.

Jennie explained that she had a couple of weeks before vacating her house but an arrangement was being considered for her to live in a guesthouse after that. "A month's time would be fine," she told Barry. "If I could see the place fairly soon, so I can plan what I need to bring?"

"Rhiannon will deal with that," Barry said gruffly, as he left the shop, leaving the tea Rhiannon had poured untouched. What had happened? Perhaps she and Charlie could take Gwyn for a walk with the dog on Sunday and visit the Griffithses. Nosy maybe, but there was also a reason: Caroline would need a friend and, Rhiannon, in spite of enjoying gossip, was well able to keep confidences.

*   *   *

Mair went to work as usual and hoped that Frank would call, but for the next two days she didn't see him. He was there, but although he watched her as she walked to and from work, he made sure he wasn't seen. He wanted to see whether she and Carl met. On the second evening he was watching the cottage when he saw PC Gregory emerge, wheeling his bicycle as though setting off for a nightshift. As before, Frank followed and, as before, he went into the house where Carl rented a room, and slipped in through the french windows.

Frank waited for an hour, but there was no sign of Gregory leaving. He had learnt from various sources that Carl rented a bedsit and that his mother lived in the same house, but with her own rooms. He had also learnt that the rooms visited by Mair's father were those of a Mrs Dreese who worked for Gladys and Arfon Weston. The woman had obviously chosen ground-floor rooms, so she could entertain without anyone being any the wiser. Well just let old Gregory start getting all uppity about him and Mair and he'd remind him of this address!

He went around and knocked on the front door, then hid, as Carl opened the door and looked at the empty step and the shadowy garden.

"If that's you, Mair, go away," he hissed. "You and I have nothing to say to each other, don't you understand?"

"It isn't Mair, it's me," Frank said, seconds before his fist contacted with Carl's face. He hurried home, rubbing his painful knuckles but smiling at the peaceable feeling in his heart. "Pretty boy no longer," he gloated.

He walked through the fields and lanes knowing he wouldn't sleep and wondering what he should do about Mair. His dream was still there, he and Mair married, and their a child on the way, but would she still marry him after his unexplained disappearance? How could he tell her the reason was that he was checking up on her father? Why hadn't he forgotten about PC Gregory until he and Mair had told everyone they were engaged? Made everything official. He would never have known about her visit to Carl and some things were better not known. Why hadn't he thought about things properly instead of going hell bent on finding out what her father was up to? How did he get in such a mess when everything was about to be perfect? Everyone else seemed to sort their life out with ease, but for Frank Griffiths, nothing went right. Still pondering the imponderable mysteries of life, he went home.

Janet almost tripped over him the following morning as she went out to open up the goats' and chickens' shed. He was sprawled across the back porch, fast asleep, his hand wrapped in brown paper soaked in vinegar.

"Our Frank's here. Been fighting again, by the look of him. Nothing ever changes," she called back to Hywel.

Jennie and Peter met a few evenings after she had accepted the job in Temptations. Foolishly, she thought he would be pleased and she went to his parents house to tell him.

"So, you have accommodation and a job. Good. That's what you wanted isn't it? To be independent and needing no one? Well I hope you'll be happy!" Peter snapped when she told him her news.

"It wasn't what I meant by independence, and you know it!"

"You certainly didn't need me."

"When I needed you you were never there!"

"That's rubbish! Mam said—"

"Don't tell me what your mam says, I don't what to know. You're still a child, Peter Francis, needing your mother to wipe your nose for you!"

"What does she want?" a voice called.

"Nothing you've got," Jennie muttered. Aloud, she said to Peter, "I just wanted to tell you I'm settled that's all, and to ask if you want any more of the china before I dispose of it."

"No, there's nothing I want," Peter said. Then his mother's voice called, "I'll have that cottage teapot, Peter."

"It's broken!" Jennie lied, determined to smash it the moment she got home.

When Jennie had left without another word, Peter was aware of life running away with him. Decisions were being made without proper thought and they were being made by Jennie and his mother. No one was asking his opinion. He didn't know whether he was pleased or not, but knew he was far from happy with the way his life was moving. Had he allowed himself to be dictated to by Mam? He'd always maintained that was nonsense, but now he began to wonder. Mam was very strong minded and looking back, she had never approved of any girl he had brought home. Jennie had been the only one who had stood up to her, and that had been flattering. But now she was gone too.

Mrs Glory Collins passed her driving test first time, and when she and Sam went out in his car, he would often stop and change places with her so she could get some practice. They explored the charming villages of the Vale and sometimes took a picnic and sat beside the river, or on a quiet beach or an isolated headland, to enjoy the tranquility of the countryside near the sea.

Sam had bought several books for the children and he helped them to identify the many varieties of wild flowers that grew in such abundance all round them. It added greatly to their outings and the children began to be quite expert at recognising the rarer species. Glory, which Sam insisted on calling her, had never imagined such happiness.

The problem with Sam's sight had not developed beyond his needing thick lenses and he had been assured by both doctor and optician that driving was not something he need give up. He knew that one day things would change but he wanted Glory to continue to enjoy their trips with her children when he could no longer drive them.

It was on a Sunday that they saw Jack and Victoria. They had locked their car and were walking towards a public house called the Sandpiper, where lunches were being served. It was not difficult for Jack and Victoria to persuade them to have lunch with them.

"We can share your picnic later, for tea," Jack said, leading Margaret, Elisabeth and Winston and carrying Montgomery towards the dining room.

It was after three o'clock when they left the Sandpiper and shared themselves between the two cars to find a place to sit and enjoy the dubious sunshine of the rather chilly afternoon. They found a bay where the children amused themselves searching in the rock pools for small fish and crabs and shrimps, stranded by the tide.

"No sign of a baby yet?" Victoria's mother asked her, when the men had gone to help the children in their search for winkles to take home for tomorrow's tea.

"No, not yet."

"And you haven't seen a doctor?"

Victoria turned away from her mother's scrutiny. "You know I can't ask a doctor about such things, Mam. I'd be so embarrassed."

"I'll come with you. It isn't embarrassing. It's the most natural thing in the world to want a child by the man you love. If you won't do it for yourself then do it for Jack," Glory pleaded.

Victoria shook her head. "We'll wait a while longer, Mam. There's plenty of time and we're very happy as we are."

She knew that wasn't true. She and Jack desperately wanted a baby but she was always so tense when they made love that she wondered if they ever would. Jack was so patient, but something about the darkened room, the almost secret way they declared their love for each other made her feel guilty, ashamed of showing her love for this man she adored. It was such nonsense, a contradiction whenever she tried to analyse it and tell Jack how she felt. She had tried to explain it to him quite recently, and he had been very understanding.

"Give it time," he had told her. "Give it time and we'll sort it out together. It's our problem and we'll find a solution. In the meantime, don't worry. Remember I love you and nothing will ever change that. Nothing at all." Yet she knew that unless she found a way of relaxing and being less guilty about the whole thing, they would never know the joy of seeing their own child.

When Sam decided it was time to leave, Jack told him that he and Victoria would stay a while longer. Victoria looked at her husband in surprise. "Where are we going, Jack?"

"Wait and see." He smiled and he put an arm around her shoulder as they waved the others off, Glory driving, showing off to her daughter and son-in-law as she manoeuvred Sam's car out of its parking place and turned it neatly into the road.

Kissing her hair, her cheeks, her neck, her lips and, holding her tight, Jack led Victoria back to the dunes. Distant sounds were muted to a soothing hum. There was only the soft murmur of the receeding tide, the soft breezes touching the marram grass and the occasional call of a bird.

Hidden from sight they began to make love.

Frank was feeding the goats when he heard the gate open and close. He hid when he saw Mair. She was coming to tell him she had changed her mind, for sure. Sidling around the corner of the goat shed he watched as she knocked on the kitchen door. Janet opened it and they exchanged a few unheard comments before Janet came down the path, calling for him.

"Frank, Mair is here and she wants a word."

"Tell her to go away, I'm out," he whispered.

Janet ignored his words and called back to Mair, "Here he is, feeding the goats and telling them how beautiful they are. Never known a man so besotted with animals as our Frank." She was smiling in a satisfied way as he revealed himself from the side of the shed. "Stay in the garden and I'll fetch some tea," she said as she disappeared into the house.

"If asking me to marry you was an impulse, later regretted, don't worry, Frank, I won't hold you to it," Mair said quietly. "We can still be friends though, can't we?"

"I hoped we'd be mòre than that, Mair, with you having my baby an' all," he said, stooping and hiding his face in embarrassment.

"I wanted that too. So, what went wrong?"

"It's that Carl Rees you really want, isn't it?"

"Carl and I finished a long time ago, I wouldn't two-time you with him, or anyone else," she said. "That's something I can promise you, Frank."

He waited, wanting her to explain the late-night visit to Carl's rooms. When she didn't, he took a deep breath and said, "You visited him though, in his house. I saw you when I was – er—"

His wit gave out then and he couldn't think of an excuse for his presence in that part of town. "When I was wandering, like," he finished weakly.

"All right, I did go and see him. He gave me up, I didn't finish it. I wanted to tell him that you and I loved each other and were going to get married, that's all."

"Do we? Love each other?"

"I love you, Frank. I'd hoped it was the same for you."

Frank didn't believe her explanation, it didn't go with the tears she had shed; but better to pretend, or he'd lose her. "Can we tell Mam?" he asked, hugging her awkwardly and kissing the eyebrow that got in the way when he aimed at her lips.

"Frank, you'll never regret marrying me," she whispered. "We're going to be real happy. Living with our Dad won't be easy for you, him being a policeman and you being too fond of a bit of poaching, but he'll soon accept you're the man I love and want to spend the rest of my life with."

"Can we tell our Mam now?" Frank's eyes were glowing.

"Mrs Griffiths, we have something to tell you," Mair said shyly, when Janet came out with a tray of tea.

"An' will you an' our Dad come with us when we tell her father," Frank said, only half joking.

Ten

J ennie was surprised when she opened the door one evening, to see Peter standing there. Since he had left the house they had shared she saw him rarely. It was strange to see him politely waiting to be invited inside.

"Peter, what a surprise! Have you come to say your goodbyes to the house we bought and furnished together?" She didn't try to be polite, didn't attempt to hide her distress at the sudden and finality of their parting. The following day, the sixth of July, was the date on which they were to vacate the property. Most of the furniture had gone, either sold or put into store. She pointed to a packing case and he sat gingerly on the edge of it.

"I wondered whether you wanted me to be here, help see the last of the furniture out and, you know, lock up and everything."

"You think it might be painful for me?"

"Yes."

"It will be painful. To see something die unnecessarily is always sad. But your mother has you back, so it isn't all bad!"

"Mam's sorry too."

"I'm sure."

"She isn't well."

"When is she ever?"

"Dad's having to do practically everything."

"Perhaps if he didn't, your mother would make a dramatic recovery." She couldn't be sympathetic. Her mother-in-law had always leant heavily on her husband and spoilt her son. This was just one of the effects of her actions. She knew she was better out of it, but it was still distressing to be abandoned because of a selfish old woman.

193

"Well?" Peter asked, and she was aware that she had said nothing for several minutes, had just sat there on the edge of another tea chest and wallowed in her misery. She was also aware that Peter had ignored her last retort.

"There's no need for you to come. I've taken the day off work and I'll see the rest of the furniture out. You'll receive your half of the money from the solicitor very soon."

"Thank you." He fidgeted a bit in a way she knew well. He was about to say something that was difficult. "What will you do? With your share of the money I mean?"

"I don't know and anyway, with the divorce under way, it's none of your business."

"Will you start another business?"

"Not for a while. I need to make sure it's a viable one and I need to save a little. The money from the house won't be much, after I've paid your mother back and settled the last remaining debts."

"Where will you live?"

"What does it matter to you?" she demanded.

"You'll want somewhere cheap if you're hoping to save," he said.

Something in his voice alerted her. He had something in mind and she wasn't going to like it!

"I might be offered the flat above the shop where I'll be working from next week. Very cheap and very convenient," she told him.

"What shop?"

"Peter, shut up!"

"You can come and stay with us if you like. Mam won't be difficult, in fact she suggested it, just while you save for your business, that's all."

"Your mother wants me to stay with you? Share the house? Why?"

"She's trying to be helpful, that's all. You are still her daughter-in-law."

"And she'll let me stay there while I save to start another business? Out of kindness?"

"Yes," he replied, but his eyes slid away from hers.

She smiled, an ironic smile and said, "And do a little house-work and perhaps some cooking? And if I could manage the laundry too? No thanks, I don't want anything more to do with you or your family!"

"You wouldn't have to work if you didn't want to."

"Stay at home all day with your Mam." She didn't try to hide the cynical expression.

"Why not?"

"Afraid you'll end up like your father, are you? Dealing with everything? Doing woman's work?" She saw at once that she had hit a tender spot. He had always complained that she wasn't behaving as a housewife should. For a while it had been a joke, but the laughter had faded, the joke had turned sour. He had never accepted her need to run a business, be something more than a submissive partner. For many women, it was enough, and they made house management into a skill, an art, but it wasn't for her. "Now," she said calmly, "if you'd please leave. I have things I must do. This chapter of my life is closed."

"If you change your mind . . ."

When she had closed the door behind him, she didn't lean against it like some weak heroine in a romantic film, she kicked it viciously.

Dora's house was busy the following weekend. They were making preparations for Rhiannon, Charlie and Gwyn to move in. A wardrobe was emptied and a chest of drawers brought from the house acoss the road to provide storage for their clothes. Their dog, Polly, had a bed in the corner of the kitchen and on that first day, they all fell over it at least once. Instead of being irritated, Dora laughed and said it was fun, wasn't it? Lewis and Rhiannon exchanged knowing looks, convinced that before the end of the first week, she'd be shouting like a cross between fishwife and newspaper vendor.

Gwyn was to sleep in the box room. Already small, it was filled with so much clutter he had barely enough room to walk to and from the window. Watching Lewis and Dora working together, he smiled contentedly. It was wonderful to have a mam and a dad, and a gran and a grandad. He remembered old Great-grandmother Maggie Wilpin who had looked after him when his father was in prison, with affection – affection and with a stab of guilt at the way he had sometimes caused her worry.

At five o'clock on Sunday, they all flopped into chairs and demanded tea. It was Gwyn who weakened first and went to make it. He carried the tray out into the garden. Polly jumped round him, not knowing what was happening but convinced it was going to be fun.

"What's that box of old newspapers doing in the kitchen cupboard, Gran?" Gwyn asked when they were sitting, enjoying a rest in the last of the day's sunshine. "Load of old rubbish it looks to me, mind."

"Oh, it's something I found in the loft. I saw that the papers had been specially saved, each one folded to show the latest developments in some court case or other. I thought it might be interesting. Ever so old they are. So flimsy you'd never believe."

"Shall we have a look then?"

Dora shook her head. "I don't think I've got the energy. Let's leave it for now."

"Tomorrow evening?" Gwyn coaxed.

"All right. Tomorrow we'll unearth the secrets of the loft of seven Sophie Street, and disturb the ghosts!" she promised.

When she came home from the cafe the following evening she had forgotten her promise, but Gwyn had not. They ate their meal, the five of them filling the table with chatter and laughter in a way that warmed Dora's heart. Lewis watched her as she waited on them all, her face glowing with the atmosphere of a busy house, which she had missed so much when the children left home. He wondered how she would cope when they went back to their own house and left the two of them alone again. Dora was one of those women for whom the family filled her life. Even working as she did, she needed people to look after. Dora was not a modern woman, and all the talk of equality simply made her laugh. "Men and women are different beings and always will be," she would remark when the subject was raised.

While Dora and Rhiannon attended to the dishes, Gwyn put a cloth over the table and carefully removed the newspapers from their box. He spread them out in chronological order and waited until the others joined him. There were a few pages of letters tucked among the papers written in scrawling handwriting that was difficult to read, and even a faded photograph or two. Gwyn glanced at them and put them aside.

At first it seemed to be the record of arrests and court appearances of a young woman called Molly Bondo, who would now be in her middle forties.

"She's quite well known," Lewis said, hesitating as Gwyn was rather young to understand such things.

"Went with American soldiers, did she?" Gwyn asked casually.

"Why blame the Americans?" Dora said. "The only reason people talk about them is that they paid better!"

"Dora!" Lewis gasped. "Be'ave yourself!"

They were putting the newspapers back in their box, Gwyn having lost interest, when Dora noticed that one of them was folded to show, not court reports, but births and deaths. Curious, she picked it up and read that Molly Bondo had given birth to a child.

"That's odd, I don't remember hearing about her having a child." Lewis frowned.

"Knew her well, did you? This tart?" Dora asked, suspicion deepening her voice.

"Everyone followed the story of Molly, love. The latest episode was read with enthusiasm in the Railwayman's, with additions from those who pretended to know from personal experience. She was mentioned practically very week at one time. Either soliciting or drunk and disorderly."

"I wonder what happened to the child? Adopted I suppose." She put the papers aside, intending to study them in greater detail later. Somewhere there was a child who might not know his true background. The thought saddened her. She put the box back in the cupboard and re-entered the room.

She looked around her, at Lewis and Charlie arguing about the assets and disadvantages of the latest cars, at Rhiannon and Gwyn laughing at something on the radio, at the fire burning low with a kettle simmering ready for their bedtime drinks. She was so lucky. And her temper and her stubbornness could have lost it for her for ever.

Barry sat looking out of the door of his flat, disconsolately wondering how to spend the rest of the day. He was lonely, and thought longingly of the Griffithses' house where there was always someone to talk to, always something going on. He watched a cat sneak over the wall in that wonderfully supple way cats have, pouring itself over the top and sliding down effortlessly onto the fence, where it sat stretching contentedly in the sun. Another cat appeared and the two of them hissed softly, each issuing a warning that the area was private property. With nothing better to do, Barry watched as they sized each other up. Without thinking, he reached for his camera and went outside, his movements were slow, his interest quickening.

The newcomer leapt at the one on the fence and knocked him off. The air was suddenly filled with growling and snarling and hissing as the cats fought for supremacy. Barry's camera clicked and the two furious animals were unaware as he sank to the ground and crawled closer. So intense was their entanglement, he had taken several shots before they became aware of his presence and ran off.

Taking his camera he went out to the van and drove to a friend's house where he had the use of a darkroom. The photographs weren't brilliant, but sufficiently interesting for him to decide to take more back-garden shots.

Making a bird table wasn't difficult as he was a talented carpenter. Buying an extra long cable and setting up a shutter release wasn't difficult either. He filled the bird table with food and spent several hours each day watching for an interesting study, prepared to click the camera when the bird table attracted the usual garden birds, but hoping for a more exciting visitor. He had been unaware of how beautiful the common species of birds were. He read books on their habits, and even a walk to the Griffithses had an added enjoyment. He made a second bird table and gave it to Joseph-Hywel together with a simple book on bird recognition, which delighted the boy.

"We'll set it up where you can see it from your bedroom," Barry told him. "That way you can see the shy ones without their being frightened."

"Binoculars for his birthday." Hywel and Janet promised, intrigued with the gift.

That evening, in the Griffiths's cottage, the fire was burning low. Janet tried to reach the grate to add fuel but Frank was stretched out, half asleep in an armchair, opposite his similarly disposed father, their legs sprawled across the hearth, jockeying for position between the cats and the dog. Janet saw that the kettle was simmering close to boiling and waited until Caroline came down, having settled Joseph-Hywel to sleep. Then tilting the heavy kettle, she made a pot of tea.

Janet was watching her daughter with concern. Caroline was frowning slightly, her round, usually happy face lost in thought. Thoughts that were not pleasant, Janet surmised, and therefore, to do with Barry Williams. She handed round the cups of tea and a cwlff – the thick slice of bread her men usually enjoyed at this time, hoping that Frank and his father would go out for a drink to the Railwayman's and allow her and Caroline to talk.

At nine, she suggested it and Frank unfolded himself and reached for his jacket.

"Come on, our Dad, I think they want to talk women's talk and we aren't allowed to listen."

"Barry and I have been talking, Mam," Caroline began, when her father and brother had gone.

Janet took a deep breath. This was what she had been expecting and dreading. She had to speak her mind, be hard on the girl and it was not going to be easy.

"Now listen to me, Caroline. You and Barry have tried being

married, got fed up, and you've come back home. Then it was on again and then it was off. It can't continue, love. It's more like a yo-yo match than a love match. If you go off and try again to live with Barry, then me and your father won't have you back. You have to make a go of it this time and not think we're waiting here to cushion you the moment it gets difficult. Go now and face the fact that you're on your own."

She told Hywel later that it was the hardest thing she had ever done and she was sure it came out wrong. "Instead of telling Caroline that she had to forget she had the family to support her, so she'd go to Barry with a real determination to succeed, and not think of the comfort in failure, I made out we didn't want her."

"What did she have to say?" Hywel asked.

"Nothing," Janet said sadly. "I didn't give her a chance. Perhaps she wasn't even going to tell me she and Barry were going to try again. Perhaps she was only going to talk about a birthday present or something. What a cruel mother I must seem. But all I want is for her to be happy, and I think she would be happier with Barry than without him, if he'd only be a little bit more considerate."

"We'll wait and see what she says when she comes home from work tomorrow. She won't think you're cruel, how could she ever think that? Let her think about what you said and see how she feels then." He stirred cocoa and sugar and milk in a cup and added hot water. "Here, love, drink this and come to bed."

In the Railwayman's, Viv told Jack, Basil and Frank about the papers found in his parents' attic.

"They all had reports on Molly Bondo's appearances in court," he whispered, aware that as they were sitting behind the partition and couldn't see the door, Molly might enter without them knowing.

They joked about the woman's career and her regular court attendances, then Viv told them the interesting news. "Seems she had a baby," he told his audience. "Mam found a newspaper item stating that Molly Bondo had given birth to a child. Never heard nothing about a child, did you?"

They all shook their heads, then Basil said, "Why would it have been in the paper if she didn't keep it? You'd have thought she'd have avoided publicity, wouldn't you?"

"Perhaps some well-meaning friend put it in."

"Enemy more like," Frank said.

Still in subdued tones they discussed this for a while, with Basil peering around the partition occasionally to make sure Molly and her friends weren't in their usual seats in the corner. They were still talking about what they knew of Molly and the oldest profession, men of the world living vicariously through the antics of others, when Frank left. Mair had invited him for supper but he had made vague excuses. Tonight he intended to follow her father again.

He walked through the fields, instinctively listening for a sound to reveal the presence of another human being, skirting Farmer Booker's farmhouse so as not to disturb the dogs. He was not intending to steal any of the farmer's rabbits but he moved as silently as possible from long practice.

Mair's father came out of the cottage pushing his bike, and closed the gate behind him. Frank followed the man to Bella Vista and watched as he entered number four through the french window of the house where both Carl and his mother had rooms. The heavy curtains opened and closed again, hiding whatever went on. Silent as a shadow, Frank moved to the window and listened. Voices, one feminine and the other the gruff tones of PC Gregory. He went around to the front door and knocked.

When Carl recognised his visitor he darted back and tried to close the door.

"It's all right, I'm not going to thump you again," Frank said as he put his size tens in the door. "I just want to know what Constable Gregory's doing visiting your mother at nights."

"What are you talking about? Mam's in bed, she always goes to bed early!" an outraged Carl hissed back. "Hush now or you'll wake her."

"In bed she may be but I doubt she's asleep, boy. Not with PC Bernard Gregory to keep her awake."

201

Carl made as though to strike Frank who lazily moved out of the way of the flying fist. "Take that back!"

"Knock on her door if you don't believe me," Frank challenged.

"No need. You're talking rot."

With a strength that surprised Carl, Frank pushed him out of the way and stepped into the hall. Guessing which door lead to Mrs Dreese's rooms he banged on it. There was a moment's silence as Frank glared at Carl, who looked alarmed. Then a small voice called, "Who is it? Is that you, Carl? I begged you not to wake me, I need my rest."

"Mam, this is important. Can I come in?"

"Open this door," Frank said in a loud authoritative voice. As the lock was eased back and the knob began to turn, he left the house and ran around to the back, just in time to catch Gregory coming out.

"Evenin' Constable Gregory."

"What are you doing here?"

"Seein' what you're up to for starters."

Carl came to join them, stepping out through the velvet curtains with Mrs Dreese wrapped in a dressing gown. Carl had an arm protectively around her shoulders.

"I had a report of a prowler," Gregory snapped. "I came to see what was up. I might have known it was one of the Griffithses!"

"You'd better go," Carl said threateningly.

"That one won't work. Can't you come up with a better excuse than that after all this time?" Frank said, ignoring Carl's words. "I followed you from the cottage, again," he said pointedly. "Suspicious I was, of all the nightshifts, see. Watched you go in and then I ran round to make sure Carl saw you as well. Besides," he added, "her son lives in the same house, for heaven's sake! She'd have knocked on his door, not gone out at this time of night to the phone box!"

"It's no use, Bernard," Carl's mother said. "I think we have to tell them."

"Tell me what?" Carl demanded. "What's going on?"

"Carrying on, more like. Him and your Mam."

"We haven't told anyone because – well, it's no one else's business." The words changed from reasonable to angry in the single sentence.

"Not even Mair's?" Frank asked.

"Or mine?" Carl said, and the two young men moved closer together, allies against the deceptiveness of parents.

Carl's mother led them into the room she occupied and, as always in a crisis, made tea.

"How long has this been going on?" Carl asked her as she gave them the steaming cups.

"Oh, quite a long time, but not before your father died, mind," she emphasized. "Soon after though."

"Why keep it a secret?" Frank wanted to know. "You're both free and you can hardly be worried about Mair and Carl? They aren't babies."

"I didn't want Mair worried. She might not like the idea of sharing a house with a stepmother."

"So it's gone that far, has it?"

"It's got to the stage where we're discussing marriage, yes." PC Gregory looked at Carl's mother with such affection, that Frank felt giggles rising uncontrollably and he went to the teapot and poured himself another cup. Quite why it was funny, he didn't know, but the thought of the pompous policeman, who rode his sit-up-and-beg bicycle through the lanes, and arrested him on a regular basis quoting the charges off by heart, didn't seem to be the type to be affectionate with a woman.

"I'll leave you three to talk about this," he said, painfully holding on to his overflowing laughter. Imagine old Gregory whispering endearments and kissing her and . . . He got through the curtains just in time and his laughter came out like a snort from a horse, as he ran through the streets and headed for the woods.

Tonight would be a good night to go poaching, he thought as he walked towards Mair's cottage. He stepped out onto the lane opposite her gate, still enjoying episodic laughter. To his surprise, he saw that there was a light on in her room. Throwing some grit up against the pane, he called, "Mair? Mair, come down, I've got something to tell you," then he collapsed into laughter again.

Mair opened the door, to his surprise she was still fully dressed. His laughter faded. "What's the matter? Are you ill?"

"No, just unhappy."

"Don't be. I've got something to tell you that will make you laugh!" She stood to let him go past her and he saw that her eyes were red with crying, her round face swollen and flushed. The story of PC Gregory forgotten, he asked, "What's the matter? What's making you unhappy?"

"Because of us, you and me," she said. "You've changed your mind about marrying me, haven't you?"

"Of course I haven't. There's something I had to sort out, a mystery and now it's sorted." He put his arms around her and held her close. "Marry me soon, Mair, we'll still give the gossips something to talk about but we won't let that worry us, will we?"

"Register office it'll have to be, a quiet affair."

"A quiet affair? With our Mam involved? What a hope." He laughed again, but this time with happiness.

It wasn't until he reached home, as dawn was creating a rich artist's palette in the eastern sky, that he realised he hadn't told Mair about her father's secret affair with Mrs Dreese. He wondered whether PC Gregory would say anything, or just hope she wouldn't find out. He would go out with his ferret and nets later, a few rabbits always sold well and he doubted whether he'd be charged if the constable saw him. He might even give him one, just to let him know they were friends.

It gradually dawned on Frank that with Constable Gregory taking a wife he and Mair would not have a place to live when they married.

"What will I do, Mam?" he asked Janet when she was cooking breakfast. "Mair and I want to marry very soon, because of – you know." He gave an embarrassed shrug. "Now we mightn't have a place to live."

They discussed the possibilities of finding rooms for a while then Frank went out to catch a few rabbits.

Frank had just left when Basil arrived, on his way to the factory.

"Worried I am," he began. "With the rent going up like that, Eleri has to work just to pay it, and she's out every evening, going off as soon as I get in from work. It's awful, Mam. She has a busy day with the boys and she should be resting, not going off to work."

"Something will turn up, you won't find yourselves out on the street."

When he had gone on his way, his ears filled with Janet's assurances, she went to find her husband. "We have to do something, Hywel," she said. "Basil, and now our Frank, and our Ernie isn't happy either, living with Gloria Gunner with her rules and rantings."

"There's that money your brother left you," Hywel said gruffly. "I don't want to tell you how to spend it, but getting the boys settled in a place of their own wouldn't be a bad idea, would it?"

"Hywel, you're wonderful," Janet said, hugging him.

"What, because I'm spending your money for you?"

"Because you knew what I was thinking."

"If we suggest they use the money as a deposit on a small place, we can probably help them all. Except Caroline, but she will be all right financially, with Barry to look after her."

"Money isn't the problem there. You're right, it's the boys who need our help, love."

"I don't know about Helen, mind, she might want something more than we could afford, but Eleri and Basil, and Frank and Mair wouldn't mind a small place."

"Don't let's tell them yet. Nice surprise it'll be. When Frank and Mair name the day will be the time to tell them all."

Frank came in whistling cheerfully, having delivered the gift of one of Farmer Booker's rabbits to the policeman. He hadn't left it on the doorstep but had knocked at the door. He was still laughing at the memory of how he had handed the constable a bag containing a rabbit and watched the man's face distorting with confusion about what he should say and do.

"There's nothing like a bit of guilt to confuse the righteous," he said to a puzzled Janet and Hywel.

"You don't think he's got religion, do you, Janet?" Hywel frowned.

Carl was not as cheerful as Frank as the night opened out into day. He knew his mother had been keeping her secret for a very good reason. Ever since his father had died, Carl and his mother had been putting money aside to clear the debts he had left behind. His mother had insisted that he was morally, if not legally, bound to pay off his creditors. He had been forced to leave college, and all hope of a career in furniture design had been left behind with his studies. Since then he had worked at odd jobs, giving a large portion of everything he earned to his mother to put aside for the wonderful day when they could announce to the world that the debts had been cleared.

He didn't quarrel with his mother over her deceit, he just quietly asked for the return of the money he had been saving. If she expected him to live a life of poverty and emptiness while she enjoyed the comfort of Constable Gregory, she was mistaken, he told her. Once he had the money in his bank account, he began working out a few changes in his plans for the future. After several phone calls, he decided his next move would be to see Frank.

Jennie called to see Barry a couple of times and, after discussing wages and hours, she agreed to take the job managing Temptations, starting a week before Rhiannon left. When she asked about the flat, Barry was evasive.

"I'm not quite sure what's happening here yet," he said. "Perhaps you'd be better to find somewhere temporarily, then we can make a decision about it later."

To hide her disappointment she remarked on the camera equipment spread on the table. He showed her the view of the garden and explained his new interest.

"Wildlife photography, eh? This week sparrows, next week condors and heaven knows what else."

"I don't think I'll find condors on my bird table."

"Nothing stopping you travelling, is there?" she asked.

"I'm disappointed about the flat," Jennie told Rhiannon one morning when she called in on her way to work. "I haven't looked for anything permanent. At present I'm in a rather shabby place called the Firs that looks about ready to fall down. There's still the room at Sally Fowler-Westons, but it's rather expensive."

Rhiannon smiled. "The Firs was where my Dad first lived when Mam threw him out," she confided.

"Really? It's an awful place. What happened to make them separate?"

"Well, I don't suppose it's a secret, not round here anyway. But don't mention it in front of Mam, will you?" She waited for Jennie's nod. "My father had a mistress, Nia Williams. When Mam found out, he and Nia Williams lived together up in Chestnut Road until she died. Nia was Barry's mother, which is why I'm telling you, so you're aware of the connection."

Jennie looked thoughtful. "But everything is all right between them now?"

"Mam couldn't cope with it at first, but somehow they've worked a way through the difficulties and, yes, everything seems to be fine now, thank goodness." She added, with a grimace, "For a while Charlie and I had Dad as a lodger. It was one of the reasons Mam took him back I think."

"Thank you for telling me. I'll never mention it, I promise."

"Dad really loves Mam, but he loved Nia Williams too. I think he was completely happy with Nia. She was so gentle and kind. Mam has this terrible temper you see."

"I thought Peter loved me but that love wasn't strong enough to escape from his mother's authority. He never put me first. Not ever."

"Come back and have a cup of tea this afternoon," Rhiannon suggested. "I used to come into the shop and do a bit of cleaning during the half-day closing, but I don't any more. Since Barry and Caroline started meeting in the flat I feel a bit uncomfortable, afraid they'll think I'm eavesdropping or something!"

"Why do they do that? They're married, aren't they?"

"Not so's you'd notice they aren't! She lives with her parents and he lives here. Crazy how some carry on, eh?"

Jennie smiled, "And there's us thinking that marriage was straightforward!"

When Jennie called at number seven Sophie Street later, Rhiannon told her about the papers Dora had found. She took the box out of the cupboard but didn't suggest looking through them. "They aren't really very interesting," she told Jennie.

"I'd like to see them though. If your mother wouldn't mind?"

"I'm sure she wouldn't. They don't concern the Lewises, and so old they are, I doubt if there's anything left to keep secret," Rhiannon said. "But I'd better check with Mam first. I'll talk to her, shall I? Then we can look through them another day."

Carl called at the Griffithses cottage a few days later and asked to see Frank.

"Sleeping," Hywel said succinctly.

"Try the back porch," Janet added.

Bemused, Carl walked through the house accompanied by three cats and a rather weary-looking dog, to find Frank sprawled on the grass under an oak tree, his body protected by a blanket to which a dog would be ashamed to lay claim.

"Frank?" Carl said, touching Frank's shoulder and stepping back quickly.

"Wha'r is it?"

"Fancy doing a bit of work for me? One night or maybe two."

"I might." Frank was cautious.

"Just between me and you."

"Oh oh, something funny, then?"

"Not really, not illegal anyway."

"Pity. I'd like to see how far I can push PC Gregory!" Fully awake now and sitting up, Frank called for his mother. "Mam? Any chance of two cups of tea? Two sugars? And some cake?"

"Get it yourself, I'm ironing," came the reply. Frank stood up and shrugged. "Worth a try," he said, ambling into the kitchen and filling the kettle. "So, what's this job then?"

"Nothing difficult, shelves mostly. I'm fitting out a shop. And time is a bit tight. Most of the shelves are already made and if you fit them on the walls, I'll get on with the rest. Okay?"

"Nights you said?" Frank frowned. "Why is that then?"

"Simply because there's so little time."

"You've given a date for finishing?"

"Yes. The place opens in less than two weeks."

"What sort of shop is it?" Frank asked.

"You'll see," Carl replied evasively. "Something and nothing, bits and bobs."

They drank their tea in silence, Carl looking around the untidy collection of barns and sheds, watching the goats who were trying to get out and join the cats who drowsed in the sun and the chickens who scratched the earth, heads on one side, looking for tidbits of food. "Nice place," he said, when he caught Frank watching him.

"This baby of Mair's. Yours is it?" Frank asked.

"No chance," Carl said quickly, too quickly. "Mair and I were never that close."

Frank thought of the times he had watched the cottage at the edge of the wood. How he had guessed what was going on inside from the pattern of lights, on and off, ending with the bedroom curtains dimly lit before that light too was extinguished. He remembered the pain of seeing Carl hurrying away from the cottage just before PC Gregory came home from his supposed night duty. It made him sad, but not sad enough to be less than thrilled at the prospect of marrying Mair.

"Getting married we are," he told Carl, watching his face intently. But if there was anything more than pleasure on Carl's face, he couldn't detect it. "Yes, in about four weeks," he added. "Haven't told our Mam the date yet mind. Suppose we'd better tell her soon, so she can start passing the news around that the Griffithses are having a party."

The thought of the party reminded Frank that he and Mair were likely to have nowhere to live. He'd better tell her about her father and that Dreese woman, get their claim in quick, before they announced their plans.

At first Mair didn't believe him and then, realising that her father was involved with Carl's mother – Carl, whose child she was carrying, it all seemed too much and she quarrelled with Frank, telling him he was a gossip and worse. He stepped back from the tirade of abuse she threw at him, then quietly took her arm.

"You're coming with me," he said quietly.

"Get lost! I'm not going anywhere. How can you do this to me? Tell stories about my father. What reason is there for insulting him when he'll be your father-in-law."

"I followed him back one night when he said he was on night duty and he went to the house in Bella Vista."

"That's where Carl lives."

"She has rooms in the same house. And your father visits her there. Come with me and we'll talk to Carl. He's working in a shop in town." She refused to go, and when he thought about it, he understood why she didn't want to come face to face with Carl.

Promising to meet her that evening and sort it out, hoping that his request for accommodation would be met by embarrassing her father, Frank went loping across the fields and into the police station. Gregory wasn't there so he left a note, untidily written with a stub of a pencil, telling him to talk to Mair and tell her the truth.

Eleven

With Terrence still calling occasionally to see his "darling daughter", Megan and Edward were uneasy. They had taken the first steps toward adopting Rosemary, but were hesitant about going further because of the threat of Terrence's presence. As Rosemary's first birthday drew near, they decided they would celebrate it quietly, and Gladys and Arfon willingly agreed to have a small family gathering in their home. They called to see Megan's grandparents one Wednesday afternoon when the sports shop was closed. They sat in the garden of the large old house and watched Rosemary determinedly taking her first wobbly steps across a blanket spread between Arfon and Edward, her plump little arms waving like windmills as she tried again and again to take more than two steps before falling into the protective arms of one of her doting family.

"The garden will be perfect for a children's party," Gladys said, happily visualising the event. "We'll have plenty of room for trestle tables and a play area, I'll get Mrs Dreese to act as waitress, we can hire a—"

"Grandmother," Megan put out a hand to stop Gladys's cheerful plans. "This has to be a quiet affair, we don't want Terrence turning up. We don't want him to come and remind us how easily he could spoil our lives. He does have a right to see Rosemary, doesn't he? And there's no way to stop him protesting when Edward and I apply to adopt her. The less he sees of her the better our case, can't you see that, darling Grannie?"

"Grandmother, please." Gladys frowned.

Edward came forward and put an arm on Megan's shoulders.

"I think we should tell your grandparents what has happened," he said.

"Terrence has more or less warned us that unless we pay him some money, he will refuse permission for Edward and me to adopt Rosemary. Can you imagine what life would be like with him turning up whenever he wanted, reminding Rosemary that she isn't Edward's child? I can't bear the thought, but I absolutely refuse to pay him to sign the papers."

"I disagree," Edward said quietly. "I think we should pay and get rid of my cousin for good."

"But would it?" Arfon leant slightly back and Gladys and Megan knew that there was a speech coming on. "As I see it, paying, giving in to this blackmail – yes, my dear," he said to Gladys, who had gasped at the unpleasant word, "blackmail it is, and if we submit, how do we guarantee that he won't come back again and again? As I see this situation, you have to appeal to the man's better nature, make him see how important it is for the child he purports to love that she has a happy settled future, and—"

"Once he signs, he won't be able to trouble us again, will he?" Edward interrupted.

"Nothing to stop him coming to see us, and no guarantee that he won't talk to Rosemary later and disrupt us all," Megan sighed.

They walked back to the flat, Edward pushing the little girl who was sleepy after her exciting afternoon in the garden among four doting adults.

"What will we do?" Edward asked.

"Nothing, just go ahead with the adoption and hope that between now and when Terrence returns to London, he will go into the solicitors office and sign the papers. He has been notified that an appointment will be made and we have to hope he keeps it and does what we want."

As soon as the young people had gone, Arfon put on his coat and announced that he had to go out. He refused to tell his wife where he was going and Gladys sat by the front window and watched him drive away. She crossed her fingers tightly, hoping he was going to sort out the situation and make sure Rosemary's future was secure.

When he returned more than two hours later he still refused to explain where he had been, but he was smiling and she felt hope and relief settle within her. Dear Arfon, he always sorted everything out. Head of the Weston family he was, and he always would be.

A few days later, when the second post arrived, Edward was serving a customer and Mair was in the kitchen making coffee. It was ten thirty, and usually the steady flow of customers slowed down then for an hour allowing them time for a brief break. Megan came down with Rosemary in her arms and casually opened the mail. She threw envelopes in the waste bin, stacked the invoices and statements in separate piles in her usual organised manner. Then she began looking at the pile of birthday cards for their daughter, smiling as she guessed the senders from the writing, frowning when she did not. Among the private mail she picked up a letter from their solicitor. When she opened it, she shouted angrily at Edward, "What have you done?"

"What is it, darling? Is something wrong?"

"You've paid him! You've paid that stupid cousin of yours and you promised me you wouldn't!"

"Megan, I haven't seen him since the time I told you about, when he asked me to reconsider and pay him. I explained that we wouldn't, whatever his threats, that no matter how difficult he made it, Rosemary was staying with us."

"Then someone has." She handed him the letter and hugged Rosemary as she waited for him to read it.

In the kitchen behind the shop, Mair heard the raised voices and she began to cry. Unaccountably the thought of Edward and Megan disagreeing frightened her. If they had problems, what chance did she have of ever being happy, starting marriage to Frank with this dreadful secret? Staunching her tears by angry rubbing succeeded only in reddening her eyes and blotching the skin around them. Would she ever be happy? Was anyone, she wondered dolefully?

"This only states that Terrence will raise no objection to the adoption by you and me," Edward said.

"Someone must have paid him. I don't believe he'd give up when he had such a wonderful opportunity to take money from us. He knows how successful the business is, he'll see no further than the constantly crowded shop and he'll imagine we are very rich. I just don't believe he'd give up such a chance. Not Terrence."

Edward said nothing more but he decided that at the first opportunity he would go and talk to Arfon. He was the only one he knew with the incentive and enough money to pay Terrence what he asked.

As Megan began to go back upstairs with Rosemary, she was aware that Mair was sobbing. She and Edward looked at each other, startled by the unlikely behaviour of their assistant. Handing Rosemary to Edward she went in and asked what was wrong. It was a while before Mair could calm herself sufficiently to talk. When she did, it all came out.

"I'm expecting," she began.

"Frank?" Megan asked matter of factly.

"Frank's promised to marry me."

"And you don't want to?"

"The baby isn't his, it's Carl Rees's and Carl won't have anything to do with it and I don't know what to do." Tears fell again and Megan whispered to Edward, took the baby from him and led the girl up to the flat.

Mair told Megan about the nights she had spent with Carl while her father was on duty, and about starting to see Frank in the deliberate intention of persuading him that the baby was his.

"We've told Frank's parents and they were so kind and, and now I can't go through with it. We'd never be happy. I'd ruin Frank's life as well as mine."

"Does Frank know yet, that the baby isn't his?"

"No, I don't think he'd guess, he isn't the sort to be suspicious." She stopped then and covered her lower face with her hands, her red, swollen eyes wide as she stared at her employer. "Oh, I'm sorry! I shouldn't be talking to you about all this. I'm sorry Mrs Jenkins, I'm sorry!"

214

"Because my husband isn't Rosemary's father d'you mean? It's hardly a secret. Edward and I love each other and we love and adore Rosemary. We aren't the first to begin our marriage in such a way."

"Should I tell Frank then?"

"You can either tell him, or risk him finding out either by counting the weeks, noting the dates, or by someone else doing it for him. Although I don't think he'd need that. Whatever you say about Frank Griffiths, he isn't so stupid he can't work it out for himself. There are few of us who cannot count to nine! There's also the risk of Carl appearing, as Terrence has done, spoiling everything with a few words. On consideration, I think it would be better to start straight and honest, but that decision is yours and only yours."

Megan sent Mair home early, knowing she wouldn't want to appear in the shop with her reddened eyes and feeling so unhappy. If anyone ought to understand how the girl was feeling it was she.

Instead of going back to the cottage Mair turned down a side street, past the shop where Carl had worked for Jennie Francis, and went along to Sophie Street. Expecting to see Rhiannon she was startled to see Jennie serving a young woman with a birthday card from the selection on the counter.

"Where's Rhiannon? She isn't ill, is she?"

"No, she's fine, but she's leaving Temptations soon. and I'm taking over. Try number seven, her mother's house. She's staying there at present. She's only gone home to put a pie in the oven. Is anything wrong?" she asked, as Mair turned to leave. "You look upset."

"It's nothing, just a bit of a tummy upset, that's all," Mair said half smiling at the irony. Her stomach wasn't upset, but her belly was getting rather full!

Rhiannon welcomed her, told her she had no more than ten minutes and went on rolling out the pastry to cover the rhubarb and apple pie she was preparing.

"I've agreed to marry Frank Griffiths," Mair began.

"Wonderful. With Basil married to Eleri who's almost my sister, you'll be almost a sister too!"

215

"How d'you make that out?"

"Well, Eleri was married to my brother, Lewis-boy, so she was my sister-in-law. But my brother died. Right? You with me so far? Then she married Basil Griffiths and although she's no longer my sister-in-law, I pretend she is and she still calls my mother, Mam. So you see, we'll be almost sisters. Isn't that exciting?"

Mair laughed for the first time for days, grateful for Rhiannon cheering her with her nonsense. "I've always wanted a sister," she said, hugging Rhiannon.

As they walked back to the shop, they were talking excitedly of how they would walk to the park together, pushing their prams, comparing notes on their and other people's children. In a happier frame of mind, Mair went home and tried to work out the best way of telling Frank the truth.

Megan was right: to start with deceit was too risky, she could lose everything with a careless or unkind word. She was surprised to realise just how much she wanted Frank's support and how anxious she was not to cause him pain and disappointment. She would have to be very careful when she told him, make him believe that it was he whom she loved and that Carl had been a brief madness.

The small family gathering to celebrate both Rosemary's birth-day and the news about the adoption had grown so that Glady's garden held most of the family. She felt her heart swell with happiness as they arrived in twos and presented the baby with a gift before sitting, talking and laughing in the shade of the tall trees. This was how families ought to be, gathered together, sharing reminiscences and being happy. Ignoring Megan and Edward's wishes, now the worry of Terrence's interference was gone, she had employed Carl's mother to help serve the food and she sat in a chair, with Arfon beside her, and beamed at the lovely scene before her.

"Only four more to come," she whispered to her husband.

Viv Lewis appeared and asked if they needed anything, walk-ing towards them holding hands with Joan. They looked happy,

Gladys grudgingly thought. Even though Viv was only a Lewis, he did care for Joan properly. She had unwillingly, but generously, invited Viv's parents to join them, even though they were Lewises and not really family at all. They had yet to arrive. Typical of the Lewises not to know how to behave. Then she remembered that the other two yet to appear, were Sally and Sian. Sian arrived at the same time as Dora and Lewis. So where was Sally?

Everyone was involved in conversation when Sally eventually came round the corner of the house and waved at her mother.

"Sally, dear. You're late."

"I had to wait for Ryan," Sally explained, and Gladys was startled and reached for Arfon's hand. "Ryan is coming here?"

"Yes, mummy. He really is much better now and wants to see you all."

Ryan certainly looked well Gladys thought, as her son-in-law came forward to kiss her and shake Arfon's hand.

"Well, Ryan, and how are you?" she asked stiffly.

"I am well, thank you, Mother-in-law. You're looking marvellous as always, and so are you, Father-in-law," he added, before turning away and reaching for a drink.

"He really is much better, Mummy," Sally whispered.

"Much better isn't enough, dear. Don't take him back, I beg you."

Ryan heard the whispered remarks and felt the anger, so difficult to control, rising to the surface. This had been a mistake. It was too soon to face them. He wondered whether he would escape before his temper erupted and ruined it all.

He had managed for almost an hour when a chance remark by Sian to Dora Lewis, tipped his fragile balance. He was walking beside Sally to where Rosemary was being coaxed to show off her new walking skills, when Sian was heard to say, "But he can never be trusted. They always revert to type, Dora, there's no denying that."

Ryan was unaware that the two women were talking about Terrence, and his attempt to squeeze money out of Edward, which was now common knowledge, after Gladys's widespread boasting about how the Jenkinses' – grand as they were – were no match for the Westons.

"What are you saying?" Ryan demanded, standing in front of the two startled women. "How do you know whether I can be trusted? Experts on everything are you? You Westons have a lot to answer for, I'll tell you that, you pompous, insensitive woman!"

"Ryan, what on earth is wrong?" Sian stepped back and grasped Dora's arm for comfort. "We weren't discussing you."

"Don't take me for a fool, Sian! Although how you, of all the damned Westons, have the affrontery to discuss my situation, with your husband living with another woman, I'll never know. Brazen you are and you haven't the right to preach to my wife about me or my marriage!"

Everyone had fallen silent and it was Mrs Dreese, employed for the day in spite of Megan's entreaties to keep the day a family affair, who calmed the situation down. She went into the sitting room and put a record on the turntable and hissed instructions to Edward and Arfon. "Start some dancing, make a bit of noise."

Her ruse worked, and within the length of the first dance tune, several couples were dancing on the lawn, and were being joined by others. Sian stood silent, still grasping Dora's arm, her face pale with shock. Her son Jack left his wife and came over to her.

"Mummy? May I have this dance?" A few minutes later, when a third record sent out its cheering melody, it was though nothing had happened.

Ryan had returned to Sally's side but he pushed her arm away as she tried to comfort him. He was terribly afraid he might strike her. Control was there, but he didn't know how long he could hold it in place, here, surrounded by the Weston family. Losing his temper and hitting poor gentle Sally had originally put him in hospital and he was still unable to be trusted to go home. Glancing down his wife now, a silly smile on her face as she pretended the incident hadn't occurred, he wondered whether he wanted to go back to her, or if a solitary life would suit him better. It would certainly be less stressful than living with this nervous woman who looked at him as though he were a mass murderer.

Why was he struggling to get strong enough to return to her, Megan and Joan, and the guesthouse that was no longer a home? To pretend that was what he wanted, that the achievement showed his success? It was a nonsense. Going back to the situation that had caused his breakdown in the first place was no longer important. Happy with the low-paid job Edward had found him, living in the flat in the basement of the sports shop, he had all he needed. Perhaps he'd ask Edward if he was allowed to get a dog.

"What are you smiling at, Ryan?" Sally asked, trying in vain to hide her nervousness.

"I'm going home," he said. "I want to buy a dog."

Convinced that his illness was causing confusion and he was not aware of what he had said, she asked, "You said a dog, don't you mean a newspaper or something?"

"What are you talking about, you stupid woman? I said dog and dog I meant." He put the glass down with a bang and hurried away from the puzzled looks of Sally and the rest. "Good riddance," he muttered as he pushed past those still dancing to find Edward. "Good riddance."

Mrs Dreese walked away from Arfon and Gladys's party still smiling from the happy hours she had vicariously enjoyed, but as she approached her rooms her smile faded. Since being discovered with Bernard Gregory, their relationship had changed. It was as though the secretiveness had been the greater part of the attraction. Now that he could knock on the door and walk in without the subterfuge of the tap on the window and the hurriedly closed curtains, he no longer felt at ease. They had little to say to each other any more. It was as though, after all these months, they had gone back to being strangers. The irony of the reversal was difficult to understand. They had been polite strangers when they had first met, after he had pulled her from the path of a car one dark evening, then there had been the slow development of friendship and the relaxed, comfortable, easy companionship. To revert to behaving like strangers, so formal and polite, was heart-breaking. She braced herself to face the fact that they were finished, that she would have to get a decent job, somewhere better to live, find a life for herself and help Carl to find his way, too.

Her brave decision to work to pay off her husband's debts would have to be forgotten. At this moment, it was that which she found most distressing. She had let them both down.

Jennie thought she would enjoy working at Temptations. In the first week she began to get to know the regulars and, with Rhiannon to fill her in on their background, began quickly to feel a part of the place. She knew her successful beginning was due to Rhiannon's kindness.

"Thank you for being such a help," she said one morning as they were opening up. "With you showing me how everything works and introducing me to the customers, I know I'm going to be happy here."

Carl was one of their first customers that day buying a small box of chocolates.

"Jennie? What are you doing here?" he asked.

"I'll be taking over when Rhiannon leaves to have her baby," she replied. "And what about you, have you found a job yet?"

"There's something in the offing, which I hope will work out," he said and there was a closed look on his face that discouraged further questions.

"It looks as if my old shop is reopening," she said, as she took the money for his purchase. "I wondered what it will be? If only I'd done what I wanted to do and not listened to Peter and his parents, I might still be there."

"Didn't you intend to sell paint and paper then?" Rhiannon asked.

Carl excused himself and left, as Jennie explained that her original idea was to make it into a gift shop selling unusual items so people would come there for birthday and Christmas presents. "I still regret not following my instincts and doing what I'd always wanted to do," she said. "Although it was an out of the way spot, I believe that if I'd selected the right stock, people would have found me and come back again and again for things they wouldn't find anywhere else."

"We sell small gifts, specially at Christmas, so perhaps you can use your ideas here," Rhiannon said.

"It won't be mine though, will it?" Jennie said sadly.

When the time drew near for Rhiannon, Charlie and Gwyn to return to their home across the street, Lewis watched Dora carefully. He wondered whether she would be upset, after seeing the house full, then slowly emptying again. She particularly loved having Gwyn there, and even though he only lived across the road she had enjoyed him being in the house, cooking his favourite meals and buying him the extra treats.

Lewis had been helping Charlie with the most urgent decorating, and he and Dora had taken a few hours off to carry back some of the furniture. At last he collapsed into his favourite chair and said, "A thousand pounds for a cup of tea, Dora love," he pleaded. "It'll have to be an IOU, mind."

As they sat drinking tea, the silence of the house settling around them, he asked, "Are you going to be all right?"

"What d'you mean all right?" Her blue eyes blazed. "Of course I'm all right!"

"We'll both miss the noisy lot, won't we?"

"There's another noisy lot wanting a home, Lewis." She looked at him, wondering how best to say what was in her mind. "Eleri and Basil have been given notice. They only have two weeks to get out of their flat and Basil hasn't found anything they can afford. In desperation, he's thinking of moving them all into the old shed place at the Griffiths's place, where Frank and Ernie used to sleep."

"So that was what all this was about, getting me to mend the fences and put up a swing, setting the lawn where I wanted to grow potatoes next year."

"It would only be for a year, while they saved for a place of their own. Eleri could work in the evenings. We'd keep an eye on the boys, if you agree. Lovely boys they are."

221

"Noisy, demanding and we'd have no peace."

"Just for a year, Lewis. We could cope for a year couldn't we?"

"Have you told them?"

"Of course not. I had to see how you felt first."

"Well ask them over for supper one night and we'll put it to them."

"Worried sick, poor Basil is. Tomorrow night?"

"Don't I even get a few days to recover from that lot?" he sighed, waving an arm in the direction of their daughter's family. But he was smiling and she hugged him.

"We could go round tonight?" she coaxed.

"Tomorrow they'll all be at the Griffithses celebrating Joseph-Hywel's fourth birthday, let's tell them then."

"Ask them you mean, they might not like the idea."

"Fat chance of them turning down a chance of some of Dora Lewis's *Maldod*, Spoil them rotten you will. The problem won't be will they come, but in persuading them to leave!"

In Temptations, when Rhiannon and Jennie were closing the shop for lunch, Rhiannon invited Jennie to go back with her.

"For a bite to eat, a sandwich or a salad?"

"Thank you, I'd love that."

"Our place is still a mess. Charlie is painting the new walls, so we're still living with our Mam."

"What about looking at those old newspapers?" Jennie suggested. "If your Mam won't mind."

In Dora's kitchen, they found a plate of sandwiches and some small cakes. Rhiannon laughed. "Mam must have known! She and Dad have been home this morning, cleaning up for us after the painting, taking the furniture and boxes back. We're moving back home at the weekend."

After they had eaten, they pulled out the box of old papers and began to browse through them, spreading them on the floor, commenting on the various discoveries. Small town news mostly, telling of fines for riding a bicycle without lights, not having a dog licence, poaching, causing an affray, house-breaking, drunk and disorderly.

"Dull stuff really," Rhiannon said. "They must have been kept for the references to this Molly Bondo woman, her name appears regularly and the pages are folded to show the cases involving her."

"I wonder who she was."

"Who she *is*, you mean," Rhiannon said. "According to Dad, she's still cause for gossip. She's a prostitute," she said in a whisper, even though there was no one else to hear. She delved deep in the box, turning the papers over with care. "There were a couple of photographs here too. I wonder – ah, here they are." Pulling out a tattered envelope she slid out some faded sepia, and black and white photographs and handed them to Jennie. "Have a look through, while I make another cup of tea, then we'll have to be going."

"Rhiannon!" Jennie gasped a few moments later. "I know these people! This is a photograph of Peter's parents!"

"That's strange. They must know this Molly Bondo, but I bet they keep that quiet!" she laughed.

"Can I borrow these?" Jennie asked. "I'll ask Peter if he knows anything about them. If I see him," she added, with a sigh.

"There's no chance of you two patching things up then?"

"Not when he does everything his mother tells him, there's not! I'd be a fool to settle for that, wouldn't I?"

"Why not phone him at the office? You could ask him to meet you and look at the photographs." Rhiannon suggested.

"I might." She packed the papers carefully back into their box. "Now we'd better open up. Typical if Barry decides to come on the one day we're late back!" She put the photographs into her handbag, debating in her mind whether or not it was worth phoning Peter. If she did ask to meet him he's be sure to make her angry by having to check with Mam first.

Barry was pleased with the first of his bird studies and taking the photographs of the fighting cats as well as the ones taken with his shutter-release method, he went to show Caroline.

"Barry, they're excellent!" she gasped. "You have a real talent for seeing the right moment to take the picture. They look almost as though they're moving. You've found something you could develop into a profitable line. Calendars and birthday cards perhaps? Even a book."

Her enthusiasm was so enormous and so unexpected, he spoke almost without a thought and asked, "Will you come back and help me? Give up your job in the wool shop and be my partner?" He was smiling excitedly at his impulsive question, but the smile faded as he saw from her expression that the answer was going to be, no.

The news of an engagement spread quickly, as Mair and Frank told their friends. The announcement was met sometimes with humour and sometimes with disbelief. Sympathy for Mair was a regular utterance, as was the conviction that neither Mair as his wife, nor PC Gregory as his father-in-law, would stop Frank's regular court appearances for fighting and poaching. There was constant discussion of how soon Mair's father would move away from the embarrassment, or even emigrate.

In the usual way, news of the engagement party at the Griffithses spread without the need for invitations. The television and any piece of furniture not needed as either seat or table, was taken out of the small living-room and stacked in the shed. Hywel and Frank made sure that there was plenty of wood for a fire, which was to be lit outside for baking potatoes which they dug from Farmer Booker's fields. Janet made food, helped by her silent daughter.

"You'd better have a bit of a chat to Frank," Janet said to a startled Hywel.

"What about? Not the birds and bees, Janet? The boy knows more than I do. He should be talking to me!"

"About responsibility, and all that. You know," Janet coaxed. But Hywel had another subject he felt he ought to discuss.

"Frank," Hywel began, wondering how to broach the subject of Mair and her baby, "I don't want to spoil things, boy, but this baby, sure are you, that it's yours?" He watched as his son continued to push and pull the saw through the lengths of wood as though he hadn't spoken. "Sorry, son. It isn't my business. But there's soon it happened. One minute it was that Carl bloke she was seeing and the next there you are, smiling like a couple of kids, saying you're getting married and having a child. I only wondered, like."

"I know it isn't mine, Dad," Frank said, when he had thrown yet another log on the growing pile. "I guessed almost as soon as she told me, but I went on acting pleased, like."

"You don't mind?"

"How else would I find a girl like Mair and persuade her to marry me."

Hywel was so upset by the plaintive, yet casually spoken words, that he couldn't speak for a long, long time. There was a hint of tears on the grizzled and bearded face when he told Janet later what their son had said. "God love 'im, Janet. I'm telling you, if that girl causes him grief I'll kill her."

"Somehow, I don't think she will," Janet said comfortingly. "I've talked to her and she is genuinely fond of our Frank. We have to support them and hope for the best."

It was a day for surprises for Janet and Hywel. When Caroline and her mother had finished preparing food for the people they expected, Janet told her about Frank's revelation. "It seems to be the pattern around here," Janet smiled. "Even those high and mighty Westons have had the same. Megan marrying that Edward Jenkins and her with a child belonging to someone else. Then there's you and Barry, now our Frank."

Then came the second surprise.

"Barry and I have decided to divorce," Caroline said quietly. "Don't start an argument, Mam. My mind is made up. We'll never be happy, I should have accepted that a long time ago instead of hanging on, hoping for some magic to transform a failure into a wonderful success. It isn't going to happen, We both know it."

"Is that why you're so quiet? So sad, love?"

"No, I'm not sad. I've been so worried about telling you and Dad. I'm happy now I've told you." She looked at her mother, her round face rosy and happy, and to Janet's eyes so gentle and so lovely. "You aren't upset, are you, Mam, having a divorce in the family?"

"Caroline, love, I'm so relieved I can't tell you! Come and let me give you a hug then we'll go and tell your dad."

The final surprise came when Lewis and Dora arrived and offered Basil, Eleri and their small boys a share of their home.

"You mean it, Mam and Dad? We can move in with you?" Eleri hugged Dora and then Lewis. "After all that's happened, you'll let me come back?"

"Losing our Lewis-boy was tragedy we'll never recover from, love," Lewis said, "but sharing you with Janet and Hywel, you still calling us Mam and Dad, like you did when you and Lewis-boy were married well, it makes our loss just a little bit easier to bear."

"Come and welcome." Dora smiled.

"And, apparently," Lewis said in mock dismay, "we've volunteered to baby-sit for you if you want to work, as well as suffering the noise of your wild boys. Kind of me, eh?" he teased, glancing at his wife affectionately.

Looking at the photographs borrowed from Rhiannon, Jennie decided to telephoned Peter's office. Predictably he sounded agitated. "Is something wrong? It isn't Mam, is it?"

"Hello, Jennie, and how are you?" she said sarcastically. "Peter, why should there be something wrong?"

"Well, you wouldn't ring unless it was important."

"I want to talk to you. Is that so unimportant? Can we meet?"

"You rang to ask me that?"

Holding her irritation in check she replied, "I rang to ask you that."

"Tonight?"

"Will you come to my room at the Firs?"

"No, better not. Can you come to the house? Mam and Dad will be there of course, but we can go in the kitchen if we need to talk privately."

They arranged to meet at seven and Jennie took the envelope of photographs with her. Perhaps, if she was in a good mood, Peter's mother might help explain them.

Very formally, her mother-in-law offered her a cup of tea. She didn't get up to make it, but nudged her husband to deal with it, Jennie noticed.

"Mother-in-law," Jennie began, "what was your maiden name?"

The woman stared at her before asking, "What's that to do with you?"

"It was Bondo," Peter contributed.

"The Lewises found some old papers in their loft, following the court cases of someone called Molly Bondo. There were photographs, too, and they might be something to do with you." Jennie pulled the photographs out, showed them to Mrs Francis, who promptly fainted.

Twelve

When his mother collapsed on seeing the photographs, Peter didn't know what to do. It was Jennie who bent her head forward and eventually got her up the stairs and into bed.

"Shall I call the doctor?" Peter asked anxiously.

"No," Mrs Francis said, "I don't want a doctor, I just want this woman out of my house."

"But Mam—"

"Best that you go, Jennie love," Peter's father whispered. "She's that upset."

"Go now, this minute, and never come back." Recovering quickly, Mrs Francis went on, "Raking up muck about us, causing trouble and getting pleasure from it. Taking revenge were you? For my son coming to his senses and leaving you? No wonder he doesn't want anything more to do with you. Spiteful revenge, that's what this is and you can't deny it! Wicked you are. Wicked."

"But I don't understand." Jennie stood in front of the woman who was glaring at her with such hatred that it was frightening. "Peter?" she pleaded. "Tell me what I've done."

"What is it, Mam?"

"Get her away from me! Coming here, determined to cause trouble. I warned you she was trouble. Didn't I warn you? Get her out of my sight!"

Seeing a distressed Jennie to the door she had entered so recently, Peter said, "Sorry about this. I'll come and explain as soon as I can."

As the door closed behind her, hardly giving her time to

229

remove herself from the step, Jennie burst into tears. What had she done to make Peter's mother hate her so? And what harm could there be in bringing a couple of old photographs for her to see? Most people would be pleased, interested at the memories evoked by some unexpected news of the past.

She couldn't face going home. She walked the streets aimlessly for more than an hour, breaking out into sobs at intervals and stiffening her resolve to forget Peter and his unpleasant mother at others. She became aware that besides being upset, she was hungry. She bought fish and chips and tore open the package and ate them walking along the road.

When she eventually reached the Firs she suddenly made up her mind to go back and demand an explanation. How dare Mrs Francis treat her so badly and call her a spiteful avenging daughter-in-law? How dare she talk to her in such a way? And why, above all, why didn't she even have the decency to explain what she had done?

Her knock on the door was loud and insistent and it was Peter's father who answered.

"I'm coming in and I'm not leaving until I have an apology and an explanation," she said loudly, as she pushed past him and walking into the living room. "Where is she? Still being pathetic in bed? I want her down here, now, this minute or I'll go up and fetch her down."

"Jennie, what's got into you?" Peter said, as he ran down the stairs.

"A bit of your mother's awkwardness, that's what! Tell her to get herself down here or I'll make so much noise the neighbours will hear me."

Mrs Francis appeared at the top of the stairs and at once, both Peter and his father ran to help her down. Jennie felt sick. Why has Peter never been so attentive to me, she wondered, as he talked soothingly to his mother and held her arm as she came down, step by slow step. Then a voice in her own head answered her, because you're too independent, Jennie Francis. A man like Peter needs to think he's the strong one, that *you* depend on *him*.

She shrugged the thought aside. This was not a moment to

suggest weakness. She stood in front of her mother-in-law and asked, firmly, "Who is Molly Bondo?" There was no response. She looked at Peter for support but he shook his head. "All right, I can easily find out. By tomorrow I'll know why you won't talk about it. Who I tell, is up to you." The implied threat succeeded.

"Tell them, my dear," Peter's father said.

"I can't. Not after all this time." Mrs Francis's face was stricken.

For the first time, Jennie felt sympathy for the woman who had ruined her marriage, and probably spoilt any chance of her son being secure in a relationship, by insisting on being his priority. The moment of compassion passed as swiftly as it was recognised. "They'll hear me in the next street, mind," Jenny warned. This had to be settled now, or it might never be sorted.

"Best that we do," Peter's father insisted gently. "Whether you like it or not, Jennie is family and she has a right to know. It will help Peter if she's here."

"Peter doesn't need someone like her!" For a moment the dislike returned, then Mrs Francis held out a hand to her son. "Peter, have you had a good life so far? Have we treated you well?"

"You've been wonderful parents," Peter was frowning, exchanging glances with his father and with Jennie. He looked almost as pale as his mother. Was she going to tell them she was dying? "Mam, you aren't ill are you? Please don't tell me that."

Getting up from her chair, Mrs Francis opened a cupboard and took out some birth and marriage certificates. "You'd better look at these," she said. Peter took them and went to sit beside Jennie while they examined them.

"But, Mam, what does all this mean?" He turned to his father. "Dad? Will you explain?"

"I think it means you were adopted, Peter. Molly Bondo is your mother's sister and she is also your real mother," Jennie said softly. He reached out for her hand and they sat waiting for further explanations.

"She was always no good, our Molly. Expecting when she was

no more than sixteen. That one died and we all thought she'd be chastened by the experience, but she was still only eighteen when you were born, Peter. Your father and I were married, so we gave you a home with us."

"Thank you," he said foolishly.

"Your mother was afraid for us to have any children of our own," Peter's father said. "I'd have loved a daughter, but it was a daughter she dreaded."

"There's always been a bad one in the Bondo family. All through the generations there was one girl who went, you know, wrong. Sometimes more than one. I couldn't face it. We had you, Peter, so we were happy."

Jennie suddenly realised the wider implications of this sad story. "That's why you were so against Peter marrying, wasn't it?" she said. "You were afraid that we'd have a wayward daughter?"

"You're very strong willed and that's what my mother used to say about our poor Molly. Strong willed and determined to go her own way."

Jennie stood up and picked up the photographs that had been left on the table. "I'll return these to the Lewises and tell them you don't recognise anyone. I think we can tear up the photograph with you and Father-in-law on it, don't you, Peter?"

"Thank you," Peter said again.

He was in shock and Jennie wondered whether he would remember clearly what had been said, or whether he was simply unable to think further than the knowledge that he'd been adopted, and had a prostitute for a mother. Those two pieces of information were more than enough to cope with. Jennie wondered with a burst of optimism, whether he would come to her to talk it out and make sense of it all. Seeing him sitting there, pale and bewildered, she hoped he would.

"I don't understand why we didn't learn of all this when we were married," she said into the silence.

"I dealt with the paperwork, remember? I presented them for you and the adoption papers never left my hands," Peter's mother said softly. "It was touch and go there, but I managed to keep our dreadful secret." She glared at Jennie, such hatred in her eyes that she frightened the girl. "Everything was all right, until you came along. Peter wouldn't have known if you hadn't persuaded him to get married and spoil it all!"

"I didn't take much persuading, Mam," Peter said, reaching out and taking Jennie's hand. "It was I who did the persuading."

Jennie smiled at him. For the first time she felt a glimmer of hope.

It was a time for revelations. Mair sought Frank out and suggested a walk. As they wandered through the wood on that late July evening, the air was warm but a slight drizzle was falling. They were more or less sheltered by the thick leaves of the trees but occasionally, the water would come pouring off the leaves like tiny rivers when it became too much for them to hold.

"Frank, I have to tell you something."

"You're calling off the wedding. I knew it was too good to be true." He tried to keep his face straight but the solemn expression showed her a sadness that would not be hidden. He would be so hurt by what she was about to say that for a moment she relented and thought she would say nothing. But she knew Megan was right. If their marriage was to stand any chance, she had to begin it without secrets.

"I want to marry you, Frank. Please believe that. I – I love you, but I didn't realise it until lately. You make me feel safe but it's more than that. I have a great longing deep inside me to make you happy, I want your love and I want us to be together for always. I want to make you a good and honest wife. But there's something you have to know, and after I've told you, I won't hold you to your promise. D'you understand me?"

"Of course I understand, Mair. I'm not as thick as all that." He tried to smile but his face was stiff, his mouth wouldn't do what he wanted it to do. He knew what was coming and wished he could help her.

"This baby, it isn't yours. I'm sorry. Tried to cheat, I did. Tried to make out it was yours. But it isn't. I was seeing Carl Rees and the baby is his." She waited for him to speak, imagining him

233

trying to work out how to be kind, as he told her he couldn't marry her.

"I know," he said finally, and she gasped.

"You knew?"

"I keep telling people – but they don't believe me – that I'm not such an idiot as I make out. Of course I knew. But, if you still want to marry me, and you can promise that you and Carl are finished, then I still want to marry you, Mair. Oh, by the way, Mam and Dad have guessed, too, so I suppose a few others will as well. Are you all right about that?"

"Oh Frank. I don't deserve you."

"I bet a few will agree with that, too." He laughed. "Marrying a Griffiths is what most fathers dread for their daughters!"

Frank was offered another night's work by Carl and although he was uneasy, knowing he was marrying the mother of Carl's child, he agreed. The extra money would be welcome now he was going to have a wife to keep. He insisted on having the money first though, just in case Carl felt any animosity towards him.

"I want you to do some fly-posting, for me," Carl told him.

"That's illegal! I'll want an extra couple of bob for that!"

"A few hours work, that's all. A hundred posters spread around the town and, on another night – if you fancy it – you can help me cover the outlying villages."

Frank didn't ask what they notices were about, he just took them from Carl and mixed up a couple of large pots of paste and went off, slapping the notices on every convenient wall or shop window. He worked fast and hoped Carl wouldn't come and check his work. He had done exactly what he'd been asked, but didn't think Carl would be pleased with the result. He got back to the cottage about four a.m. and, as the night was warm, he slept in the porch, where Janet found him when she went to open up the goats and chickens in the early morning. She wondered why he was smiling.

Jennie arrived in Sophie Street early that morning and, as it was not time to open Temptations, she walked back to look again at her shop, curious to know what it would sell when it reopened. She didn't look very hard at the posters that had sprouted overnight, simply noting that they were red in colour and impossible to read. She saw the shop window as she reached the corner and as she drew closer she gasped in dismay. It was a gift shop, just like she had imagined opening! Her first thought was disappointment, closely followed by the second, which was anger that Peter and his family had ruined her hopes of owning such a shop, pushing her into a paint and paper store. Even that had been taken from her by Peter's mother's demand for her loan to be repaid.

She went to the shop door and peered in and saw Carl inside.

"Carl? Are you fixing shelves for the new owner?" she shouted. "Who is it? Someone I know?"

Unlocking the door, Carl smiled hesitantly. "You know him all right. It's me."

She stared in disbelief at the shelves packed with glass and china ornaments of every size. There were wooden items too, made, she guessed as revelation dawned, by Carl. She saw toys and ornaments hand crafted and beautiful. The shelves had been painted in patterns of flowers and fruits, the walls and ceilings used for ornamentation and displays. The whole effect was so magical, so attractive that she felt disappointment swelling inside her: a balloon of misery. "But you stole my idea! You should have at least told me!"

"What would be the point? You weren't going to do it, so I did."

Forgetting Temptations, she ran to Peter's office. He stood up in surprise and asked at once what was wrong.

"It isn't your mother so don't worry!" she snapped.

"Which mother would that be?" he asked with a shrug. Her expression softened and she touched his arm in silent sympathy.

She told him that Carl had stolen her idea and had opened a gift shop. "I gave him addresses of stockists that offered the best variety and best prices. Everything he needed to start him off. He's added some of his own work: wooden toys, ornaments, small kitchen items. It will be a success, Peter, and it should have been mine. Whatever problems your mother had, she didn't have to ruin my efforts." She was close to tears.

Peter wanted to help and he sensed that this was a rare time when she wouldn't brush his concern aside. Arranging for the day off, he walked home with her and they sat side by side on the worn couch, in the dark living-room of his mother's house.

"We won't be disturbed," he said soothingly. "You can shout, scream, cry, hit me, anything. Mam and Dad are out shopping and won't be back for at least an hour."

"I don't want to do any of those things. I just want to sit and let everything simmer down. Then I'll make my apologies to Barry for being late, and go to work."

Peter put a cushion under her head and coaxed her to lie back. "This brings back memories," he said. "We did a lot of our courting here."

"Yes, with your mother listening from the landing!" she said, then the anger faded and they smiled.

His arms wrapped her against him and they kissed; a sweet, gentle kiss that left them both shaking. A second kiss offered hope and they held each other close, each afraid to speak and spoil the moment. Until the voice from the landing called, "I'll have a cup of tea if you're making one. I didn't feel well enough to go with Dad this morning."

Helpless with laughter, Jennie and Peter hugged each other once more, before getting up and creeping from the house.

Later that morning Carl stormed into Temptations and demanded of Jennie, "Did you do this? Did you persuade Frank to mess up my posters?"

"What are you talking about?" she asked, frowning. Then she remembered seeing some posters that morning as she had wandered back to look at her old shop. "Oh, are those red ones yours? The ones that are hard to read?"

"I paid good money for Frank to distribute them. So why did he paste them back to front?"

"I don't suppose it's any surprise to you, Carl, but you aren't the only person in Pendragon Island to cheat occasionally!" The revelation lightened her mood and when Peter came to meet her at five thirty, she was quite cheerful. She was even happier when Peter suggested going back with her to The Firs to share a meal.

When Frank and Mair went to the register office to exchange their vows, there was a crowd of people outside. Among the mass of excited onlookers Frank recognised Jack and his wife, Victoria; Viv Lewis, dressed in a smart suit and sporting a rose buttonhole, with his wife Joan, and a group of children and young people gathered around Jack and Victoria who he realised were Victoria's brothers and sisters. Why had they all come? He was pleased though. "Better than no one at all," he confided in Basil, who was to be his witness.

"They aren't here for you, you fat-head." Basil laughed. "Look who's coming." A car stopped and a shy Mrs Glory Collins stepped out to be greeted by her family. Stepping forward from where he had been waiting, was Sam Lilly, with his sister beside him. "You aren't the only one getting wed this morning," Basil said. "And I told you we were too early!"

The wedding party went inside amid fluttering hands and shouted good wishes. Then Frank saw the rest of his family and friends gathering. By the time Glory and Sam Lilly had come out with their small party and stood with the new arrivals, the pavement was packed solid.

The crowd parted when Mair arrived, dressed in a blue, mid-calf-length dress with flowers in her hair, accompanied by her father. For once, Bernard Gregory was not in uniform as he approached Frank Griffiths. Instead of the usual glowering disapproval, he smiled and offered his hand before following him through the doors. The cheering crowd of well-wishers, many unknown to either of them, settled to wait. Some ran to buy boxes of confetti, happy to be able to celebrate the joyful occasion.

Sam and Glory Lilly went to the small house in Goldings Street for their celebration meal. "Fancy having to stand there and hear the registrar say my name for everyone to hear, 'will you, Gloriana Fleur Collins.'" Glory laughed.

"Even your children were surprised. I think you're in for some teasing, don't you?"

Outside, fixed to the window frame, there was a 'house for sale or rent' notice. As soon as they were able, the couple, plus Glory's children, would make their home together in the house on Chestnut Avenue, with Sam's sister sharing the house until she could find a place of her own.

For Frank and Mair there was the certainty of an all-night party in the Griffiths's small cottage. Who would come no one knew, but they did know that the house would groan with the size of the party and that the food would last until the cockerel declared a new day had begun.

Barry watched as people crossed the fields and headed for the cottage, laughing as they hurried towards the welcome they knew would be there for them. There was regret in his heart. He would love to have been a part of that unconventional and contented family, but he knew that he lacked that special indefinable something, that was needed to make him belong. Time to look away and search further afield for whatever life had in store for him. Two marriages today, and on Monday he would see the solicitor and tell him to get on with breaking up what was left of his.

Rhiannon and Charlie had planned a day out for the Sunday after the weddings. Mr Windsor from the garage had offered to lend Charlie a firm's van to take his family out for a drive and to buy tea somewhere.

"It will probably be the last outing before the baby arrives," Charlie coaxed as Rhiannon showed slight hesitation.

"Then I think we should," she said but there was still doubt revealed by the slight frown. "Gwyn would love to go somewhere different. We don't get out nearly often enough, do we?"

"We'll get a saddle for my crossbar just as soon as the baby's old enough and we'll go off on our bikes again. We all enjoyed that, didn't we?"

As she packed the picnic, Rhiannon was thinking that with

238

only three or four weeks to go before the birth, she didn't want to be too far from home. "Perhaps we could go to Dinas Powys and walk on the common. I love wandering down the green lane," she suggested.

"I've got something better in mind," Charlie said. "But don't ask, because it's a secret. Right?"

"Not too far, though, Mam and Dad have invited us for dinner, remember," was all the doubt she showed. How could she spoil Charlie's surprise?

Dora and Lewis's day had been planned. A morning making sure the rooms were all ready for Eleri and Basil and the boys to move in. Then, after a snack lunch, the van bringing their new lodgers' belongings would arrive, followed by the family. "I expect the whole Griffiths clan will be here as well," Dora sighed. "Lucky I made plenty of cakes."

"They won't be here for ages yet and the place is so clean you're wearing it out," Lewis said as he put the last bed precisely into its allotted place. "We've got time to go and see Mair and Frank, give them that gift you bought."

After a cup of coffee, and having made sure everything was as ready as they could make it, they left the house at eleven o'clock to call on Frank and his new wife.

Basil brought the Griffiths's old van to a halt outside the flat in Trellis Street and waited for Eleri and the boys to get in. They were going to leave the children with Hywel and Janet, while they used the van for the removal to 7 Sophie Street.

"Not sad, are you, love? Leaving our home like this?" Basil asked, as he pressed down the clutch and put the old van into first.

"I wish we could have stayed," Eleri replied. "But if we have to move, I can't think of anywhere better than sharing with Mam and Dad Lewis. They were so kind to me when I was married to Lewis-boy and they've never changed since. I love your parents, Basil, you know that, but I love the Lewises too. They'll always be a part of our family."

"We're pretty lucky all round, aren't we, love?"

239

"I should say we are." She touched the heads of their two small boys as she spoke, then looked at her tall, boyish-looking, loveable husband. "I love you, Basil Griffiths. More than I can tell you." She stretched up and tried to kiss his cheek.

"Hang on," he warned with a laugh. "We'll be causing an accident and where would our luck be then? If I damage this ol' van, our dad'll kill me!"

Sam had suggested taking the children for a run as the weather was fine. They were surprised when four of them refused. Albert and George wanted to explore the area around their new home in Chestnut Road. Elizabeth and Margaret had been invited to a nearby house to play with some new friends, so it was with only the two youngest, Winston and Montgomery that the couple finally set out that Sunday morning.

"What about calling for Victoria and Jack?" Sam suggested. "We'll be back for lunch, but they might like an hour and a pint somewhere."

"Shall I drive?" Glory asked, and when Sam nodded agreement, she slipped into the driving seat, a cushion at her back, and fiddled with the seat adjustment to be able to reach the pedals comfortably, and they were off.

After they had picked up Jack and Victoria, they decided instead of going for a drive into the country, that they would take them back to Chestnut Road to see the changes taking place there.

"But we could go through the lanes instead of the road, make a bit of an outing of it," Sam suggested. "If you don't mind driving through the lanes, dear?"

"Of course I don't mind. It's no different from driving through the busy streets after all. In fact it can be easier as no one tries to overtake, and people drive more slowly."

"So, back to Chestnut Road, but by the scenic route."

On that Sunday morning, Jennie was sitting in her small bedsit wondering where she would be a year hence. So much had happened in the past six or seven months that it was impossible to guess. Would she and Peter be together, or would they go ahead and divorce? To be back with him was what she wanted, but with conditions, she mused. She wanted Peter without his parents too near, or at least without his interfering, over-possessive mother. His father she thought she could manage without much difficulty. He was one of the 'anything for peace' type and wouldn't try to run Peter's life for him.

She understood a lot of her mother-in-law's behaviour now she knew about Peter's parentage, but she still couldn't face living a life with her clinging to them and insisting that everything was done to suit her. No, if she and Peter remained married, it would have to be a long way away from Pendragon Island.

A knock at the door surprised her. She hadn't had a single visitor until last night, when Peter had walked her home. She remembered how he had stared with some discomfort at the single iron bedstead, situated so close to the small sink and scarred old cooker in the room she now called home. She thought it might be Peter now, braving a second look, and hurriedly smoothed back her hair and checked her face in the mirror, adding a touch more lipstick before calling, "All right, I'm coming."

It was Peter, but his words were not cheering. "I've got the car outside, with Mam and Dad in it. We thought you'd like to go out for lunch," he said.

"To lunch? Me? With your mother?" She regretted the sarcastic response as soon as it was uttered, but was unable to take it back.

"Please," Peter said. "Mam wants to try and make amends for – for – well, you know," he finished lamely.

Putting on her summer jacket Jennie regretted not washing her hair. She went into the bathroom she had to share with four others and cleansed her face and neck, and reapplied her make-up. She looked at her thick hair, dull and with a hint of greasiness. She was ashamed of her neglect that morning. She combed it through with cotton wool in the comb to which she had added a few drops of cologne. Not perfect but it would have to suffice.

Peter insisted she sat beside him, which she did, in spite of a few complaints from his mother, and he drove in an uneasy silence along Sophie Street up to the main road and on towards the quiet lanes that eventually would take them westward.

"I thought Tenby would be nice," he said cheerfully. Jennie agreed, wondering how she was going to cope with this awful journey and wishing she hadn't answered the door. Peter's father was pleased. He loved Tenby and hadn't been there for years. Mrs Francis said nothing. She sat looking out of the window, stiff-lipped as though hating every moment. So much for making amends for her behaviour, Jennie thought grimly. What a dull boring day this was going to be, she silently sighed, as they passed the end of Chestnut Road.

Chestnut Road was on Lewis's mind as he drove towards the Gregory's cottage tucked into the edge of the wood. Perhaps it had been the talk of Frank and Mair's wedding that had begun the train of thought. He had married Dora when they were very young and, like Mair, she had been expecting a child, a baby they had lost. For years he had thought he was happy. Although there had been a few lapses on his part and many quarrels, he had believed he and Dora would spend their lives together. For most people, even now in 1956, when the number of divorces was increasing, that was still the expected thing.

Meeting Nia Williams had changed all that. For many years he had wanted to leave Dora and go to her, but Nia wouldn't agree. Their loving relationship had lasted undetected for many years. They had had a child, Joseph, who had been brought up by Nia as Barry's brother. When Joseph had been killed in the same accident as Lewis-boy, their affair had been revealed. Then he had left Dora and gone to live in Chestnut Road with Nia. When Nia had died in a stupid accident in her garden, he had not imagined anything more unlikely than his present happiness with Dora.

Dora had changed, he had changed and together they had found a contentment he had once thought impossible. It wasn't the strong passionate love he had known with Nia, nothing would ever replace that. He was thinking then of the moments he had shared with the quiet, softly-spoken Nia, the woman who had been the real love of his life, when a car hurtled out from a side lane right across his path.

"Lewis!" He heard the warning, and it was Nia's voice he heard. But he heard it too late.

In Sam's car, Glory's reflexes were not fast enough to stop the car as the van Barry was driving crossed in front of Lewis and Dora. Sam grabbed the wheel and pulled in towards the side where a ditch was hidden by ferns and grasses that grew there in profusion. Barry was wide-eyed with shock as he ran straight into Sam's car, at the same time being shunted sideways towards the edge of the lane by Lewis's car.

Charlie heard rather than saw the accident and his foot was already on the brake as they turned a corner and came upon the three vehicles. Even though his speed was not great he found himself moving inexorably towards them. A protective arm across Rhiannon, he waited for the bump that would certainly come.

Basil, in the Griffithses van coming up behind him, was unaware of the crash. Charlie and Rhiannon were bewildered and frightened when the bump they expected came, not in front of them, but from behind. When the van came to a stop and they had recovered from being thrown forwards and backwards, Basil and Eleri sat stunned as both children began to cry.

The sound of the tormented metal which filled the air finally ceased, and there was only the sound of crying, accompanied by the slow regular drip of escaping petrol and an unidentified clicking.

It was Charlie who reacted first. Carefully opening the passenger door he helped Rhiannon out and made her sit on the grass near a gate set back from the road, away from the cars. When he turned back, people were emerging slowly, stiffly as if dancing in some strange ballet. Their movements were accompanied by low moaning and wails and the occasional shrill cry of a child. He recognised Lewis and Dora who were standing

staring as though bemused by what had happened. He couldn't
know that Lewis was looking around him, expecting to see Nia.
Basil carried the two boys, while a tearful Eleri held his arm and
walked beside him to sit with Rhiannon. He exchanged a few
words of reassurance before running to see why no one was
getting out of one of the other cars.

Peter was sitting in the driving seat and beside him, Jennie was
frantically trying to open her door, but her side of the car was too
close to the bank and Charlie opened the driver's door and
dragged Peter out. With Jennie out and helping, he half carried
Peter, and left him with the women. He saw to his relief that her
mother was with her, and went back to Peter's car. Peter's
parents were in the back, Mrs Francis wailing softly, a shivering
kind of moan that chilled him.

"Don't worry, Missus, we'll soon have you out of there. Just
get you all away from the cars, then we'll go for help."

"It's my husband," she whispered. She looked bewildered. Her
voice was trembly and weak. "Help him, will you?"

Charlie leant into the car and looked at Peter's father. His
head was at an awkward angle and there was absolutely no
movement. He checked that Peter had turned off the engine, and
holding back his panic, concentrated on opening the back door.
"Come on, Missus. Let's get you out of there, shall we? Give
your husband a bit more room, is it?" He was no expert, but he
didn't think the man had survived the crash.

He helped Mrs Francis out, groaning as she leant on her dead
husband to do so, wanting to scream with the horror of it,
wanting to get back to Rhiannon, filled with some atavistic dread
of being so close to a dead body. He wanted to run back to the
gateway, hug his wife, make sure she was safe and unharmed,
longing for the live, healthy warmth of her. At the same time
ashamed of his abhorrence, of his lack of pity for this man, and,
for what the woman would have to face.

When he was sure that apart from Mr Francis, no one was left
in any of the vehicles he ran back to the gate and hugged
Rhiannon. "Are you all right, my darling girl? I'm sorry I
had to leave you but we had to get everyone out. You do

understand, don't you? You don't think I should have stayed with you?"

"Charlie, you did all the right things and I'm so proud of you," she said tearfully.

Dora nodded, watching her daughter for any sign of distress. After a few seconds allowing relief to spread through them, Rhiannon asked for details of what had happened. He avoided mentioning Mr Francis, but told her the rest.

"Will you help me up now, please, Charlie? I want to make sure Jennie is all right."

"Basil has gone for help and Jennie is with Peter and his mam," Charlie told her. "They're all right. Don't worry, help will be here soon."

Dora left them then and walked back to the crossroads looking for Lewis. When she realised he wasn't there, shock took away her composure and she began crying and talking to herself. Rhiannon was talking to Eleri but seeing her mother was upset, hurried as fast as her ungainly body would allow and hugged her. "Where's Dad?" she asked.

"He was here a minute ago, all wide-eyed and upset, then he vanished. I don't know what's happened to him."

"Gone for a pee for sure," Charlie whispered, "most of the men have done that, mind."

"Some of the women too," Rhiannon confided, trying to help Charlie cheer her mother. Sam took out the picnic basket and shared the contents while they waited for the police and ambulances to arrive. "Carbohydrate is good for shock," he told them as he offered cakes and pasties to them all, coaxing them to eat.

"I'll see that your husband has some," Charlie said quickly, when he saw Mrs Francis going towards her car. "You just sit and wait quiet. Leave it to me."

"Where is Mr Francis?" Rhiannon asked.

"He looks in a bad way and I'm afraid to move him," he said. Best not to say more than that. He might be wrong and either way there was no point upsetting her any more than necessary. He held out his arms. "Come here my lovely girl and give me a hug."

Dora became frantic as Lewis did not reappear and the rest of the victims were taken by ambulance to the hospital for check-ups. Jennie held Mrs Francis as the body of her husband was removed from the car and taken away separately from the rest. Peter watched as the vehicle drove away, staring after it in disbelief. "How could such a thing happen?" he kept asking Jennie, who tried to hush him, pointing at the distraught figure of his mother. Mrs Francis pulled away from Jennie's arms and stood up, her body trembling as though her legs could no longer take her weight.

"I should have gone with him," she said. "Why did you stop me? I should be with him. He'll wonder where I am. You shouldn't have stopped me, you wicked girl."

"Mam," Peter said soothingly. "You heard what the ambulance men said, he's past our help, all we can do is let him rest in peace."

"He isn't dead! Don't talk as though he's dead! D'you hear me?" Mrs Francis said angrily.

Dora and Rhiannon were refusing to go to the hospital until they had found Lewis. When Charlie pleaded with Dora to help him persuade Rhiannon to go, she seemed unaware of the situation.

"Where's Lewis? I can't lose him now. Where is he, Charlie?" It wasn't until Charlie held her by the shoulders and spoke sharply to her, and reminded her that Rhiannon was eight months pregnant, that she came out of the confusion of the accident and the loss of Lewis and grasped what he was telling her. She knew that her daughter might need help.

She managed to tell her daughter, in brief moments of clarity, that she owed it to Charlie and Gwyn to go and have a check-up with the rest.

"Come on, Mam, come with us, please."

"I can't, love. Not yet I can't. Where's your dad gone?" She looked around at the slowly changing scene: cars being pulled out of the way to allow approaching traffic to pass, people sitting, limbs still shaking, waiting for their turn to be taken to hospital, and from all directions, men, women and children gathering from the nearby houses, coming across the fields and down the lanes to see what had happened.

Several times Dora thought she recognised Lewis, and she would begin to run, only to slow down and stop, disappointment painful as she realised her mistake.

When everyone else had gone, the ambulance men insisted on her going with them.

"Most probably find your husband there, Mrs Lewis. Taken there by a passer-by maybe. Let's go and have a look-see, shall we?"

After an examination, Dora went home, taken there by a concerned Basil and Eleri and the children, who had all been declared unharmed, apart from a few bruises. An hour passed and another and at five o'clock, Dora refused their entreaties to stay and wait for Lewis to return, and announced she was going out to look for him.

"Where will you go?" Eleri asked. "If Lewis comes back we don't want him going out to search for you, do we?"

"I'll come with you," Basil insisted.

"No, I'll go up to the cemetery, I think he might be at Lewis-boy's grave. If you need me that's where I'll be. You wait here and we'll have a cup of tea when I get back." She pulled a face. "Sick of tea I am, that's all we seem to have done today is drink tea, but I'll have one when I get back."

They let her go and Basil watched as she set off along the road, running a few steps and then slowing again to a walk. "I'll soon find her if Lewis gets back first," he told Eleri. "Go on the bike I will."

"It's in the van," she reminded him, "and the van's in the ditch."

"Our Dad'll kill me," he said.

Dora was hurrying as she went up the hill towards the cemetery. There were several figures there, bending over graves, attending to flowers, and she felt guilty, remembering that she hadn't been to change the flowers for poor dear Lewis-boy for several weeks, not since Easter Sunday in fact. Then the cemetery had been so busy it looked like a picnic outing, children in best clothes, flowery dresses besides the flowery bouquets for the dead.

There was no one beside her son's plot and she walked over to stare down at the bedraggled blooms and the dead foliage of her most recent offering. Death was so final. Sobbing for Lewis-boy and his father, she removed the debris and tidied the area, pulling out a few determined clumps of grass and one or two daisies that were able to root, sprout, flourish and flower in such a short time. Then she just sat and thought about Lewis. Where would he have gone? Then she knew.

She went to the bus stop, thankful she had remembered to pick up a purse, and caught the bus up to Chestnut Road, where Lewis had lived with his other love, Nia. That was where he would have gone, she was sure of it. The realisation didn't anger her, she felt a deep sadness, but not for herself. Her sadness was for Lewis, and for Nia who had died. Death was so final.

Glory and Sam were allowed out of hospital and they left with Jack and Victoria. They went by taxi, first to Jack and Victoria's house in Philips Street, not far from Sophie Street, then on to Chestnut Road.

Sam's sister Martha was surprised to see them back so soon. The plan had been an evening with Victoria and Jack. "What happened? You surely didn't run out of food!" she joked. Then they told her about the accident.

"Oh, then that might explain him," Martha said, pointing a thumb towards the big tree in the garden.

Sitting on the ground, his back against the thick trunk of the oak, was Lewis. Beside him was a tray of tea but it was untouched.

"He hasn't moved an inch in the hours he's been there," Martha told them. "I tried talking to him but he seems lost in a dream. Asked about someone called Nia. I thought I'd call a doctor if he doesn't move soon. D'you think we should call one now?"

"I think a doctor might be a good idea," Victoria said. "When the accident happened, he was in a car with his wife and he disappeared. It's obvious he's in shock."

Sam agreed and as Martha went towards the telephone, there was a knock at the door. She opened it and Dora stood there, her bright-blue eyes wild with anxiety.

"It's all right, Mrs Lewis, your husband is here and he's safe."

Dora didn't refer to the incident once Lewis was home and had been examined by a doctor. He had slept the clock around and a couple more hours besides and Dora sat with him, dozing a little herself, watching him and hoping that when he woke he wouldn't tell her he couldn't stay with her, that he still loved Nia that living with her in 7 Sophie Street made him feel disloyal.

When he did wake it was nine o'clock at night. He sat up, rubbed his eyes, peered sleepily at the clock and demanded to know what was he doing in bed at such a time.

"There was an accident, love, don't you remember?"

He frowned as he concentrated on her explanation. Then he gasped, "Hells bells, I do remember. Is everyone all right? What about Rhiannon?"

"We're all fine." She'd tell him about Mr Francis later, she decided. He didn't mention Nia or going to Chestnut Road and she hoped the memory would remain hidden for ever.

Once he was up, bathed and fed, she went across the road to tell Rhiannon that her father was all right, but there was no reply to her knock. At once panic set in. Rhiannon had been harmed, she was going to lose a baby again! She opened the door with the key given for emergencies and went in. The house was empty. Something dreadful must have happened. Then the back door opened and young Gwyn walked in.

"Congratulations, Gran," he said, with a wide grin. "You've got a granddaughter and I've got a sister!"

Jennie and Peter worked together to deal with the Peter's father's funeral and all the time they wondered how they would deal with the bigger problem of Peter's mother.

"Will you reconsider, Jennie, and come and live with Mam and me? We could be happy. Mam has changed, hasn't she? She's talking to you normal, now. No complaining at everything you do. Please, Jennie, let's give it another try?"

"If I thought for one moment that you wanted to try again because you loved me, and wanted me, over and above your need to look after your mother, I'd say yes," she said, calmly and quietly. "But all you want is someone to make sure the household runs smoothly. Well, your mother didn't want me to have you and now she's got you back. So let's leave it at that, shall we?"

Peter told his mother that he had tried, but Jennie refused to come back.

Mrs Francis replied that he hadn't tried hard enough. The following day she went to see Jennie in the sweetshop. It was just before lunchtime and she persuaded her to go with her to the Bluebird cafe in town.

"I'm not here to persuade you, Jennie," she began, when they had ordered their meal. "I don't think I'm the person to do that. But what I want to tell you, is that now my dear husband is no longer with me, I can choose how live the rest of my life. I can go downhill and be utterly dependent on Peter, or I can start a new life. I'm free of most of my commitments, I have a house I can afford to stay in which I can manage easily on my own. I can go out and shut the door behind me and not worry about what time I get back. That's exciting. I'll probably visit some friends I haven't seen for years, and I've always wanted to learn to play bridge and now, with no one else to consider, I can."

"Peter thinks you still need him."

"Then it's up to you to tell him different, isn't it?"

That evening, Jennie decided she would go and see Peter. His mother had explained that he would be on his own, that she was going out with a friend to see whether she could join a bridge club. Today might be a new beginning for them all.

She passed 7 Sophie Street as she left Temptations and heard laughter and shouts coming from the open front window.

Inside, Dora and Lewis were trying to feed Basil and Elerie's family while entertaining Rhiannon and Charlie and Gwyn with the new baby, who was to be called, Mary Jane Bevan. The house was so full, Dora had to bend down and burrow her way through bodies to reach the kitchen where she had food cooking, enough for them all.

Lewis was happy. When he had woken on the day of the accident and found himself in Nia's garden, he had expected Dora to be upset, but she had said nothing, presuming perhaps that he was unaware of what had happened to him. He was grateful for the happiness he had been able to recapture.

Filling the house had been a good idea. By the time Basil and Eleri were ready to leave, the new grandchild would be enough to keep Dora busy. Busy with family and friends was what kept Dora happy and it worked for him too. The baby began to whimper and at once Gwyn jumped up to see to her, to help Rhiannon by picking up Mary Jane to be fed. To make room for Rhiannon to leave the table, everyone moved like a party game, carrying their plates with them. Ronnie asked why the baby didn't have a cup like he and his brother Thomas, and every one laughed. Dora and Lewis smiled at each other above the chaos and nodded. This was what 7 Sophie Street was built for. Loving families having fun.